Shoulda, Woulda, Coulda

Shoulda, Woulda, Coulda

La Jill Hunt

Dedication

In loving memory of Mario Joyner,
who brought so much laughter and humor to so many
lives.
Although you are not with us in body, the smiles you
continue to bring to our faces and the wonderful
memories you left us with, will always allow you to be
with us in spirit.
We love and miss you, SupeRio!!!

Shoulda, Woulda, Coulda

Urban Books
74 Andrews Ave.
Wheatley Heights, NY 11798

ISBN 0-7394-6092-7

Printed in the United States of America

*This is a work of fiction. Any references or
similarities to actual events, real people, living, or
dead, or to real locals are intended to give the
novel a sense of reality. Any similarity in other
names, characters, places, and incidents is
entirely coincidental.*

Acknowledgements

As always, I have to start by thanking God for continuing to keep his hand upon me and allow me to succeed in this endeavor. Lord, I thank You; Your grace is more than I can ever ask for.

To my daughters, who keep my smiling and working hard. I have to especially thank Alyx, who stepped up her game and took on more than her fair share so Mommy could finish. I'm so proud of the young lady you are becoming.

To Pastor Kim W. Brown and Elder Valerie Brown, thank you for your continual love and guidance. None of this could be possible without you or the Mt. Lebanon Missionary Baptist Church family. My family owes you more than we will ever be able to repay.

To the future Dr. Marshall B. Hunt, III. Thank you for always having my back. Especially over the past year. I am proud to be able to call you my cousin.

To those special people that stay in my corner and are always there when I need an encouraging word. This journey is certainly a difficult one, but knowing you are there for me makes it a little better: Yvette Lewis, Robin LeBron, Cherie Johnson, Mechellene Moore, Pamela Green, Cheryl Pleasant, Shantel Spencer, Saundra White, Joycelyn W. Ward, Tonya Kabia, Toye Farrar, Roxanne Elmore, Norell Smith, and Robilyn Heath.

To Selena Johnson, thank you so much for being you. You were there for me before I even called to say I needed you. Without a doubt, you are truly my friend.

To my brother and mentor Carl Weber. Your continual faith in my talent and abilities inspire me and I strive to make you proud. I know I frustrate you to no end, but I hope it's all worth it. LOL.

To Martha, the one and ONLY editor that can do what you do! I have learned so much from you and I can't thank you enough for not only being my editor, but being my friend. You are one of a kind and without you, your knowledge, your kindness and patience, none of my books would be the same.

To Chris Young, otherwise known as Big CTY. Thanks for all the insight and allowing me to use those distinct characteristics and "wonderful" original adages. LOL. You are definitely one of a kind!!

To the readers and book clubs that have shown me so much support. Thank you so much for sharing your thoughts and opinions. It makes writing even more enjoyable when you know it's being enjoyed by others.

To Dwayne S. Joseph, Roy Glenn (you too, Arvita!), Nikki Turner, and K Elliott, thanks for being there for a sister when she needs an empathetic ear.

I've tried to remember everyone, but if there's someone I forgotten, I apologize. Again, I thank everyone who has been with me along this journey. It definitely hasn't been easy, but I know there was a purpose behind it (I Cor. 2:9-10). Keep praying for me!!

Feel free to email me at MsLajaka@AOL.com

Prologue
(the beginning, where it starts, read this first!)

"I've never liked you."

Tell me something I don't know, Paige thought. Instead of saying it, the words, "That's fine, Ms. Lucille. I accepted that fact a long time ago," came out of her mouth.

"All my life I worked hard so my son could have nothing but the best in life. From the moment he was born, I knew he was destined for greatness. I bust my ass working two and three jobs and never took a handout from nobody, not even his sorry-ass daddy before he decided to make this world a better place and die. There's nothing I didn't do for him—nothing! And when he got a full scholarship to school, it made me the happiest mother in the world and I knew that all my hard work paid off. He went off to college and everything was going fine, until you came and ruined his life. You snatched my son and his future away from him."

Paige listened as Marlon's mother continued to ramble about how much she disliked her. It came as no surprise. His mother had given her the cold shoulder from the moment they met. Granted, the first time they laid eyes on each other was the day Paige and Marlon graduated from college, which also happened to be the day Marlon told his mother that Paige was carrying his child, but that was almost seven years ago. The feelings between them had not gotten better, as a matter of fact, they were worse.

But knowing how his mother felt was not enough to keep Paige from attending Marlon's sister's graduation. Unlike his mother, Camille had developed a close relationship with Paige and wouldn't hear of her not attending the ceremony, and then coming to the party they were having at the house. Not wanting to hurt the girl's feelings, Paige agreed, thinking that Ms. Lucille would remain civil since there would be guests at the house. Everything was going fine until Myla spilled punch down the front of her dress. Paige rushed her daughter inside to clean her up, only to find herself face-to-face with Ms. Lucille. She tried to excuse herself and walk by, but Ms. Lucille blocked her entrance to the bathroom.

"Myla, go ahead in the bathroom. Mommy will be right there." She looked down at her beautiful daughter, who was hesitating. Paige nodded, signaling to her daughter that it was okay for her to walk past the mean old woman standing in front of them "Ms. Lucille, I just need to get my daughter cleaned up. Can you please excuse me?"

Paige thought that by using the polite approach, she would get some sort of cooperation from the woman. The party wasn't even in full swing, but Paige could see that Ms. Lucille was already tipsy.

"Excuse you? Please, I ain't even invite you!"

"That's fine, we can leave. I just need to get Myla," Paige remained calm, smoothing the skirt of the off-white dress she was wearing. She was ready to leave anyway. The small house was slowly filling with guests and she wasn't in a social mood. She only wanted to get her child, find Marlon and leave. She went to walk by Ms. Lucille when suddenly she was pushed by the woman.

God, please just get her out of my face before I swing on her, Paige began to pray. *I just want to get my child and leave, that's all. Coming here was a bad idea. Help me get my child so I can get out.*

"The door is that way. Get the hell out my house!" Ms. Lucille demanded.

Paige swallowed and regained her composure, determined not to let this woman get to her. Her heart began pounding so hard, she was sure she could hear it and so could Ms. Lucille.

"Mom, come here!" Myla called out to her.

"I'm coming, baby," she yelled to Myla. "Ms. Lucille, I need to get Myla. Just let me get her and I promise we will leave. I don't wanna be here anyway."

"You little bitch." Ms. Lucille stepped toward her. Music began drifting in from the backyard, which was slowly filling with people. Marlon was manning the grill and acting as security, so she knew there was no-way he was coming in.

Paige realized that the easiest thing for her to do would be to just walk away and send Marlon in to get Myla. She turned and headed for the front door. She had almost made it when she felt the hand on her shoulder. Refusing to turn back around, she snatched away and opened the screen door. Before she could step out, Ms. Lucille grabbed her by the hair and pulled her back in. She squealed, unable to get away from her grasp.

"Let me go!"

"Mama!" Camille yelled. Paige was relieved to see the pretty girl standing near them, holding an armload of gifts. She tossed the gifts on the sofa, rushing toward them. "What is wrong with you? Let her go!"

3

"Go back outside, Camille. I need to have a little chat with Ms. Thang here. It's been a long time coming."

Paige twisted, but Ms. Lucille kept a grip on her hair, which hung to the center of her back. The more she pulled, the tighter Ms. Lucille tugged, causing her to flinch. Her anger was building moment by moment, and she could feel tears stinging in her eyes. "I'm telling you to let me go, Ms. Lucille. You told me to get out and I'm going."

"Mommy, what's going on?" Myla's voice quivered. Paige hated the fact that her daughter had to witness the madness that was unleashing.

"Ms. Lucille's ring got caught in my hair, that's all. Go tell Daddy to come here for a minute," Paige told her. Myla went running out the door, Camille right behind her.

Paige tried to reason with her attacker once again. "Ms. Lucille, there are people right outside. You need to let me go so you won't cause a scene."

"This is my house. I don't give a damn about them free-loading hood rats. Don't nobody pay shit around here except me. I can cause all the scenes I want to." She laughed in Paige's face. The alcohol smell was so strong that it burned Paige's nostrils. In her fit of amusement, Ms. Lucille stumbled, her clench loosening enough to give Paige a window of opportunity to escape. She jerked away and regained herself. Ms. Lucille lunged at her again, but this time, Paige was prepared. She reached for Ms. Lucille's throat, holding her at arm's length.

"Paige! What the hell are you doing?" Marlon yelled.

4

"Get her, Marlon. Get your mama before I hurt her!" Paige's eyes remained on Ms. Lucille.

Marlon walked over and pulled his mother away from Paige, standing between them. "Are you all right, Ma?"

"Yes, baby. I'm fine," Ms. Lucille answered, rubbing her neck. Her playing the victim was no surprise to Paige. She looked at Marlon comforting his mother, making sure she was okay. Camille walked in, still confused by what was going on.

"Paige, what the hell is wrong with you?" he turned and asked.

"Ask her! I came in to help Myla get cleaned up and she went the hell off. I knew coming here was a bad idea."

"You damn right, it was!" Ms. Lucille replied once again, stepping closer to Paige.

"You know what? I'm outta here!" Paige rolled her eyes. "You really need to think about getting her some help, Marlon. But at this point, she needs twenty-four steps rather than twelve."

Without warning, the unthinkable happened. In a flash, the saliva spewed from Ms. Lucille's mouth and into Paige's face. Paige closed her eyes and prayed that when they opened, she would be waking from some horrible nightmare. But when she did open them, Ms. Lucille was standing in front of her with a sick grin, and Marlon was motionless. Paige tackled the woman with no regard. The two women screamed as they wrestled. Marlon grabbed Paige and pulled her off his mom, restraining her as he backed her away.

"Come on, tramp! I been waiting for this for a long time. I been wanting to kick your ass for years!" Ms.

Lucille screamed, rushing toward them. Marlon continued holding onto Paige and she had no way of defending herself from the blows coming her way.

"Let me go, Marlon! Get the fuck off me!" Paige screamed, struggling to get out of his grasp.

"Shit! Cam—Cam, get her—get her!"

Camille tried to grab her mother, but Lucille was too quick and landed blows to Paige's face. Thinking fast and unable to take anymore, Paige kicked Ms. Lucille in the stomach and she doubled over. Marlon released Paige and she reared back with all her might. Her hand formed a fist which connected with Ms. Lucille's nose. Blood began spewing everywhere and Camille began crying loudly.

"Mama! Oh God. Camille, get a towel, quick!" Marlon looked at Paige with a hatred that caused a chill to run up her spine.

Paige wasted no time. She grabbed her purse and ran, fleeing out the back of the house, past the crowd which had formed outside the door to see what the commotion was. She spotted Myla standing near the fence and she called for her.

"Mommy, can we please go now? I don't wanna be here anymore! It's not right!"

"Let's go then, sweetie. We're outta here."

Ignoring her ripped dress and aching feet, which still wore three-inch ivory sandals, she took Myla by the hand and they ran to Marlon's car. Paige reached into her purse and took out her keys, quickly unlocking the doors and screaming for Myla to get in.

It will be a cold day in hell before I ever step foot into that house again, she thought speeding off down the street without looking back.

1

"Mama, is Ms. Lucille crazy?" Myla asked as her mother tucked her in.

Paige thought about how pitiful it was that Myla had to call Marlon's mother Ms. Lucille rather than Grandma or anything remotely close. Granted, she referred to Paige's mother as Darling from the time she could talk, but that was a hell of a lot more affectionate than Ms. Lucille.

"I don't know, Myla. I really don't know." Paige kissed the top of her daughter's head. The battle lines between her and Ms. Lucille had been drawn a long time ago, and tonight, Marlon had chosen his team. "Go to sleep. We gotta get up early so I can take you to Darling's house."

"Goodnight, Mama."

Paige went into her bathroom, located in the master suite of the house. She turned on the hot water and began to undress. Glancing at her reflection in the mirror, she noticed the bruises which decorated her mahogany skin with shades of purple and red. She pulled her long hair into a bun at the top of her head, wanting to cut it now more than ever. Marlon refused to let her, often commenting about how he loved to run his fingers through it as he played with her thick tresses.

If my hair was short, that wicked wench wouldn't have had anything to grab on to.

She stepped into the shower and allowed the steaming water to massage her skin and ease the tension, which seemed to be embedded in her shoulders. She held her head down as the thoughts and images of Marlon and his mother swirled in her head.

He held me down as she beat on me. Was he really trying to help her or am I imagining he was? He asked her if she was okay and asked me what the hell was going on. He ran to her side when she was the one that attacked me.

Her anger was no longer toward Ms. Lucille, it was aimed straight at a new target—Marlon. By the time she got out of the shower and dressed for bed, she was livid. She cut off the lights and climbed into bed. Too mad to even think about sleeping, she began channel surfing.

"Paige," Marlon called her name as he walked into their bedroom. She glanced at the clock and was surprised that it was after midnight.

"What?" she answered, sitting up and folding her arms. He reached for the remote and muted the television.

"We need to talk about what happened."

"Your mother is a crazy alcoholic who attacked me. That's what happened." She knew Marlon hated to talk about his mother's drinking problem, but she had tiptoed around this issue long enough, and after what happened, she wasn't walking lightly anymore.

"Look, let's not even go there, okay? I want you to tell me your version of what happened."

"My version? Oh, I get it. She already gave you her version. I bet she told you I hit her first, huh? Or better yet, I grabbed her by the hair. Well, we know that can't happen because she wears a wig." Paige laughed sarcastically.

"Paige, please."

"Okay, Marlon. Here's what happened. I pushed her down and Myla held her while I slapped her in the face. Uh, no, that's what you did to me!" Paige's voice was loud and an octave higher than normal.

"I was trying to hold you back before an all-out fight broke-out and someone got hurt."

"I was already hurt! She had been pulling my hair and grabbing on me for ten minutes before your ass even came in the house. She spat in my face! And you were holding me back while she continued to whip my ass!"

"Stop yelling, Paige, before you wake Myla." Marlon began pacing the floor like an expectant father.

"Believe me, Myla's not 'sleep. She's lying in her bed right now wondering why the hell your crazy mama went off on me. Thank God she was outside while you were assisting your mother in kicking my behind or she really would be confused."

"I still can't believe this. You broke my mother's nose."

"Whoop-dee-damn-doo! What? Am I supposed to feel bad? I don't think so."

"You know she wasn't thinking right, Paige. She had been celebrating Camille's graduation."

"I thought about that when she first grabbed me. That's why I didn't fight back. I've been dealing with her bull for years, Marlon, and tonight it all came to a head."

9

The phone rang, interrupting them. He answered it and from the conversation, she knew it was his mother.

"Yeah, Ma. Yeah. Yeah. I know. You're right. Okay. You need anything? You take the medicine they gave you? I'll tell her. Now? All right, I'm on my way. See you in a minute."

Paige made a disgusted face as Marlon headed out the door. "Where are you going?"

"To get my mother. Camille is gone out and she doesn't need to be alone."

I don't believe this. She hopped out of bed, chasing down the steps behind him. "Wait a minute. Then you go over there and spend the night. Don't bring her to *my house!*"

Marlon stopped and turned toward her, "First of all, it's *our* house. Second, that's my mother and I don't give a damn how you feel about her. As long as I got breath in my body, wherever I lay my head, she can lay hers too. Now, you need to be ready to apologize for what happened by the time I get back."

Paige was speechless as he walked out the door. If she didn't know anything before, she knew now that there was no way she was going to apologize, nor was she going to be there when he and his mother got back.

Seven years. That's how much of her life she had given him. *Seven whole years.* That was 2,545 days, roughly eighty-four months, and enough time for the Discover Card she ran up while she was in college and never paid to fall off her credit report. Funny, it seemed like an entire lifetime.

After meeting at a basketball game, they had only been dating for a few weeks when Paige knew without a doubt she was in love. She gave him everything: her heart, her body, her soul and her virginity. Myla was the result of her generosity. Despite his mother's obvious disappointment in their relationship, Marlon stayed by her side and was there for her and Myla.

The first two years of their relationship had been pretty rocky. Marlon seemed to talk a good game, but he still wanted to go out and party, spending money on clothes and rims for his car. Paige waited it out, and her patience paid off. A month after Myla's second birthday, Marlon decided it was time for them to get a house and start building a serious future together. For the past five years, life with Marlon was rocky, but Paige stuck it out in an effort to hold their family together. Like all relationships, they had their issues, such as his refusal to even discuss marriage, and his mother's constant disrespect of her. But overall, things could be worse, and Paige told herself that they were happy.

She went back to school, got her master's degree and began working as a librarian, but after becoming pregnant with their second child, Marlon encouraged her to quit, so she did. Being a stay-at-home mom was okay, but she liked working and having her own money. Marlon was now the sole breadwinner, and she was wholly dependent on him, which she didn't like. He had all the control.

Their lives took a drastic turn the day she gave birth to their son. Paige went into labor at two-thirty in

11

the afternoon. She called her mother first, then her doctor, then Marlon. Everything was going according to plan. Her mother was on her way to pick Myla up from daycare, and Marlon was there within minutes to take her to the hospital. She was admitted into labor and delivery and they happily anticipated the arrival of their son. Paige's labor was a painful one, and Marlon stayed by her side. Her blood pressure became sky-high and suddenly, the baby's heartbeat stopped. The medical staff quickly rushed her to do an emergency caesarean, but it was too late. Her son was gone. It was the most painful experience Paige had ever endured. She went through nine months of pregnancy, six hours of labor, and had nothing to show for it.

Two days later, Paige, Marlon and Myla, along with her parents, a few close friends and Camille, had a graveside ceremony to bury Myles. Ms. Lucille never even acknowledged their loss. She called their home late that night demanding Marlon come and take her to the grocery store. Paige was too exhausted mentally, physically and emotionally to even protest as he rose out of their bed and left. It was at that moment that she began to feel numb. Instead of dealing with their grief, Paige and Marlon began to just coexist within their own lives.

Marlon began working even more. The times he wasn't traveling and was at home, things were so strained between them that they didn't even enjoy each other anymore. He would snap about the slightest little thing, and she found herself beginning to dislike him more and more. His mother constantly called, demanding for him to come to her house for any reason, and when she called, he went running.

Paige tried not to get frustrated, but it was beginning to take its toll on her. Fed up with the loneliness and emptiness that seemed to dwell in their house, she decided that she needed a change. Her mother's house was a welcome oasis as she drove into the night.

2

"So, you hit her?"

"Yes, Mama, I hit her. What was I supposed to do?" Paige asked her mother. They were sitting in the cozy living room of her mother's house and she was exhausted. The usually short hour-long drive seemed to have taken forever, especially since the events of the night before continued flashing in her head like someone had filmed them and kept pressing repeat.

"You could've walked away, Paige. You knew she was drunk. You should've turned the other cheek." Her mother shook her head.

Paige knew her mother was going to be critical of her reaction to Ms. Lucille. Whenever she even mentioned Ms. Lucille and her evil ways, her mother constantly told her to pray for her.

"Mama, she had me by the hair. I could barely move . . ."

"You didn't have to hit her so hard that you broke her nose, Paige. I hope you know you've only made things worse. You know how much Marlon loves his mama. What did he say when you left?"

"He wasn't home when I left. He was gone to get his mama."

"You didn't even tell him you were leaving? You'd better call him. I bet he's worried sick." Her mother got up and pointed to the phone.

"Ma, Marlon ain't stupid. He knew I was coming here tomorrow anyway. And he's not that worried. He didn't even call me on my cell phone to see if I was all right. He's too busy playing nurse maid to Ms. Lucille. Her head is probably about to bust right about now between the hangover from being drunk and the concussion I gave her." Paige couldn't help laughing.

"That's not funny." Her mother didn't even crack a smile. "I'm gone to bed. You'd better be thinking about how you're gonna straighten this out. And you got my poor grandbaby in the middle of all this mess." Paige's mother reached down and lifted Myla off the recliner where she had curled up and gone to sleep.

"I can get her, Ma."

"No, I got her. She can sleep in the bed with me."

"Well, goodnight."

"Goodnight." Paige sat in the living room and looked around. She pulled the crocheted blanket and curled under it. She inhaled scents of vanilla and fabric softener, leaning into the comfort of the sofa, drifting off to sleep.

The stream of sunlight coming through the curtains beamed across her face, waking her up. She looked around, confused, and then remembered she was home. She loved this house. It was the one she grew up in. Memories of dancing along with Salt & Peppa videos and arguing with her cousin that Ronni DeVoe was the finest member of New Edition caused her to smile. For a moment, she was so caught up in the nostalgia of her childhood years that she forgot about the chaos of Marlon and his mother. But the pain shooting up the side of her neck quickly brought her back to reality.

She slowly got up and walked into the bathroom. She was sore and didn't even want to look at her reflection in the mirror, but she forced herself. There was light bruising on her cheeks, and the marks which were previously pink-and-purple, were now black-and-blue.

"Mommy, are you in there?" Myla's voice called out.

"Yes, I'll be right out to make you some cereal."

"That's okay. Darling is making me some eggs and grits."

"Great, great," Paige said sarcastically. She washed her face and checked the rest of her body for bruises. The more marks she came across, the angrier she got. She wanted nothing more than to drive home and yank Ms. Lucille out of her house. She didn't try to stop the tears that were flowing down her face. She had been through so much over the past few months that she was drained emotionally.

"Mommy, breakfast's ready. Darling says come on."

Paige forced herself to get it together for her mother and daughter's sake. She washed her face and walked into the kitchen. Myla was sitting at the table, smearing what looked like an entire jar of jelly on a piece of toast.

"Good morning," she announced. "Myla, you know that's too much jelly."

"Leave that chil' alone. Good morning to you. Why did you sleep on that lumpy sofa when you got a big old bed back there in your room?"

"I fell asleep, Mama, that's all. And you know I love that sofa anyway. It's more comfortable than any bed around here," Paige answered sitting at the table and reaching for a piece of bacon.

"What time are you leaving, Mommy?" Myla asked.

Paige looked up at her mother, not knowing what to say. She didn't know when she was leaving. The ringing of the phone saved her from having to answer.

"Hello," her mother sang into the receiver. "I'm fine. Yes, she's here. Hold on."

Paige didn't even have to ask who was on the other end, knowing it was Marlon. She sat at the table, not moving. Still seething with anger, she didn't want to talk to him, especially if his mother was there.

"I don't wanna talk to him!" she told her mother.

Her mother looked at her like she was crazy, passing the phone to Myla.

"Hello." Myla spoke loudly. "Hi, Auntie Meeko! What are you doing? Where's Uncle Stan?"

Paige dropped her eyes into her plate, picking at her food. She listened to Myla chatting with her cousin. Meeko was the daughter of her mother's sister. She was the closest thing Paige had to a sister while growing up. Lord knows if Meeko had been at Ms. Lucille's house, things definitely would've turned out a lot different. Not only would Ms. Lucille have had a broken nose, Marlon would be the one all bruised up this morning.

"You want some coffee or some juice?" her mother asked.

"Juice," Paige answered, suddenly feeling fourteen.

"Auntie Meeko, Mommy had a fight with Ms. Lucille!"

"Girl, give me that phone." Paige snatched it. "Hello."

"Oh, hell naw! You put her back on the phone," Meeko demanded.

"I will not. What's up?"

17

"What do you mean what's up? What was she talking about? Did you have a fight with Ms. Lucille?"

"Meeko, please, it was nothing."

"Oh no, I don't even wanna hear this one over the phone. I'm on my way! Tell Aunt Jackie to save me some grits!"

Paige passed her mother the phone. "Hang it up."

Her mother took it out of her hand and stood up. "Let me put another pot of grits on the stove. I know Meeko is on her way."

Paige was unloading Myla's bags when the gold Mercedes CLK pulled into the yard, horn blaring. She closed the back of her Cherokee and shook her head. Meeko hopped out of the car and ran to her. She looked great. Marriage certainly seemed to agree with her. She looked great as usual, dressed in white capris and a multi-colored halter top. Her auburn-tinted hair was in its usual bob style, framing her face, and she still wore auburn, wire-rimmed glasses.

The more things change, the more they stay the same, Paige thought.

"Wow, you're glowing," Paige told her. "Are you pregnant?"

"Have you lost your mind? You must've forgotten who I was. Pregnant? Don't make me fall the hell out!"

"I'm saying. You are married now. You and Stan got that great big house and you aren't working anymore."

"I do work. I'm focusing on my music full-time now, that's all," Meeko replied matter of factly. Meeko had always dreamed of being a song writer. Paige had to admit that she was talented too. Meeko had written a couple of ballads for her best friend, Isis, who, in Paige's opinion, could've easily gotten a record deal.

Both women were now living the married life. Isis had snagged Tobias Sims, otherwise known as DJ Toby, one of the finest men around. Meeko had surprised everyone, including Paige, and married Stanley Winston. How her cousin, who was known for dating fly-guys and bad boys, wound up with a typical, run-of-the-mill nerd like Stanley was beyond Paige. But married they were, and he spoiled Meeko like she had never been spoiled before.

"Your husband still treating you like a goddess, huh?" She pointed to the diamond-and-platinum tennis bracelet glimmering in the sunlight.

"And I'm still treating him like a king, so shut-up." Meeko helped her with the bags. "Come on, now tell me what the hell happened yesterday."

"Lucille was drunk as usual, and she swung on me, so I swung back," Paige said.

"Good for you. It's about time you stood up to that old bat. I can't believe you waited this long to do it. I tell you this much, I woulda let her have it a long time ago, that's for sure. I know Marlon had a fit, huh?"

"Yeah, he was pretty pissed at me."

"At you? Tell me you're lying. You said she swung on you, right?"

"Yeah, but he said that since I knew she was drunk, I should've walked away. That's why I left and came here."

"Walk away, my ass. You did what you were supposed to do. I'm glad you left him. And I hope it's for good this time. I am sick of him and his mama," Meeko said.

"I am too," Paige said as they dragged the bags into what was now Myla's room. It was decorated in all shades of lavender, accented with mint green. Her mother had really outdone herself.

"Wow, your mama never decorated the room like this when it was yours." Meeko laughed.

"That's because she never woulda kept it clean," Paige's mother said, walking up behind them.

"Hey, Aunt Jackie. How are you?" Meeko walked over and gave her a big hug.

"I'm fine, Miss Meeko. It sure is funny the only time I get to see you is when Paige comes home."

"I know, Auntie. But I don't know your work-schedule, otherwise I would drop by more often."

"You need to stop lying, Michelle. You know I retired two years ago."

Paige looked at Meeko, who was suddenly engrossed in taking Myla's clothes out of one of the suitcases and putting them into the drawer. She knew her cousin was in hot water when her mother called her Michelle.

"But you work full-time at the church now, Aunt Jackie. Isn't that a job?"

"I'm surprised you even know that I'm working at the church. We ain't seen you there since the day you said *I do*."

Paige couldn't hold her laughter in any longer.

"What are you laughing at, Paige?" Meeko playfully shoved her cousin. "I can't help it if Stan and I are still honeymooning."

Soon, all three women were cracking up and it seemed like old times. Curious as to what was so funny, Myla came bursting in the room. "Aunt Meeko!"

"Hey there, Ms. Myla. Look at you, getting so big." Meeko twirled the little girl around. "And still beautiful like your Aunt Meeko."

"She looks just like her mother." Paige rolled her eyes.

"I look like my Darling." Myla ran over and hugged her grandmother. "Darling, can I go over and play next door?"

"You sure can, precious. Just don't cross that street, do you understand?" Paige's mom gave Myla a kiss on the forehead.

"I won't," Myla promised and skipped out the room.

"You know you played right into that, right?" Paige looked at her mother, still beaming as she walked over to the window.

"Played into what?" her mother asked defensively.

"You had already told her she couldn't go out until she unpacked her stuff."

"Well, Meeko already unpacked for her. I gotta go clean this kitchen. Meeko, if you want something to eat, you'd better come and get it now!"

Paige and Meeko looked at each other, both amazed at how lax her mother was when it came to Myla. When they were that age, they couldn't even think about going outside until the entire house was clean.

"You're a good one! There is no way I woulda just left. When he got back with her, I woulda been standing at the front door, waiting with a gun!" Meeko said between forkfuls of grits.

"Shut up, Meeko." Paige shook her head. "Granted, I *do* wanna kill her."

21

"See, that's the wrong attitude for you to be having. I keep telling you to pray for that woman. She got a whole lotta pain up inside her and she's just lashing out," Paige's mother said. Paige looked over at Meeko, both women thinking the same thing: That's crazy.

"Mama, my praying for her won't do any good."

"Nope, what she needs is an exorcist," Meeko added. "My friend Connie has a spiritual advisor who may be able to help. You want me to call her?"

"No, Meeko," Paige replied, staring at Meeko as she ate.

"The only spiritual advice we need is the one that's in that Bible over there."

"I'm just trying to help." Meeko shrugged.

Paige's cell phone began ringing. Taking her time, she walked into the living room and answered it.

"Hey," Marlon said.

"Hey."

"Are you at your mother's?"

"Yes."

"I figured that's where you were when we got back last night and you were gone," he said. She didn't respond and there was an awkward silence. "Where's Myla?"

"Outside playing."

"Oh. Well, when are you coming back home?"

"I don't know."

"So, you're going to stretch this thing out and throw a tantrum and run to your mother's instead of coming home?" He sighed.

"Throw a tantrum?" Paige couldn't believe he had the nerve to have an attitude.

"What's the point of your being up there, Paige? We're going to have to deal with this sooner or later."

"Deal with what? Your mother's alcohol abuse?"

"Don't go there. Everyone can't have a Bible-toting, scripture-quoting mother like yours, so don't judge mine."

"Have you lost your damn mind? Do you even realize what's really going on? Your mother has treated me like shit for years and you never had the backbone to say anything to her about it. Yesterday, you held me down while she beat me up. You questioned what I did to her. You've chosen your mother over me for years and I allowed it to happen. You've taken money out of our account and given it to her. There were times you paid her bills before you even paid ours. You think I don't know about it? I know, Marlon. I just never said anything. The times we had to cancel plans because she was passed out somewhere and you had to go get her. You're leaving out in the middle of the night to go rescue her. You're there for her more than you are there for me. Not anymore. I refuse to deal with it anymore. And now, you wanna criticize my mother for being the kind, gentle-hearted person that she is? You can go to hell, Marlon."

"That's not what I meant, Paige. Come on, don't start tripping. I know you and my mother don't see eye-to-eye . . ."

"Don't see eye-to-eye?" Paige laughed. "Your mother is blind. But this really has nothing to do with your mother, Marlon. I'm tired. I'm tired of playing house. I'm tired of pretending like everything's fine between us when it isn't."

"Things are fine between us, Paige. Look, just come home so we can talk about this. No, I'll come there and get you."

"No, Marlon. Maybe we need some time apart. Some time for you to spend with your mother and to think if being with me and Myla is what you really want."

"Are you saying it's over? You don't love me?" His voice cracked.

"Yes, Marlon, I love you. But I can't keep living like this. It's just too much. I'm tired and I need a break to think about things."

"Paige, baby, just tell me what you want."

"I want you to marry me! I want to be your wife! Can you do that, Marlon? Can you give me that?"

Marlon took a deep breath and she waited for his response. His head dropped and he replied, "You know I love you with all my heart, Paige."

"Are you gonna marry me?"

"No."

"So how long were you gonna string me along?"

"I'm not stringing you along, Paige. I gave you everything you ever wanted. We have a good life together. We have a nice house, cars, we vacation, the ring you're wearing right now on your right hand is worth more than any wedding ring. What more could you ask for? Can a piece of paper make me love you any more or do anything more for you?"

"So, let me get this straight. I'm good enough for you to lay up with or better yet, shack up with. I'm good enough to bear your children. I'm even good enough for you to buy a house with, even build a future with. But I'm not good enough for you to

24

marry." Paige laughed sarcastically. "Why not, Marlon?"

"Because I'm not ready to make you my wife, Paige. You know that. Not right now, anyway. I mean, things may change in the future. My mother . . . she . . . just not right now. It's not time yet, Paige. And if you think giving me an ultimatum is going to change that, think again."

"I'll talk to you later, Marlon." She clicked the phone off, wondering what she had just done. It was as if someone else had jumped into her body and actually said the words that she had been wanting to say for months. She was tired, and it was time for her to get it together. Hopefully, Marlon would take her advice and do the same.

3

One month later, Paige was having lunch with Nina Seymone Taylor, her best friend since first grade. There wasn't anything Paige wouldn't do for her and she knew that Nina felt the same way. Next to Meeko, Nina was the closest thing she had to a sister.

"I think you're right about taking some time, Paige. You've been through a lot and maybe what you and Marlon need is to be apart for a while. Maybe with your being gone, he'll realize how much you mean to him," Nina told her. "You'll see how much you mean to each other."

"You sound like you want us to be together," Paige replied.

"I want whatever makes you happy. I know how much Marlon means to you. How much your being a family means to you. That's why you've put up with him and his crap for so long. His mother, especially. I don't know how anyone can deal with that mess. But you do, so that shows how much you love him."

Paige thought about what her best friend was saying. She did love Marlon, but she was finally beginning to realize that there was something missing in their relationship. "I don't know, Nina. I don't know what I feel right about now. Marlon is calling and begging me to come home. I know I'm not ready to go back yet, though."

"Then don't go. Don't let him pressure you into going, either, Paige. Stay here for a while. I've missed you. Besides, didn't you say you've already started looking for a job?"

"I put in an application at the city for a librarian position they have opened at the downtown branch. I haven't heard anything yet, though."

"The downtown branch? Boring. No one ever comes in there."

"It's a library, Nina, not the club."

"Speaking of club . . ."

Paige giggled, picking through her chicken salad. She really hadn't had much of an appetite these days.

"Okay, but I was thinking maybe we could hang out at Jasper's tonight. I heard it was nice on Thursdays."

"A club? Come on, you know I don't do clubs, Nina."

"It's not really a club. It's more like a restaurant, but with a dance floor. Paige, you've been home for weeks now and we haven't hung out. It'll be fun." Nina tilted her head and waited for Paige to say yes.

"I'll have to see if Mama will . . ."

"She already said she would keep Myla and Jade. I'll pick you up at seven-thirty."

Paige saw the excitement in Nina's eyes and didn't want to disappoint her. It had been a while since they had hung out and had fun. Paige had been withdrawn since she lost the baby and her relationship with Marlon became stressed. She thought about the days when they would get all dressed up and party. She ran her hand along her hair, which was pulled into a ponytail.

"But my hair's not done. And I don't even think I have anything to wear."

"Please, you know you got that Indian stuff. Blow it straight and call it a day. We can swing by the mall and get you something cute."

"Uh, hello. I don't have a job, remember?"

"But I have a credit card. Hurry up and eat, we've got a lot to do," Nina squealed. She reached into her purse and pulled out her phone. "Meeko, Paige and I are coming. Leave our names at the door."

After an hour of blow drying, Paige didn't know what made her angrier: Nina, for talking her into straightening her hair or herself for listening. Her arms were beginning to ache and her hair was still damp.

"Mom, Miss Nina's here!" Myla yelled.

Aw hell, Paige thought. She looked at her watch and saw that it was indeed quarter to eight. She wasn't anywhere near being ready.

"Paige! Let's go, come on," Nina called out to her.

Paige stuck her head out the door and saw that her best friend was posed in the hallway mirror, looking stunning in ivory pants, a lavender shirt which hugged her thick body, and lavender stilettos. Nina was a size sixteen and proud. She had never made an attempt to be a skinny girl, saying she liked to eat. Her chin-length hair was crimped and her makeup was perfect. Paige was jealous. In a matter of three hours, Nina had transformed from drab to fab, and Paige still looked a hot mess.

"I'm not going," she whined.

"What?" Nina's heels clicked on the floor as she rushed toward the bathroom door.

"I can't get my hair right and I'm not even dressed."

"Move out of the way, Paige. Jeez, sit down and let me help. Why are you hanging on to all this hair if you don't know what to do with it?"

"I don't know. Marlon always threatened that if I cut it, he would leave." Paige laughed, then flinched as Nina pulled her hair to the top of her head.

"Well, you left him, so we can go ahead and chop it," Nina commented.

"I didn't leave him. We're taking a break."

"Whatever you say." Nina twisted and twirled her hair, reaching for hairpins, the brush, comb and gel, all at the same time. In a matter of minutes, she stood back and announced, "Voila!"

"You're done?"

"Yes, now come on and get dressed. Let's go."

Paige stood up and looked in the mirror, amazed at what Nina had done. "Wow, Nina, I look so nice. Thank you."

"Shut up. You know you slow-poked and fumbled with your hair, hoping I would show up and do it. You've been pulling that trick for years, Paige. Go put your damn clothes on."

"Ohhhh, Ms. Nina, you said a bad word," Myla sang.

"Say sorry." Jade joined her.

"Sorry, girls. But I'm going to say something worse if she doesn't hurry up."

"I'm going, I'm going." Paige rushed into her room and pulled on the black slacks and sleeveless wrap-shirt they had found at the mall earlier. She put on some mascara and eyeliner, dabbed some gloss on her lips and after adding her silver accessories, she was ready. They said goodbye to the girls and her mother

29

and for the first time in a long time, Paige set out for a night on the town.

"I need to stop at the ATM," Paige announced over Jaheim singing over the radio. "They have one inside the convenience store."

"I got money, girl," Nina told her.

"Just stop. I wanna get some mints too."

"Yeah, we don't need for you to have stank-breath." Nina laughed, pulling into the parking lot of the small store. They got out the car and walked in. The store was fairly empty with the exception of a middle-aged woman buying a lottery ticket and a tall, handsome man who Paige noticed checking her out. He smiled at her and she smiled back as she walked past him down the aisle.

"My man, can I use your restroom?" the guy asked the clerk.

"In the back, down the hall and to the left," the clerk told him. Paige couldn't help watching him as he walked to the back of the store.

"Looks like someone's caught your eye," Nina teased. "I don't blame you. He's fine."

"Girl, please. I don't think so." Paige walked to the side of the store where the ATM was located and inserted her card. She got forty dollars out and looked at the receipt. *I gotta get a job*, she thought as she looked at her available balance. Her savings was depleting fast. She folded the small piece of paper and placed it inside her pockets along with her card and the money. The lottery woman was gone. She spotted Nina looking at magazines in the corner of the store.

"Now this haircut would look so good . . ."

"Give me the fuckin' money—NOW!"

They turned to see two masked men standing in front of the register, aiming guns at the man behind the counter. Paige could feel her heart pounding and stood frozen, not knowing what to do. Her eyes remained on the robbers, who were both screaming for the man to open the register. The store clerk began fumbling with the drawer.

"Don't fuck with me! Hurry up and give me the money!" The sound of the gun blasted, causing both Paige and Nina to scream. The men turned and looked at them, and fear gripped her.

"I thought you said wasn't nobody in here!" The spokesman yelled to his partner.

"I ain't see them!"

"Shit!" He seemed nervous that they were there. "Get the fuck down! I ain't playin'!"

"And stay down, too!"

The women hit the floor without having to be told twice. The gun blasted again, and a screech escaped Paige's mouth. She squeezed her eyes shut and began to pray. *God, please help me. I don't want to die. Please don't let them kill me. Help us.* Gunshots continued to ring out.

"Let's go! Let's go!" She heard someone yell. She kept her eyes closed, afraid that if she opened them, she would be facing the barrel of a gun. She could hear a lot of commotion, but she remained on the floor, too scared to move. There were voices: men talking and shouting orders. Someone was pulling her up, and she screamed.

"It's okay. Open your eyes."

"Are they gone?" She looked up and found herself face-to-face with the darkest, most intriguing eyes she

31

had ever seen. It was the guy that had gone into the restroom.

He smiled at her and gave her a look of assurance. "Yeah, they're gone. I called the police and they're on their way. Come on, I'm gonna help you out of here."

She could feel his arms around her as she was lifted off the floor. Her eyes finally opened and she looked over at Nina, who was already standing. She was safe and more importantly, she was alive.

"Let's go," the deep voice told her. Paige leaned into him as he led them out of the store. She couldn't help glancing over at the counter where the clerk had been standing. She was relieved when she didn't see a dead body. Hopefully, the man was still living. When they got outside the store, he was there, nervously smoking a cigarette.

A few minutes later, the parking lot was full of police cars. As she gave her statement of what happened, Paige began to cry. *I could have died. My life could have been taken and Myla would have no mother.* She cried tears of joy, sadness and anger all at the same time. It was as if everywhere she turned, another wall was crumbling, and there was nothing she could do.

"The good thing is no one was hurt, ma'am. You're all safe," the officer tried to comfort her.

"Wh—where's my girlfriend?" she asked.

"She's right over there. Are you sure you're okay?"

Paige nodded and looked around the chaos of the parking lot, wondering what happened to the man who helped her. He was gone.

4

It had been two weeks since the robbery. The police didn't have any leads or suspects, but they assured her they would keep her informed if anything changed. She knew the chances of that happening were slim-to-none.

"Paige, I want you to come home." Marlon ran his fingers through her hair. They were in her room and her mother had taken Myla to the park. Over the past few weeks, he had been coming to visit often. He was attentive and they had been talking more than they had in years. Their relationship seemed to be mending.

"I know you do, Marlon. You tell me that every five minutes."

He sat up and looked her in the eye. "Then come home. I've been thinking about this, Paige, and I want us to try and have another baby."

She was shocked. It was the first time he had mentioned a baby in months. The subject had been avoided since their son's death. Somehow, she believed Marlon blamed her, but never said anything.

"I don't think I'm ready for that."

"That's okay, I understand. How about this? We can go on a vacation. Anywhere you want to go. I want us to be like we used to. Remember the plans we made to go on the cruise? We never went, Paige. We can go now." He ran his hand along her cheek. She looked at him and smiled. It was like he was the old Marlon, they were in college and time had never passed.

33

"Marlon, I hear what you're saying, and I promise, I'm thinking about it."

"I almost lost you. You could've been killed. I don't ever wanna feel that way again. I love you." He kissed her tenderly. She loved the feel of his lips on hers, soft and full. His kiss was one of the reasons she fell in love with him.

"I just need a little more time, Marlon. I love you too. Camille called me this morning. She sounds good."

Marlon's sister decided to spend the summer with her girlfriend in Myrtle Beach. Paige knew that she didn't need much of an excuse to get away from her mother, and Paige didn't blame her. Camille often mentioned that after she finished high school, she would be on the first thing smoking out of town. Paige admired her decision.

"Yeah, I talked to her earlier. She acts like she's not even coming home before she leaves for school. Mama's lonely without her." At the mention of his mother, Paige stiffened. Marlon looked at his watch. "Look, I have a meeting in the morning, so I need to hit the road."

Paige nodded. "Call me when you get home."

"I will, I promise. I love you."

"I love you too."

Lying back in her bed, she thought about going home. Maybe this would be the opportunity for her and Marlon to rebuild their relationship. *I could use a vacation, too, after all this I've been through.*

The doorbell rang and she went to open it.

"Daddy?"

"Hey, baby girl. How ya doing?" Her father smiled. Although she had spoken to her father over the phone, she hadn't seen him since she had been home. With the exception of a few more gray strands in his wavy hair, he was still the handsomest man she had ever seen.

"I'm fine, Daddy. Come on in." She held the door open and he walked inside. She hugged him and they sat across from each other on the sofa. "You look good, Dad."

"You do too. I know I should've called before coming, but I wanted to check on you. I hope it's not a problem." His eyes glanced toward the back of the house.

"It's okay, Dad. You know you're always welcome here when I'm home. How've you been?" Paige had always had a good relationship with her father. Her parents had split up when she was an infant, but he played a significant role in her life growing up. He had always been there for her. Even still, Paige wished her parents had stayed together and that was partly the reason that Paige worked so hard at staying with Marlon. She wanted Myla to have both a mother and a father in the house.

"I've been doing all right. Working hard, that's about it. Where's Ms. Myla?"

"She went to the park with Mama. They should be back in a little while."

"Is Marlon here visiting too?"

She looked at her father and shook her head. "No, he's back at home."

"You finally wised up and left that joker?" Her dad grinned at her. Although her dad was accepting of

35

Marlon, he often commented on him not being good enough for her.

"No, Myla and I just came to spend some time with Mama, that's all. I'll be leaving soon."

"I'm telling you, Paige, life is too short to be wasting it on someone that don't have your best interests at heart. How long you and him been together? You know my motto. If you been with him for five years and he ain't gave you no ring, he ain't giving you one."

"That's not true, Daddy. Marlon has given me plenty of rings." She pointed at the jewelry she wore on her fingers.

"That's not what I'm talking about and you know it. Has he given you a ring to show his intentions?"

"He bought me a house to show his intentions, Daddy. Isn't that enough?"

"No, it ain't enough. Paige, I know you're smarter than that. If a man . . ."

Her father was interrupted by the sound of the door opening. Myla came running in with her grandmother behind her. She stopped when she saw her grandfather sitting with her mother.

"PawPaw?"

"Hey there, sweetness, come give me a hug." He stood up and lifted Myla into his arms. His attention went to her mother. "Jackie, how've you been?"

"Fine, Wendell. Just fine," Jackie said.

"Is Daddy gone?" Myla asked.

"Yep, he left a little while ago," Paige answered.

"Guess what? Darling says I can go to Bible school next week. Isn't that good?" Before anyone could answer, she hopped out of her grandfather's arms and was headed out the living room saying, "I'm gonna call Jade and ask her if she wants to come with me."

"Well, I guess I should be going. I'm just glad to see that you're okay. And don't forget what I told you about that joker. Five years is enough time for any man to decide."

"Decide what?" Her mother raised her eyebrows. Paige tried to rush her father out the door before her parents got into one of their debates.

"To decide if he wants to keep the car he just paid off or trade it in and get a new one." Her dad winked at her.

Her mother was not fooled. "If it's already paid off and working fine, why should he get another car note? That's stupid."

"He may need to get something with a warranty that runs a little better." He folded his arms and remained in front of the door.

"Runs better, huh? Don't you mean looks better?"

Paige looked from one parent to the other, enjoying the conversation. Both of her parents were so headstrong, she knew neither one would be outdone. It had been like this her entire life.

Jacqueline and Wendell Michaels had been married for a year before Paige was born. Her father was a hardworking man who took good care of his family and was determined to make them happy. He did require at least one night a week to relax, and on Fridays, he would occasionally stop at the local bar and have a drink or two. Her mother never had a problem with that. As long as he never spent up his paycheck or came home drunk, she was fine.

The problem she did have erupted when one Friday night she received a call from a friend who told her to get down to the Groove Shack because Wendell was there hugged up in the corner with a woman named Lovey Brown. Jackie thanked her friend, called a neighbor to watch two-month-old Paige, rode down to the club and peeked in. She didn't make a scene, and Wendell didn't even know he had been seen dancing with the woman. He got home that night to find his wife and daughter gone, and all the fly collars cut off his shirts and suits.

They never divorced, and they never reconciled. Wendell continued to take care of them. Jackie never dated another man, and Paige had never seen her father with another woman. He always said Jackie was his one true love and if he couldn't be with her, he'd rather be alone. Jackie said he was full of it.

"Ain't nobody said nothing about looks, Jackie. I'm talking about security and knowing that if something breaks down, you got coverage."

"So, you admit, even new cars break down, huh, Wendell? Even the finest ones out there?" Her mother smirked.

"Jackie, you're crazy, you know that? But what can I say, huh? Your mother had a Mercedes, but she wanted to walk instead, so cars don't hold no value to her anyway." Wendell opened the door. Before Jackie could respond he added, "You ladies be blessed and have a nice night."

He hustled out the door, leaving both of them to think about what he just said.

"Your daddy got issues, Paige, and I wanna apologize for making him your daddy," her mother teased.

"Mama, you need to stop. Y'all both got issues. You need to stop fronting like you're not still in love with him. I know you are."

"No, I'm not. I love him, but that's about it. That man is crazy. I hope you're not taking any relationship *or* car advice from him."

"You know Daddy has to put his two cents in just like you do."

"Paige, listen to me. I love you more than I love myself. And I hate to say it, but there is something your father is right about. You need to decide if being with Marlon is what you really want. I know you love him and he loves you, but is that enough? Is living with him enough or do you want more? Don't you think you deserve more? I can't tell you how to live your life, but you need to be happy."

Paige looked at her mother. "I'm not moving home, Mama."

"Honey, that's not what I'm talking about. You know that you can stay here for the rest of your life. I just want you to look at the big picture. For years, you and Marlon have been playing house. This past year has been rough on all of us with everything that's gone on, not just you two. You all need to consider your daughter in all of this."

"We do consider her, Mama. That's why we're trying to work things out." Paige sat down, not really wanting to have this conversation. Unlike her father, her mother usually didn't comment on her love life. Each time Paige had come home because she and

Marlon needed a break, she was always welcomed with open arms.

"But what are you working on?"

Paige didn't have an answer to that question. Myla walked into the living room and sat next to her, laying her head in Paige's lap. Paige began stroking her daughter's hair, thinking about what her mother told her. If Marlon wanted her to come home, then some change needed to be made, starting with his dealing with his mother.

5

Paige pulled up to the mailbox, getting the mail out before she pulled into the driveway. The box was full of letters and advertisings, letting her know that Marlon hadn't checked it in several days. She fumbled with the keys, letting herself into the home she had been missing. Walking in the door, she glanced around, surprised at how clean it was. Marlon wasn't all that neat, but he had obviously been doing a good job since she had been gone. Everything was in place. Even the den was straight, and it was usually the junkiest room in the house. She went upstairs and entered their bedroom. She smiled when she saw that only Marlon's side of the bed was rumpled. The other was still tucked as if it had never been slept in. Her side. She sat down and took a deep breath. Her side of the dresser was still empty, it was as if he was waiting for her to come home. She flipped through the pile she was still holding, noticing a pink envelope.

Don't go looking for nothing. You might just find it, her mother's voice warned. But she ignored her, and smelling the strong scent of perfume coming from the envelope, she snatched it open. Her heart began racing as she read the chicken-scratch handwriting which was inside.

Dear Mookie,
Just a note to let you know how much I enjoyed
our weekend together. It was so much fun

spending time with you and Lucille. She is wonderful. I hope we'll be able to have more good times like that now that you're spending more time at home. We all flow together just like we were meant to be. See you when you get here.

Love,
K

That bastard, was the only thing Paige could think. Her instincts kicked in full blast, and she continued looking through the mail. Marlon's cell bill was among the envelopes she had already laid on the bed. She picked it up and ripped it open. Her eyes quickly scanned the telephone numbers, recognizing her cell phone and mother's home number several times, in addition to his office and other familiar numbers. But something else soon caught her eye as she looked further and turned to the dates of the previous weeks. There was another frequently dialed number that she didn't know.

She hopped off the bed and entered the walk-in closet that held the filing cabinet, which housed their old bills and receipts. She found the bills from the previous months, and found the unfamiliar number once again. Not as frequent as on the current bill, but there nonetheless. The fact that she didn't know whose number it was didn't bother her. It was the times that the calls were made or received. There were several calls received at two and three in the morning, when she was asleep in the bed next to him.

In a moment that seemed to add fuel to the already brewing fire in her chest, the phone rang, startling her.

She looked at the caller ID and saw that it was the same number that she had noticed on his bill. In a moment's hesitation, she convinced herself that it was still her house and she had every right to answer the phone.

She picked up the phone after the second ring, not speaking at first.

"Marlon, baby. Are you there?" the female voice on the other end told her.

"Who is this?" Paige demanded.

"Uh, I—I think I dialed the wrong number," the woman answered.

"No, you didn't dial the wrong number. And don't play games with me because I'm not the one. Now, again, who is this?"

"I'm not playing games with you. I was trying to reach someone else."

"Who were you trying to reach?"

"Marlon Taylor."

"He's not here. Who's calling?" There was silence on the line. "Who the hell is calling?"

"Kasey," the voice on the other end finally answered, after inhaling so loud Paige could hear it.

"Who?" Paige asked. She wanted to make sure she wasn't hearing the name wrong. There was no way in hell that she could've said Kasey. If she did, it had to be another Kasey, and not the same one Paige was thinking of.

"Kasey, Paige. It's Kasey Towsend."

Kasey Towsend, the tramp from across the street. Paige knew Kasey had a thing for Marlon from the moment they moved in. She had even gone so far as to come over and welcome *Marlon* with a plate of

43

homemade cookies one day within minutes of Paige leaving the house. It was *Marlon* that Kasey spoke to when they both got out of the car and she happened to be outside. It was *Marlon* that she called when her porch light needed changing or her garage door wouldn't open. Being the typical man that we was, Marlon told Paige she was being paranoid and he thought Kasey was just needy. Paige saw right through her and tried to warn him about the funny, horse-looking girl with big lips and grey eyes—obviously, his dumb ass didn't listen.

"So, you're still after Marlon, huh?" Paige sighed.

"I don't know what you're talking about, Paige. I'm calling Marlon regarding a business matter."

"Is that also what he and you've been talking about at two and three o'clock in the morning?"

"I don't have to explain to you what Marlon and I talk about."

"You do have to explain what the hell you were doing spending the weekend with him."

"I don't know what you're talking about." Kasey giggled.

She thinks this shit is funny.

"I got your little card." Paige forced herself to remain calm. She knew Kasey was only trying to push her buttons and piss her off. "You couldn't wait until I left so you could have your ass all in his face, could you?"

"You're crazy. Look, I called for Marlon, he's not there. I'll try to reach him at his office. Oh, and Paige, I think I left my earring the other day. Can you check and see if it's there? Bye-bye."

The sound of the dial tone let Paige know that Kasey had hung up before she could cuss her out. She stood up and screamed, accidentally dropping the phone. She leaned over to pick it up and throw it across the room, but something caught her eye. There in the carpet lay a shiny object. She reached and plucked it out, her heart pounding as her fingers clamped around the gaudy, obviously fake gold earring. For some strange reason, she smiled. She didn't understand why. Maybe it was because she always thought that if she one day caught Marlon cheating, it would devastate her. She wasn't devastated, she was mad as hell, and for the first time in her life, she knew exactly how her mother felt when she saw her dad with Lovey Brown that fateful night.

"So, when do you think you'll be able to start?" the perky, blonde woman asked.

"Immediately." Paige smiled as she answered. With everything else she had going on in her life, she had almost forgotten she had even applied for the position at the downtown library. She wanted to tell the personnel director that she couldn't interview this morning, but she knew that she needed to get a job as soon as possible, now that leaving Marlon was definite.

"Then I guess I'll see you Monday morning."

"Thanks a lot, Ellen. I look forward to it."

Paige walked out of the building and tried to be happy about her new job. But her anger at Marlon dampened her spirits, which made her even angrier at herself for allowing him to make her feel this way. She had yet to confront him with her revelation the day before.

I should be on cloud nine, ready to celebrate the fact that I just got a great job with a full benefit package and instead, here I am thinking about his cheatin' ass and how I'm going to let him know that I know. She walked over to her black Pathfinder and climbed in. She saw Meeko had called her on her cell and dialed her number.

"Well? Did you get the job?" her cousin asked.

"Nope."

"Stop lying, you trick. When do you start?"

"What makes you think that I'm lying, Meeko?"

"Not only are you probably the only person that applied for that boring-ass job, but you have a degree, you're black and you're a woman. I know for a fact you got the job unless you went into that interview and did something utterly stupid." Meeko sighed. "Now, when do you start?"

"I start on Monday, Ms. Know-it-All." Paige smiled, glad that her cousin called to distract her thoughts.

"Then this weekend, we must celebrate. Don't make any plans for Saturday."

"What are you talking about?"

"Just leave Saturday open. And tell Nina too. I'll even spring for the babysitter."

"And just how much will you be paying, Mama?" The two women laughed, and by the time Paige turned onto her mother's street, she felt a heck of a lot better, until she saw Marlon's car in the driveway. Anger consumed her as she parked and got out. As she slowly began walking toward the house, praying every step of the way, the front door opened and Myla came running toward her.

"Mommy, Daddy came to take us to dinner. He said we can go to Jillian's and I can play the boxing game!"

Paige looked at her daughter, hating to disappoint her. "I don't think so, sweetheart."

The joy on her daughter's face slowly faded and Myla frowned. "Why not? We've been waiting for you to come home all day."

"Myla, I've only been gone a few hours, so that's not true. I'll take you to Chuck E. Cheese this weekend."

"I don't wanna go to Chuck E. Cheese. I wanna go to Jillian's. And I want Daddy to go!" Myla raised her voice, causing Paige to raise her eyebrows.

"Myla, you better watch who you're talking to! I'm not having this conversation with you. You go to your room and stay there until you lose that attitude," Paige commanded.

Myla huffed and stormed past her mother into the house. Paige entered behind her to find her mother and Marlon sitting in the living room, talking. He was wearing the yellow Polo shirt she had given him two years ago, jeans and his Timbs. His hair had just been cut, and he looked damn near perfect. She tried to fight the urge to kiss his clean-shaven face.

"What's the matter with her?" Marlon asked.

"She doesn't like being punished, as usual. What are you doing here?" She rolled her eyes at him, deciding not to mask her attitude.

"Paige, I'll take Myla out for a while so you and Marlon can talk." Jackie touched her on the shoulder.

47

Her mother had been very disappointed in Marlon when Paige told her about his apparent affair with Kasey, but Paige knew she wasn't going to say anything to him. "Did everything go okay at your interview?"

"Everything went fine. I start on Monday."

"Interview? Job? When did all this happen?" Marlon questioned her.

"I got a job at the downtown branch, not that it's any of your business."

"What? For the summer?" He stood up.

"We'll be back in a little while." Her mother excused herself.

"No, it's a permanent position." Paige slipped her feet out of the baby-blue mules, that matched her rayon blouse perfectly.

Marlon began walking back and forth. "Paige, what in the world would possess you to take a permanent position knowing you're coming home in a few days."

She laughed. "You're funny, you know that."

"What are you talking about?"

"I am home. But I guess you're talking about the house where you live. I'm not coming back there."

Marlon's face now wore the same look of disappointment that Myla's wore a few minutes earlier. "Paige, we decided that you were coming home and we were gonna spend some alone time."

"Well, I thought about that, and then I began to feel bad."

"Feel bad about what?"

"Well, I didn't want to stop you from spending time with that bitch Kasey, since she's spending so much time with you at home."

"Paige, don't be ridiculous. Kasey told me about what happened. That card from her meant nothing. You know she's just a needy woman, a worry-wart who—"

"Don't do this to me, Marlon. Please don't. I have put up with a lot of things from you over the years—you putting everything in front of me and Myla, including your job and your mother, your inability to commit to me, your constantly leaving crumbs all over the kitchen when you make any type of meal. But I won't put up with your lying to my face," Paige walked over and looked him in the eye. "You've never lied to me. It's the one reason I have a teeny bit of respect left for you."

"Paige, I . . ."

"It's over, Marlon. It's been over for a while now. The card was just the last nail in the coffin, the straw that broke the camel's back, the end of it all, thank God. It's over, and time to move the hell on," she told him. As the words came out of her mouth, she realized just how true they were. No matter how much she loved him, it just wasn't going to work. She was tired of forcing it.

"Don't be stupid, Paige. I love you."

She reached into the pocket of her skirt. "If you loved me, Marlon, that bitch's earring wouldn't have been under *our* bed." She threw the cheap metal at him and he looked down at it as it hit the floor. Paige reached out and pulled at his shirt. "Come on, don't play me like I'm some weak chicken-head who believes everything you say. At least have more respect for me than that."

There was silence, and they just stared at each other. After a few moments, he finally spoke. "You want to throw all that we've built over the years away over a bunch of bullshit? You need to have more respect for yourself than that. Damn, Paige, I know our relationship hasn't been perfect, but it was good. Look at all we've done. We're good for each other. You don't want for shit!"

"I do want! That's the problem. What I want, you can't give me.

She could no longer tolerate his presence. "I need for you to leave. Now! Just get out."

Marlon looked as if he wanted to say something else, but he was smart enough to walk out the door without saying a word. Paige went into her bedroom and changed clothes. She sat on the side of the bed for what seemed like hours, not moving. She heard the front door open, and soon Myla came walking into her room.

"Mommy, are you still mad at me?"

"No, sweetheart."

"Then why are you crying?"

Paige didn't even realize the tears were present until her daughter pointed them out. She looked down and saw that some had fallen, leaving wet spots on her shirt. "Because I am happy that I got my new job, that's all."

"I'm happy too, Mom."

"Go on and get ready for bed. I'll be in there in few minutes to tuck you in." Myla scurried out of the room. Paige looked up to see her mother standing in the doorway.

"You okay, Paige?"

"Yeah, Ma. Just a little hurt, that's all."

"Believe it or not, that's a good thing."

"How so?"

"The hurt now leads to the healing later."

Paige prayed that her mother was right, because she felt as if Marlon had just stabbed her, ran over her with a Mack truck and left her for dead all at the same time.

6

Partying was not a mood Paige found herself in when Saturday arrived. She tried everything under the sun to get out of going with Meeko, but she wasn't hearing it. Nina picked her up and they arrived at the mansion which Meeko called a house. They rang the doorbell and she came to the door, wearing a black kimono robe and holding a glass of wine.

This chick is taking being the woman of the house a little too far.

"It's about time you both got here. We've been waiting for our guest of honor," Meeko greeted them.

"And who is that?" Paige asked, following her inside the massive home. She admired the marble floors in the foyer and the cathedral ceiling.

"You, crazy girl. Come on. Everyone else is back here." They continued through the house until they arrived in the large family room. Paige was surprised to see Isis, Meeko's best friend, Anjelica, a pretty girl who had been a bridesmaid in Meeko's wedding and Celeste, their very distant cousin by marriage, all sitting around chatting.

"Hey there, Paige." Isis gave her a big hug. Paige always thought she was the most beautiful girl she had ever seen in her life. She was half black, half Asian with skin so flawless that she looked like she stepped out of the pages of a Cover Girl ad.

"Hey, Isis, I am so happy to see you. You're looking beautiful as always," Paige told her.

"Doesn't she? I keep telling her she should quit that spa and model full-time." Anjelica laughed. "How've you been, Paige? I heard about you and Nina's encounter at the corner mart. I'm glad you weren't hurt."

"Thanks. That's the last time I listen to Nina and Meeko when they convince me to go out, though, you know that."

"Oh, please. None of that was my fault. Don't even try it. Besides, I'm making it up today by throwing you this little soiree," Meeko announced.

"Oh really? And what is up with that swanky robe you got on? This soiree isn't good enough for you to put on clothes?" Nina asked.

"Where is Stanley at?" Isis asked.

"He and Shawn went to some golf tournament, or so she says." Anjelica shook her head.

"He is. Ladies, ladies, the afternoon is still young. I have a lot in store for all of us. But first, we must toast the occasion. Would you like mimosas or wine?" Meeko walked over to the bar located on the far side of the room.

"Mimosa for me," Nina answered.

"Same here." Paige shrugged. All eyes were on Meeko as she poured champagne into the crystal flutes then added orange juice.

"And what's the occasion again?" Celeste finally spoke. She had been sitting so quietly, that Paige almost forgot she was in the room. Her cousin was known for being anti-social, and Paige was actually surprised that Meeko had even invited her to this small gathering.

"This is a celebration of all sorts for Paige—her new job, her return home and her new life." Meeko handed a glass to Paige and Nina. She got her own and raised it. "To a new beginning."

"Here, here," Nina, Isis and Anjelica all said. "You go, girl."

"You're moving back home. What about Marlon?" Celeste's eyes lit up.

"Marlon and I are no longer. I got a job at the library downtown and I'm moving back here," Paige told her.

"Wow, Mr. Perfect must've really messed up for you to leave him after all this time." Celeste smirked.

Paige looked at her and decided not to respond to her comment. There really was no need, since all in all, Celeste's life was pathetic in itself. She was older than Paige but younger than Meeko. All of their lives, she had been the odd girl out, not wanting to hang out when they invited her, and complaining when they did things without her. While they went to college and finished, Celeste dropped out mid-year, saying that it was too hard and she just wanted to work. It took her two years to find the part-time job as an office aide for an insurance company, where she had remained for the past three years—still working part-time, still living with her mother, still satisfied with her life. Paige didn't understand it, but never questioned it.

"I don't know where you got that idea from, but Marlon was far from perfect," Paige told her. "That's why we're not together."

"So, this is some *Waiting to Exhale* type, male-bashing girls night out because Marlon got busted and Paige moved back in with her mama? Damn, when me and Cofie broke off our engagement, you didn't even offer to take a sister to dinner."

Paige looked over at Meeko, who gave her a look which told her, *Let me handle this.*

"Don't be a hater, Celeste," Anjelica commented.

"I ain't hating." Celeste rolled her eyes.

"Well, Celeste, while we were all saddened when your fiancé received his fifteen-year sentence for armed robbery last month, We were glad that your mother talked you into *not* marrying him. But whenever we even brought it up, you were so defensive that I thought you didn't even wanna talk about it. The only reason you're here right now is because you're picking these dishes up for your mother and I asked you if you wanted to stay. Now, if you want, I can have a soiree for you next week. But today is Paige's day, and we're about to eat, drink and be merry."

"I heard that," Anjelica agreed.

"Bring on the food," Isis added.

Meeko laughed and walked behind the bar, picking up a remote. She clicked it on and music filled the room as Kool and the Gang sang "Ladies Night."

"I'll be right back." She waved as she floated out of the room.

They began dancing and clapping to the music like they really were having a party. Anjelica began doing old school dances like the Prep and the Cabbage Patch. No one noticed the three men who had entered the room and were watching.

"Ahem." The first one cleared his throat to get their attention. He was a tall, bald brother whose head was so smooth and shiny, Paige's first instinct was to touch it. That was until her eyes traveled to his chest that was just as appealing. He was beyond fine, and so were the other two guys standing beside him. The first one was as dark as night and had the body of a Greek god. He easily stood six-foot-five and weighed about 250 pounds. He smiled, and his teeth were so white and straight that she had no doubt that he wore braces as a child. The third guy was smaller, but he was just as sexy as the other two. He wore long dreadlocks which were pulled back. His muscled shoulders let them know that he worked out on regular basis.

"Oh my God, she hired strippers!" Isis clapped.

"I did not!" Meeko responded. "Come on, fellas, everything's all set up out back. Ladies, if you'll follow us."

They followed Meeko and her male companions into the backyard, which held the deck and swimming pool. Meeko and Stanley had been saying they were going to install a Jacuzzi, but Paige guessed they hadn't gotten around to it. She looked around the area and noticed a padded table, a chair with a foot tub in front of it and another smaller table holding a manicure set.

"What in the world? Are they gonna strip out here?" Anjelica asked.

"They're not strippers. Ladies, I would like to introduce Amir, Jacques and Dominic, otherwise known as The Total Package. They will be pampering us this afternoon. Jacques will be doing our feet, Dominic will be doing our hands, and Amir, with his fine-ass, will be doing our bodies—I mean, our massages. I have to go in and finish with the food. Paige, since it's your day, you pick your pleasure first. What'll it be?"

56

"Choices, choices." Paige smiled. She looked over at Amir, knowing that she wanted to save him for last. "Let me start from the bottom up. I'll start with my feet."

Without hesitating, Jacques whisked her into his arms and placed her into the chair. There was a pitcher of steaming water near him, which he tested and then poured into the foot bath. He slipped her feet out of the sandals she was wearing and slowly put each one into the tub. She glanced over at her friends, who were arguing about who was going where.

Soon, Isis ran into the house, emerging a few moments later wearing a kimono. She was lifted onto Amir's table, and Anjelica was giggling with Dominic, deciding which color to paint her nails. Nina went in to help Meeko with the food, and Celeste was pouting in the corner.

By the time Paige's hands and feet were done and her body massaged, she was walking around in a daze. She was feeling so good and relaxed. Between Meeko refilling her mimosas every five minutes and the warm feeling she got every time she looked over at Amir, she didn't know if she could contain herself. She decided to eat before she drank any more alcohol. Meeko had prepared a spread large enough to feed at least twenty-five people. There were steamed shrimp, salad, roasted potatoes, lobster and rolls. Everything was wonderful. She even had a *Congratulations Paige, Moving up and Moving on* cake with strawberry filling, her favorite.

"This was the bomb, Meeko," she said, licking the million-calorie icing off her fingers and not caring.

"It was nothing. You deserve it." Meeko smiled, looking over at Nina, who was enjoying Amir's wonderful hands. "Celeste, are you sure you don't want to partake of The Total Package? I got them for another hour."

"No, they already have their hands full with the divas. I think I'll pass. As a matter of fact, I need to be going."

"Suit yourself, honey. I ain't begging. I'm about to get another pedicure myself. Oh, Dominic," Meeko sang as she stood up.

"Uh, Meeko, Dominic does manicures. Jacques is the one that did the pedicures." Paige giggled.

"Hell, I don't care. All of them are fine. I just want a refill. Celeste, you can show yourself out."

Celeste rolled her eyes at Meeko, who was singing along with TLC's "Baby, Baby, Baby" and making her way to Dominic and Jacques, who were both chilling in the pool.

"I'll walk you out," Paige told her.

"I don't need you to do that. You just stay and enjoy all of your pampering. I mean, this all is for *you.*" Celeste sighed.

Paige looked at the plain Jane girl. Celeste was pretty enough, but she never had any get up-and-go about her, just like in her life. She wore wire-rimmed glasses instead of contacts, and she never ever wore makeup. She was a little on the big side, but so was Nina. That was no reason to be as frumpy as she was.

Paige tried to reason with her. "Celeste, it's not even like that. You know Meeko just needs any excuse to be a hostess. You should at least get your feet done or like Meeko said, a massage. I'm telling you, these guys are off the chain."

"I don't think so. You all go ahead. My head is hurting anyway."

Paige sat down and tried not to feel sorry for the girl, which is exactly what she knew Celeste wanted. "Celeste, listen. I'm sorry things didn't work out between you and Cofie. Maybe we can start hanging out now that I'm moving back home. We're both going through a rough time, and we can get through this together."

Celeste looked at her like she was crazy. "I ain't going through nothing. That's you that's having a five-star pity party because you couldn't hold on to Marlon anymore. I am fine, and I will be fine."

"You really are pathetic." Paige shook her head and turned to go back inside.

"Glass houses," Celeste called out to her. It took all of Paige's self-control not to turn back around and smack her cousin. She reminded herself that Celeste was a hopeless cause and went back to join her party, which was still in full swing.

An hour later, the Total Package departed along with Isis and Anjelica. Paige, Nina and Meeko chilled in the den, as Tyrese serenaded them by asking "how you gonna act like that?"

"Where the heck did you find those guys?" Nina asked.

"Girl, at the For Sisters Only convention," Meeko replied. "The line for their booth was wrapped damn near around the convention center."

"I see why." Paige laughed. "I probably would've stood in line twice."

"They would've seen my big ass even more than that!" Nina shrieked.

"Y'all are so stupid. I don't know what I would do without either of you. I would probably be home moping over Marlon." Paige sighed. She felt the heaviness began to creep back into her heart. "Do you think I made the right decision?"

"Do you feel like you made the right decision?" Nina asked.

"I mean, I love Marlon, but . . ."

"But you know you and he weren't headed anywhere. Come on, Paige. I'm not gonna let you sit here and mope over something that you knew was a dead end. You've been saying for months that you and Marlon haven't been happy. You know that deep down inside you've wanted him to be your husband, and you have every right to want that. If he won't step up and get off his mama's tit and marry you, then the hell with him!" Meeko shook her head.

"Meeko!" Nina tried to stifle her laugh, but Paige still noticed it.

"No, no, no. Paige, you are smart, beautiful, intelligent, and fine as hell. There are men out here that will marry you tomorrow if they had they chance. The hell with Marlon. He doesn't deserve you."

"Meeko, you're drunk," Paige told her.

"I'm not drunk, I'm honest. What you need to do is get yourself together, starting with that damn ponytail . . ."

"Amen, Meeko!"

"Whoa, hold up. What's up with y'all hating on my ponytail?" Paige ran her hands along her thick waves. "Don't hate because I have Indian in my family, skanks."

"Well, it's time for you to get scalped. Hand me that phone behind you, Nina. I swear, if I don't act quickly, you're gonna be as frumpy as Celeste."

"Who are you calling this late?"

"Fool, it's only eight-thirty." Meeko stood up. "I don't know why I didn't think of this earlier. Don't move."

"Meeko, we gotta get home," Paige called after her. She didn't want to stay out late, knowing that Mama would be waking her up bright and early for church.

"Just chill. Have some more cake, listen to Tyrese." *How ya gonna act like that?* Meeko's heels clicked on the floor as she ran up the steps. Paige tried to make out what she was saying into the phone, but she was muffled.

"What is she up to now?" Paige tossed her head back.

"Ain't no telling. I think your coming home excites her. And I have to admit, I'm glad you're moving back too. I just want to make sure you're cool with this. I mean, is this really it?"

Paige inhaled. "I don't know. I don't know. I've loved Marlon for so long that I can't imagine life without him. I don't want to imagine life without him. From the moment I saw him, I wanted him. I went after him and I got him."

"Paige, you said the same thing about Black Mike." Nina laughed.

"Oh God, Black Mike. Lord have mercy, that boy was beautiful."

"And fine."

"Girl, wasn't he fine?" Paige thought about Mike, her boyfriend when she first went off to college. His

61

skin was the color of a Hershey bar the special dark
kind, and whenever Nina and she would talk about
him, they referred to him as Black Mike. Paige was on
the path to thinking he was "the one" until she found
out that he not only had two baby mamas, which he
didn't tell her about, he also had two strikes and was
well on his way with his third. Dating a convicted felon
was definitely not something Paige was ready for.

"I wonder where he is."

"Probably in somebody's jail cell." Paige giggled,
thinking about her old flame. "He may not have been
the brightest boy on the block, but he was the finest."

"Ain't that the truth. But I still don't understand
how you carjack someone and not be able to drive a
stick shift. Dumb ass."

"Stop it! I can't take it. I'm gonna pee on myself,"
Paige was laughing so hard that her side was hurting.

"Hey, come up here." Meeko's voice interrupted
them.

Nina stood up and reached over to help Paige.
"Come on, let's see what she's done now."

"Where are you?" Paige called out, still thinking
about how blessed her cousin was to live in such
opulence.

"In the guest room, to the left."

They walked into the room and found Meeko
standing in the doorway of a walk-in closet. There were
piles of clothes on the bed, and shoes lying on a
nearby chair.

"What in the world?" Nina walked over and picked
up a navy blue jacket with gold buttons.

"You invite us over here, feed us and pamper us so
we can help you clean out your closet?" Paige smirked.

"Ha, ha. You're so damn funny. I'm not cleaning out my closet. I'm trying to come up with a decent wardrobe for your new job. I know if you had it your way, you would be wearing dark slacks and white blouses every day." Meeko put one hand on her hips. "I can't let that happen."

"Let what happen?" Nina asked, still picking through the clothes on the bed.

"Let her turn into a homebody. It's bad enough she's moving back in with Aunt Jackie. I can see a Celeste fiasco unfolding before my eyes, and I love you too much to let that happen."

"You're crazy," Paige told her. "I can't believe—"

"Believe it. It's Meeko. Nothing she does should surprise you. Wow, this is fly. Go try it on." Nina held up a black-and-white pinstriped suit. Paige knew it would fit, just by looking at it. She and Meeko had always worn the same size. Although she hated to admit it, her wardrobe did need a bit of a tweak.

"I'm not trying that on," Paige said, eyeing the suit, deciding that she would definitely be taking it with her when she left.

"She doesn't have to try it on. That heifer knows that if I can fit it, she can fit it," Meeko said. They continued going through the clothes and reminiscing over old times. Soon the doorbell rang. Meeko rushed down to answer it then waltzed back into the room. Another woman followed her, carrying a large black duffel bag.

"Hi." The woman smiled.

"Hello," Paige replied.

"Paige, I'd like you to meet Veronica Black, the woman that's about to transform you so that your inner goddess can shine!"

"You have lost your mind!" Paige shook her head.

"I'm not saying all that," Veronica laughed. "Nice to meet you. But please, call me Roni."

"And this is my best friend, Nina. I apologize for my cousin's behavior. It's not hereditary," Paige assured her.

"That's okay. Meeko is my girl. I don't mind at all. So, what's the hair emergency?"

"You can't see it? Look at that mop of hers." Meeko reached over and pulled at Paige's ponytail.

"She has beautiful hair. Meeko, you need to stop! I came over here thinking you tried to color your own hair again and it came out pink or something." Roni laughed.

"Ha ha. That only happened once. Don't even play," Meeko warned. "But seriously, Paige is starting a new job on Monday and she needs a new look."

"What's wrong with how she looks now?" Roni asked, dropping the bag on the floor.

"There's nothing really wrong with her look." Nina interrupted. "She's beautiful inside and out. We're just trying to give her a little more flavor than she has right now."

Paige felt like she was being ambushed. "I'm trying not to get pissed right about now."

"Come on, Paige. Let the woman work her magic. You know you've been wanting to rock a short style for a while now." Nina nudged her arm.

"You can use my bathroom, Roni. It's big enough. Nina and I will get these clothes together for you."

Meeko smiled at her and Paige knew she wasn't going to win this fight.

Roni put her arms around Paige's shoulder and whispered, "I promise I won't do anything that won't make you look fabulous. Trust me, I have my master's in diva style."

Paige reached up and touched her hair, thinking about how long she had wanted to cut it. Marlon had been adamant about her keeping it long and somehow it seemed only fitting that she get rid of it. They were right, it was time to let it go too. She pulled the ponytail holder out, and the mass of curls came falling into her face.

"Then let's go diva me up, Roni." She laughed.

7

Paige still could not believe how different her life had become. It had been over a month since she and Marlon had parted ways, and although she had to admit she missed him, she didn't feel empty. The previous times they had split up, she had felt as if something had been drained out of her. This time, it was different. Maybe it was because she had found a job that she enjoyed going to every day. Or maybe it was because she was enjoying the time she spent with her mother and daughter. It could've been due to the girlfriend time she shared with Meeko and Nina, and occasionally, Celeste, something she had missed for a while. She realized that being Marlon's pretend wife had consumed her life, and she missed being Paige.

She looked in the rearview mirror of her truck and admired her new look. True to her word, Roni had turned her into a true diva. That night at Paige's, she had cut an amazing amount of hair, all of which was donated to Locks of Love, an organization that made wigs for cancer patients. Her naturally wavy hair was now short, curly and manageable, something she was thrilled with. Not only had she departed with a new hairdo, she also had a new corporate wardrobe, complete with shoes, handbags and belts, compliments of Meeko, who had previously been the branch manager of a bank. Paige couldn't help smiling as she drove home, singing along with Will Smith's "Summertime."

Today was payday, and she decided to treat Myla to a new pair of sneakers, followed by dinner at the mall. She blew the horn when she pulled up to the house, and her daughter came bouncing out.

"Hi, Mom. Are we going shopping now?"

"Yes, Myla. We're going shopping," Paige answered. Myla hopped into the truck and immediately pushed the CD button. Will was quickly replaced by Beyonce's "Crazy In Love."

"Uh, excuse me, but I was listening to that."

"Oh, sorry," Myla said, and kept bobbing her head to the music. Paige looked over at her daughter, looking just like Marlon, "Where are we gonna eat at?"

"At home."

"Mom! You said we were going out to eat," Myla whined.

"I said we were going out and then we're gonna eat. And we will, at home," Paige teased.

"You're not funny, Mommy. Can we go to The Great Steak?"

Paige thought about the pricy restaurant her daughter suggested then quickly remembered the bills that had been piling up. She made a point not to touch any money in the joint checking account she shared with Marlon, with the exception of using the check-card for items for Myla. Therefore, he couldn't even think she needed him. He called her cell phone daily, and each time he did, Paige would pass her daughter the phone without even answering it. When he would come and pick Myla up from the house, Paige would conveniently not be at home.

"Um, why don't we go to that Chinese restaurant you like?" Paige suggested.

"Okay, that's good."

The mall held its normal Friday night crowd. Paige and Myla walked along the mall until they came to the Foot Locker. Myla wasted no time picking out several pairs of shoes she liked.

"Myla, you're only getting one pair."

"But, Mommy, look at these. Aren't they cute?" Myla held up a pair of pink-and-white Reeboks that lit up on the bottom.

"Yes, are those what you want to get?"

"But I like these too. They're just like Jade's only hers are blue." She held up another pair, this one white with red hearts on the heel.

"Then get those."

"Why can't I have both?"

"Because I don't have money for both. Pick one and you can get the other pair next time."

"I want them now. Just call Daddy. He can give you some money."

"Myla, I'm not gonna stand here and debate this with you. Pick a pair of sneakers so we can go."

"Can I help you beautiful ladies?" The baritone voice startled Paige. She turned and saw that it was one of the employees. He was dressed in a black-and-white referee's uniform and a pair of black-and-white Jordans. His nametag bore the name Eli. He smiled at her, and the attraction was instant. He was slightly taller than she was, and had a nice build. She wondered if he could be half Puerto Rican due to the reddish undertone of his dark skin and the thickness of his hair. He smiled and she noticed the deep dimples in his cheeks.

"My daughter is being a bit indecisive," she told him.

"Well, let's see if we can't help her out. You're so beautiful. You look just like your mommy. What's your name?" He kneeled down and asked. Paige knew the compliment was aimed at her.

"Myla." She sighed, still looking at both shoes she was holding. Paige knew her daughter wasn't impressed by the compliment because it was something she'd heard all of her life.

"Well, Myla, you like both of these, huh? Good choices. Beautiful and good taste." He looked over at Paige. "I think I have a solution for you. I'll be right back."

They waited a few moments and soon he returned carrying a box. He kneeled back down beside Myla and presented it to her like she was Cinderella and he was Prince Charming. Myla opened the top and squealed with delight as she pulled out a pair of white-and-pink Adidas which lit up and had hearts on the heel.

"Yes!! These are the ones I want. Can I get these, Mom?"

"Yes, Myla. Get them." Paige smiled.

"Can I wear them now?" Myla asked Eli.

"That's up to Mom." He looked at Paige for an answer.

"They're your shoes. You wear them if you want."

Myla pranced around the store in her new shoes while Paige walked back to the register to pay for them. "Thanks a lot. Because you know I was on the verge of leaving, and she wasn't going to get any shoes."

"That's why I came over when I did. There was no way I was gonna let you leave outta here without buying something and getting your number." Eli smiled.

"Oh, really." Paige handed him the cash.

"That's right. And now that we've got the sale taken care of, do you think I can have your number and call you sometime?"

Paige smiled. It had been so long since a man had asked for her number that she didn't know how to respond. She thought about it. *Well, he has a job. He seems to be good with kids, and he's cute. Why not?* She reached into her purse and took out a business card, writing her cell number on the back. She held it out for him and his fingers brushed hers as he took it out of her hand.

"Now that's funny," he said, reading the card.

"What is?" she asked, confused.

"You're a librarian and your name is Paige."

She couldn't help laughing because she had never realized it until Eli said it.

"That is funny, Mom. You get it? Book . . . Paige . . . like pages in a book. And you work in the library." Myla giggled.

"I get it." Paige shook her head at her daughter. The store began getting crowded and Paige didn't want to be any more of a distraction than she already was. "I'll talk to you soon."

"Definitely." Eli smiled and waved, placing the card in his pocket.

Talking to Eli on the phone each night was something Paige began looking forward to. It had been a week since she met him, and she agreed to meet him for drinks at Jasper's. She had a feeling that she was in for an enjoyable evening. He was waiting in the lobby of the restaurant, which was known for its great food and smooth jazz.

"Wow, you look wonderful," he said when she walked through the door. "Stunning is more like it. Green is definitely your color."

"Thank you. You look nice yourself," she told him. He was wearing a casual yet bold white shirt with royalblue and yellow stripes, jeans and a pair of black shoes. It was what she referred to as the Kanye West look—casual yet dressy. She was quite comfortable in a green sleeveless pantsuit, compliments of the Meeko makeover bag. She gave him a brief hug and they walked inside.

There was a small combo playing and the ambiance was warm and inviting. The only lighting in the room came from the candles in the center of each table. People were grubbing on plates of everything from catfish and collard greens to steak and potatoes. It was a mixed crowd of black and white, old and young. Everyone seemed to be having a nice evening. He led her to a small table in the corner and held her chair as she sat down. A waitress came and took their drink orders. He ordered a rum and Coke, while she decided on a glass of Zinfandel.

"Have you been here before?" he asked, looking at the menu.

"Yeah, a couple of times." she nodded.

"I've heard about this spot, but I've never been here. I usually chill down at State Streets."

"I've been there a few times, too." She shrugged.

"Oh, so you get around, huh?"

"I'm not saying all that. But when I would come visit every now and then, I would hang out."

Suddenly, there was applause and Paige looked up to see Isis walking to the front of the small stage.

"Hello, everyone. Welcome to Jasper's. I hope you're having a great time. I didn't know I would be singing tonight, but Uncle J is threatening not to let me eat if I don't sing one song. So, I'd like to send this one out to my wonderful husband, Tobias. I love you, baby." She blew a kiss and from the corner of her eye, she saw Toby standing at the bar, raising his drink.

The small band, consisting of a piano, a saxophone, bass and a drummer began playing. Everyone in the room became mesmerized as Isis sang "Anytime, Anyplace" better and more sensual than Janet Jackson had ever done live in concert. She was followed by a saxophone solo like none Paige had ever heard. By the end of the song, everyone in the restaurant was on their feet, and people were whistling and clapping long after Isis had departed the stage.

"Wow, that was awesome!" Eli said, his eyes still on Isis.

"Yeah, I keep telling her she needs to drop an album." Paige nodded. For some reason, she thought that Marlon would really like this place.

Stop it. You're on a date with another man. Don't even think about him, she scolded herself.

"You know her?"

"She's my cousin's best friend. Her husband's family owns this place. Uncle J is Toby's uncle."

"Oh, so we can eat free since you got the hookup." Eli smiled.

Paige wondered if he was serious. *Please don't tell me he's cheap. I know he doesn't think I'm gonna ask for a hookup.* She was relieved when he added, "Just kidding."

The rest of the evening went on enjoyably. Eli, whose real name was Elijah, talked about working at the store and the customers he came in contact with. She told him about working in the library and the lunchtime story program she was in the process of implementing, as they dined on chicken wings and potato salad.

"The key is to get some of the business big-wigs downtown to read stories during their lunch to the kids," she told him.

"Sounds like a great idea, but how are the kids getting to the library?"

"Well, we are actually contacting local daycares and community centers who have their own buses and vans. It's just in the planning stages, so I haven't really ironed all the kinks out. My goal is to get both the community and the businesses to start utilizing the library and its facilities."

"I'm sure it will be a success. You are very insightful." He reached across and grabbed her hand. It felt strange having another man's hand on hers. She wanted to remove it, but she didn't want to offend him.

"I appreciate the compliment, but I wouldn't say all that." She laughed. The waitress came and asked if they'd like dessert. "None for me. I couldn't eat another bite if I wanted to."

"None for me either," Eli said. He paid the check and left a tip on the table, then asked if she was ready to go. She told him yes. They were almost out the door when she heard her name. She turned, and Isis and Toby were waving.

"Hey there, you two," she told them. She took Eli by the hand and walked over to where they were standing. "Toby, Isis, this is my friend Eli. Eli, this is Toby and Isis."

"Nice to meet you. Man, you've got a voice on you. Your performance was nothing short of amazing," Eli said.

"That's my wife—amazing." Toby leaned over and kissed Isis on the cheek.

"Shut up. It's a shame I have to work for food around here, isn't it?" Isis asked. "Girl, you look fabulous. That hair is fierce. Who did it?"

"Some friend of Meeko's. Her name is Roni. I think she dates Stanley's brother, Sean."

Isis and Toby looked at each other and laughed. Paige instantly wanted to put her foot in her mouth. "I'm sorry. I didn't mean to—"

"Girl, stop apologizing. Veronica Black. That girl is talented. I don't know why Toby didn't marry her when he had the chance." Isis nudged him.

"Probably because she was dating Stanley's brother, Sean behind my back." Toby shrugged.

"Look, we should be going before I say anything else. It was nice seeing both of you." Paige hugged them and they said goodbye.

"What was that all about?" Eli asked as he walked her to her truck. She told him the story of Roni and Toby, who were engaged when he caught Roni cheating with Sean. "And she's the one that does your hair? And you mentioned her name to him *and* his new wife?"

"I didn't mean to. Jeez, this is all Meeko's fault. Out of all the hairdressers she knows, she had to pick the ex-fiance of her best friend's husband to do my hair."

"Wow, sounds like you, your cousin and all your friends got a whole lotta drama going on."

"You haven't heard the half of it." She giggled. "I had a nice time. This was fun."

"I'm glad you did. Does that mean we can go out again?" He took a step closer to her.

"I'd like that." She put her arms around his neck and hugged him. When she released him, he looked down at her and kissed her gently. It was a simple kiss and she appreciated the fact that he didn't try to put his tongue in her mouth. She wasn't ready for that. "Call you later."

"I'll be waiting," he said and watched her as she drove off.

She looked at him in the rearview mirror and smiled. She liked him. She had survived her first date post-Marlon, and had enjoyed a great evening. Life wasn't so bad after all.

8

"What time is your dad bringing you home?" Paige asked Myla. Marlon had picked her up Friday evening, and it was now Sunday night and he still hadn't brought her back. He usually dropped Myla off early Sunday evening in order to beat the traffic going home.

"I don't know. Let me ask him. Hold on," Myla said. After a few moments, she returned to the phone, "Auntie Camille is gonna bring me. She should be here in a few minutes."

"Okay. I didn't know she was home this weekend. Did you get to see her?"

"Yeah, she took me to the mall and the movies yesterday. She bought me some shoes and a T-shirt too."

"You are too spoiled, you know that?"

"No I'm not, Mommy. Oh, Daddy says he's gonna curse you out, too," Myla said innocently.

"What? What did you say?" Paige asked, hoping she had heard wrong.

"Daddy says he's gon' curse you out. I told him you were going on a date with Mr. Eli and he got mad. Then he said, 'I'm gonna curse your mama out for having you with her while she's out meeting men!'"

"Myla Taylor, how many times have I told you what happens when you're with me is none of your father's business?"

"I know. But he asked me about my sneakers and I told him about going to the store and Mr. Eli and how nice and funny he is."

"Put your father on the phone." Paige tried to remain calm. She could not believe how ignorant Marlon was. How could he say something like that to Myla? Now her daughter thought she had done something wrong, when she hadn't.

"Hello," Marlon said into the phone.

"Have you lost your damn mind?"

"What are you talking about, Paige?" Marlon sighed like she was wasting his time.

"How dare you send some stupid-ass message about you're gonna cuss me out? How could you even say something like that to my daughter?"

"How dare you get your flirt on while my daughter is standing right there? What? Were you trying to get a discount on shoes, Paige?"

"You know what? I'm not even going there with you with your cheating-with-the-whore-across-the-street ass. You just stay out of my business, and if you have any other threats for me in the future, Marlon, you had better damn well make them yourself!"

"Whatever, Paige. If I find out about you having strange men around my daughter, believe me, it won't be a threat."

"Go to hell."

Instead of answering, Marlon hung the phone up in her face. Paige wanted to jump in her truck and drive to the house just to slap him, but she restrained herself. Instead, she put on some shorts and a tank top and decided to go running, something she hadn't done in a long time. She ran through the neighborhood, reliving childhood memories and trying to keep her mind off Marlon. She hated this. Every time she got to a good place and things were going well, he always had a way of pissing her off. And every time she became angry with him, it made her feel like he had some type of hold on her. Her legs pumped up and down as her feet hit the pavement. The pain she felt in her calves let her know that she should be running more often. Sweat trickled down her face and between her breasts as she sprinted. She didn't know where she was going, but it felt good, so she didn't stop. The faster her heart beat, the faster she ran until finally, she was at the back of her high school. She panted and bent down, trying to catch her breath. Not wanting her legs to cramp up, she began walking. She was almost three miles from home and it was nearing dark. She picked up the pace and sprinted back.

Paige had just gotten out of the shower when she heard a car door outside. She peeked out of her bedroom window and saw Camille and Myla getting out of Marlon's blue Camry. She quickly got dressed and went to open the door for them.

"Hi, Mommy," Myla greeted her.

"Hey there." Paige pulled one of her daughter's long ponytails.

"Where's Darling?"

"She went to evening service. Is Camille coming in?"

"Yeah, she's talking to some boy on the phone. She bought me a new game for my Leapster. I'm going to play it in my room," she said and skipped down the hallway. Paige stood in the doorway waiting for Camille as she walked up the walkway.

"Wow, look at you! Oh my God. That is so fly!" Camille squealed. "I can't believe you cut it off. I know you and Marlon must be over for real."

"Be quiet, you," Paige said. She was glad to see Camille and hugged her tight. "Look at yourself. You look good. They must be feeding you well, because I see you picked up some weight." Camille was usually model-thin, but now she was looking rather curvaceous to Paige.

"Yeah, I can't front. A sister has been getting her grub on."

"So, tell me all about Myrtle Beach," Paige demanded, pulling her to sit down on the sofa.

"Oh, it's wonderful and so pretty. I can't believe how much fun I'm having. I'm working at one of the hotels, and the people are really nice. I never thought life would be this good for me."

"I'm glad. I told you there was a whole world out there for you. Now you see first hand."

"Yeah, you were right. Mama's not too happy, though, but I don't care. I can't go back home, not now anyway. It's just too . . ." Camille girl looked down and Paige knew what she meant. Camille had a rough life living with a woman like Lucille. Most of the girl's life was spent caring for her alcoholic mother. Paige told Marlon that wasn't fair to her, but he acted like Paige didn't know what she was talking about. Now, it seemed that Camille had discovered her first taste of freedom and wasn't going back to that jail of a home, and Paige was glad.

"You don't have to tell me, Cam. I know."

"I still don't understand what went wrong with you and Marlon, though. I feel like this is all my fault. If I

79

wouldn't have had that party, you two would probably still be together."

"None of this is your fault, Camille. I don't even want you to feel that way. Your brother and I just grew apart, and that was just one of several incidents that had the domino effect on our relationship, so to speak."

"Well, do you think you will get back together? I know Marlon loves you, Paige. He always has. Don't you love him?"

"Yes, I will always love your brother, but I can't say that we'll be together. Not like we used to. Things between us are really complicated."

"I can't believe he's mad about you going out with another man when that cow of a neighbor is up in the house every chance she can get. She's already walking around there acting like she owns the place. She even had on your house shoes! You know the ones I gave you for Christmas. I can't stand her. And Mama acts like she's the greatest thing since sliced bread. It's sickening."

Paige knew she was referring to Kasey. "Well, he's entitled to his friends the same way I am. I have no say in that matter."

"I can't believe he's taking her to Cancun next week."

"What?" Paige frowned, confused by what Camille was saying.

"Yeah, they're going on some cruise. And he has the nerve to be dogging you out about going on a date. She was bragging that she's moving in after they get back. He's stupid."

Paige began biting her bottom lip. She could not believe that not only was Marlon taking Kasey on a cruise, but he was allowing her to move into their house. There was no way that was going to happen. "He's an asshole."

"You got that right." Camille nodded as she took her ringing cell phone out of her pocket. "It's him. He's just calling to see if I left yet. He had the nerve to tell me not to even get out of the car and come in. He just wanted me to blow the horn and let Myla out. I told you he's stupid."

"You are crazy, Camille." Paige tried to manage a smile. "You be careful. I'm glad you're having fun this summer. Call me if you need anything."

"Thanks, Paige. I love you. And even though my brother is stupid, I'm glad he had sense enough to get with someone like you. Although he was dumb enough to mess it up, and now he's dealing with a cow."

"Don't worry about your brother. You just take care of yourself. When does school start anyway?" Paige walked her to the door. Camille had accepted a full scholarship to Spellman.

"Another month."

"Well, I certainly hope I get the chance to see you before you leave for Atlanta."

"Most definitely. You know you are my sister, and I wouldn't think of leaving without spending time with you and Ms. Myla."

Camille's phone began ringing again. Paige shook her head and said, "You'd better get outta here before Marlon comes looking for you."

She watched as Camille got into the car and pulled off. Walking back into the house, she picked up the phone and dialed.

"Your sister is on her way," she said.

"I've been calling her for the past twenty minutes and she hasn't answered the phone. I thought maybe something had happened."

"Something did. She had enough decency to come inside and talk for a minute, against your advice, of course. I can't believe how much of an asshole you are, Marlon."

"Don't start tripping, Paige. I just wanted her to get on the road as soon as possible. You now how bad that traffic can be."

"Whatever," she snapped. Deciding to mess with his head, she asked, "What time are you picking Myla up next weekend?"

"Uh—I—I've been meaning to talk to you about that. I have a convention in Jersey, so I'm not gonna be able to get her. I'll be gone for a week."

"A convention, huh?"

"Yeah."

"You're such a liar, you know that? I don't know why you find it necessary to lie to me. I know all about your little cruise to Mexico that you and that ugly-ass heifer are going on. And you tried to trip about me going on a date?"

"Paige, I don't give a damn what you do. I just don't want it done in front of my daughter. As far as the cruise, I asked you about going on vacation months ago when you first left and you said no. And I'm not taking Kasey. I'm taking my mother. Kasey just happened to be booked on the same ship. We even have separate cabins."

"And you really expect me to believe that? Then why would you lie about going to a convention? Why lie, Marlon?"

"Because I *am* going to a convention. In Miami which is where the ship leaves from. I'll be there for three days before we sail."

Paige couldn't take it anymore. She didn't want to deal with him. She kept the knowledge of Kasey possibly moving in to herself, not wanting to hear any more lies. It was as if he was trying to make her think she was crazy, and she knew she wasn't. She hung the phone up without saying goodbye.

He's taking her on a cruise, along with his mother. She tried to tell herself that she didn't want to go anyway, that she no longer gave a damn about Marlon or what he did. But deep inside, she was hurt. Not so much by Marlon, though. She hurt herself because that after everything she just learned, she knew she still loved him, and it made no sense.

"Well, I guess we need to go get your stuff."

"What? What stuff?" Paige asked Meeko. They were in Paige's office having lunch. Paige told her cousin all about Marlon, the cruise and his soon-to-be new roommate, Kasey.

Meeko plucked a tomato out of the chef salad she was eating and popped it into her mouth. She took a sip of her tea and replied, "Your clothes, furniture, all of your stuff. Whatever belongs to you that's still in that house."

"You want me to go rob my own house?" Paige laughed, breaking her tuna sandwich into little pieces. "I need to talk to him first. The furniture belongs to both of us—both Marlon and I. We both paid for it."

"You both paid for the house, too, but he didn't find it necessary to consult you before letting another woman to move in. You're gonna let her have your house and your stuff too? Oh no, that's crazy. Not only did he cheat, but the woman he's cheating with is about to move into your house. Don't be stupid, Paige. Go and get your shit. I'm telling you, you'd better go get it before that heifer throws it away when she moves in. I don't understand why you've waited this long to go and get it anyway."

Paige knew Meeko was right. She had been putting off going to get her stuff for weeks. She didn't really have a reason not to, other than the fact that she knew that when she did, it would mean that she and Marlon were truly over.

"I don't know. I mean, do you know how pissed Marlon would be if he came home and all of me and Myla's stuff was gone?" A big grin spread across Meeko's face. "Meeko."

"What?"

"I don't like the way you're looking. Like you have something up your sleeve."

Meeko reached into her purse and took out her keys. She fumbled and removed a single one, passing it to Paige, "Here, you got your own place now."

"What is this?" Paige frowned.

"It's the key to my townhouse."

"I thought you were selling it."

"Well, now I'm renting it. And don't make me come looking for my money. The painters are there now and the carpet is new too. We can go get your shit tomorrow." She smiled and put another forkful of salad in her mouth. "Can you get the day off?"

Paige's original plan was to go to the house and get Myla's bedroom set, most of her toys and all of their clothes. But as they passed Kasey's house, she saw a FOR SALE sign in the front and it confirmed what Camille had told her. Infuriated, Paige went along with Meeko's plan instead. It took all of four hours for Paige and her moving staff, which consisted of Meeko, Nina, Stanley and his brother Sean, to pack up all of Myla's and her belongings and load them into the two large U-Hauls she had rented. When they finished, Paige looked around, admiring their handiwork. The only thing which remained was the sofa in the den, which was so worn, she didn't want it, the big screen television, although she took the thirty-two inch one from their bedroom and the two other smaller ones— one from Myla's bedroom and the one from the guest bedroom. She took all of the small appliances: the toaster, waffle iron, George Foreman grill, and smoothie maker. She took towels, linen, even cleaning supplies. In addition to the house shoes Camille told her Kasey had worn, she also left the bedroom set. She could never be able to sleep in it anyway, knowing Marlon and Kasey had been in it. The house was basically empty.

"He's going to be so pissed," Paige said aloud.

"Who cares?" Meeko shrugged. "Come on, we still have to unload all of this."

"So, this is it, I guess." Paige sighed, picking up a few of the pictures of Marlon, Myla and her. It was the one they had taken last Easter. They were all wearing green-and-white, and Paige was still pregnant.

"Paige, I know this is hard, but it has to be done. You have to make a life for you and Myla now. Leaving your stuff here to linger would only prolong the inevitable." Nina rubbed her back. "You're doing the right thing."

"I know." Paige nodded. "Besides, they can just move all the stuff from that cow's house over here."

"Now you're thinking!" Meeko laughed and they shared a group hug.

Paige's mom was waiting at the townhouse when they pulled up. She had the place spotless and all ready to move in, and they began unloading.

"Where's Myla?" Paige asked.

"With your father. She's gonna spend the night over there. I can't believe Marlon let you take all of this stuff. I'm glad to see you all making this an amicable breakup. I knew you two were mature enough to handle things the right way."

Paige looked up from the box of towels she was unpacking, she looked over at Meeko who was walking through the door with a box. "Uh, yeah, Mom. You know Marlon's doing whatever he can to make the transition easy for Myla's sake."

"That's wonderful." Her mother smiled. "I'm sure going to miss you and Myla, though. I was beginning to enjoy having you in the house."

"Oh, Mama, please. You know Myla and I will be over there almost every day anyway. We're only two neighborhoods away. You act like we're moving out-of-state."

"Well, when Meeko lived here, she hardly ever visited, so I wouldn't know."

"Uh-oh, that's my cue to leave," Meeko said, putting the box down. As she turned to leave, she bumped right into her husband.

"Oh, baby, I'm sorry," he said.

"No, it was my fault. I was running from Aunt Jackie."

He leaned over and whispered, "What do you want us to do with this stuff?"

Meeko looked into the box and realized why he was whispering. It held the baby items that they had removed from what used to by Myles' nursery. Paige put her heart and soul into making sure everything in it was perfect, from the crib to the small toy chest. When they were packing the house up, she had insisted that they remove everything from that room as well. Meeko wondered what Paige wanted to do with it. She glanced over at her cousin and called her name softly.

Paige looked up.

"Hey, uh, what do you want us to do with the baby's things?"

A deafening silence fell in the room, and all eyes were on Paige. She walked over and peeked inside the box, lifting the thick baby-blue-and-white comforter, which used to be on her son's bed. The bed he never got the chance to sleep in. She inhaled its scent, tears coming into her eyes. Myles would have been eight months old. Her mother walked over and put her arms around her.

"That's a good question. I think that's part of the reason I've been putting off going back to the house too. I knew I was going to have to clean that room out." Paige looked at Meeko standing beside Stanley and suddenly knew what to do. "Take them to your house."

"Huh?" Meeko tilted her head.

"Take them to your house and make a nursery for your baby."

"Our baby?" Stan's eyes lit up and he grabbed Meeko.

"Boy, don't even think about it. You know I'm not having a baby." Meeko saw the look of disappointment in her husband's face and quickly said, "Not yet, anyway."

"But you know you will be in the future. You both have given me so much. I can't think of anyone else I would want to have all of this. So, it's yours."

"Oh, Paige, baby. I would be honored to have it. And one day, it will be put to good use, I promise." Meeko hugged her.

"We really appreciate this, Paige. You know that, right? I guess we'd better hurry and get finished so we can go home and—"

"Stanley!" Paige and Meeko both said at the same time.

"What? I was gonna say so we can go home and unload the truck and get it back to the U-Haul." Stanley shrugged. He laughed all the way out the door.

By midnight, Paige was all moved into her new place. She got into what used to be the guest bed and lay back on the pillows. It had been years since she lived alone. It would take some getting used to. She reached over on the nightstand and picked up the phone, dialing Eli's number. He had offered to help her move, but she assured him she had enough help.

"Hey, you all moved in?" he asked.

"Yep, pretty much. I have some little things here-and there to pick up, but for the most part, I'm done."

"That's good. So when do I get to see the place?"

"When do you wanna see it?"

"How about now?"

"I don't think so. I'm already in bed."

"That's all the more reason for me to come over. You're all alone—in bed. I don't want you to be scared." He laughed. She knew he was teasing.

"I'm fine."

"You sure? I can be there in like ten minutes. You said it's over on Fairfield Manor, right?"

"Yep."

"That's a really nice area. You must be paying a grip for rent."

"Actually, my cousin is renting me the place, so it's reasonable."

"That's cool. It's really nice to have family that looks out like that." He sounded kind of distant. As often as they talked, Eli had never mentioned his family.

"Yeah, you're right about that. Do you have family here?"

"No, my family lives near Philly."

"How many brothers and sisters do you have?"

"Two brothers and one sister. I'm the youngest. All teachers, even my mother and father."

"Wow. You didn't want to be a teacher?"

"I didn't want to do the work in college. Had a full football scholarship, too, but wasn't interested enough to go to class. Needless to say, I'm the black sheep of the family." he laughed. "The embarrassment of the family."

"Well, I like sheep. Even black ones," she told him.

"And I like Paige in the library." The way he said it made her blush. The more she got to know him, the more she liked him. They talked for a while longer and by the time she fell asleep, she was glad to be in her own home.

9

"Mommy, I have to ask you a question," Myla announced to her mother.

Paige looked into the rearview mirror at her daughter. It was Monday morning, which was always a struggle for her. She had gotten used to her mother taking Myla to summer camp, but now that they'd moved out, the responsibility fell back on her. She sat in the early morning traffic, trying not to get frustrated at the people who seemed to be driving like they really didn't have anywhere to be and didn't care that she was running late.

"What is it, Myla?" she asked, hoping it had nothing to do with Marlon. Since they had moved into their own place, it seemed like Myla wanted him to be the topic of all their conversations.

"How does PawPaw go to the bathroom?"

Paige was puzzled and turned the radio down. "What?"

"How does PawPaw go to the bathroom?" Myla repeated, meeting her mother's stare in the mirror.

"What are you talking about? I don't know what you're asking." She sighed as she put her blinker on and tried to merge into the exit lane. A woman driving a Taurus station wagon looked straight ahead like she didn't even see her and pulled up so Paige couldn't change lanes, "You stupid . . . I know you see me trying to get over!"

She lay on the horn and the woman still refused to look. Luckily, a blue Honda behind the woman flashed its lights and the driver motioned for her to come over. She waved half-heartedly as she jumped into the lane.

"Now, what are you talking about, Myla Seymone?"

"How does PawPaw go to the bathroom through his *peanut*? I was 'sleep, but then I had to go to the bathroom and by accident, I walked in while he was in the shower and I saw his peanut. It was big . . . almost to his knees. And I ran out really fast. He didn't see me, so he didn't yell at me. I was really fast, Mom. But when I got back in the bed, I was trying to figure-out how does he fit it in his pants, and how does he go to the bathroom when he does number two?"

Paige didn't know what to say or how to answer her daughter's question. She tried to think of a logical parental answer, but couldn't. "He just does, Myla. The same way you do."

Myla nodded and seemed satisfied with her mother's reply for a few moments, but then said, "Well, can you ask him? Don't tell him I saw his peanut in the shower. He might get mad because he tells me I'm s'pose to knock first if the door is closed, but I forgot. Just tell him you saw it and you wanna know. Okay, Mom?"

Paige sped to Lighthouse Academy where Myla attended camp and pulled into the student drop-off area. "Hurry, sweetie. Mommy's running late."

Myla opened her door and grabbed her lunchbox. She paused long enough to give her mom a kiss and whispered into her ear, "I love you. Don't forget to ask PawPaw."

Paige shook her head as she watched her daughter skip off into the building. She looked at the clock and figured that with a little strategic driving, she could muster up enough time to stop at 7-Eleven and grab a cup of coffee. She weaved her way through traffic and pulled into the parking lot. She ran inside, prepared her drink, paid and was headed back to her truck in record time when her cell phone began ringing. It was the call she was expecting.

"Hello."

"Where the hell is my stuff?"

"Good morning, Marlon. You just missed Myla. I already dropped her off. I'll have her call you this evening," Paige said, sounding overly cheerful. She knew he was pissed, but she was prepared.

"Don't play with me, Paige, because I'm not in the mood."

"What are you talking about? It's Monday morning and you know I don't play on Mondays. Come on now."

"I'm on my way there, and I'm getting all my shit back. How the hell I go out of town and you rob me? What kind of shit is that?"

"If I recall, that stuff was mine, too, so you can drive all the way here if you want, but it'll be a wasted trip."

"You did this out of spite! You're mad and jealous that I went on the cruise, and not by myself."

"I don't give a damn about where you went or who the hell you went with. I came and got that stuff to make our child's house a home."

"She already had a home, but you chose to leave it. Don't give me that bullshit."

Paige could feel her blood pressure raising to the point that she thought she was going to have a heart attack. Before she knew it, she was screaming to the top of her lungs. "I hate you, Marlon! It's taking everything in my being not to wish you were dead. You have been playing these mind games so long that I don't even fall for them anymore! Leave me the fuck alone and I mean that!"

She kicked her truck into reverse and hit the gas without even looking. The sound of a bump and a crash caused her to suddenly stop. She put the car into drive and eased back into her parking spot.

God, what now? I can't deal with anything else. She jumped out to see what happened. As she walked to the back, she found a guy kneeling next to a motorcycle. She looked at the back of her truck to assess the damage. There was a slight scratch and dent in her tailgate, but nothing major. She was relieved, and walked over to the guy who was still fumbling with the bike.

"Are you okay?" she asked, folding her arms. She still couldn't believe he had hit her.

He looked up and nodded. Although it was a humid July morning, he was wearing a black leather jacket and boots. Even though he was leaning, she could tell he was tall. There was something familiar about him, but she couldn't place it. She could hear her phone ringing, but ignored it. She stood watching him as he picked something off the ground and tried to fit it back on the bike. It was his sideview mirror.

"Damn," he huffed. He stood up and looked at her. "I guess you were in a rush. That, plus you were on the phone."

"Uh, yeah," she admitted. He removed his sunglasses. Her eyes met his and she saw that he recognized her also.

"Well, let me get your insurance info and you can be on your way," he said, unsmiling.

Insurance. Oh, hell no. She and Marlon were on the same insurance. If she reported it, he would find out, and she didn't want that to happen. "Come on. Do we really need to report this? Look, let me get my checkbook and we can settle this right here."

"Are you for real?" He didn't seem to think she was serious, so she went and got her purse.

"Okay, how much do you think the damage is? Fifty, sixty dollars?"

"Oh, hell naw. I know you're kidding now. Try more like two, three hundred dollars."

"For a broken piece of plastic and a mirror? And why shouldn't we be splitting the damage? After all, you were parked behind me just sitting there."

"Was I? If I recall, I was waiting for the person next to you to leave the parking space, and my blinker was on, clearly indicating that fact. It was you who failed to check in the rearview mirror to see all of that because you were too busy screaming at someone on the phone."

Paige looked at him, too stunned to move. She knew exactly where she knew him from. He was the guy who helped her out in the store the night of the robbery.

"Why are you looking at me like that?" He frowned.

"I know you. You saved me and my girlfriend."

"Huh?"

95

"The store was robbed. My girlfriend and I were inside. We were on the ground and then you came and helped me up."

His face softened and he smiled. "Yeah, I knew I knew you from somewhere. You look kind of different. Your hair."

She reached and touched her curls, secretly flattered that he noticed the difference. "Yeah, I cut it. Look, I'm really sorry about your bike. You're right, I wasn't paying attention."

He exhaled loudly and looked back at his bike, "Accidents happen. But no one was hurt. My boy has a body shop not too far from here. I'll just take it over there and let him check it out."

"Oh good." Paige was hoping that meant that he was going to let it slide. She was wrong.

"Give me your number and I'll call you with the estimate. And you better believe it'll be more than sixty bucks," he said matter of factly.

"I really don't see how, but okay." She reluctantly took a business card out of her purse and wrote her home number on the back. He passed her a card out of his pocket. For some reason, she checked to see if he was wearing a wedding band. He wasn't. She read his name off the card he gave her: "Quincy Westbrooke."

"Paige Davis." He smiled. Nervously, she looked at her watch and realized she should have been at work thirty minutes ago.

"Well, call me when you get the estimate. And since he is your boy, can you please try to get a good deal?"

"I will. I'm not trying to break a sister."

"And I'm not trying to be broke, either," she told him as she turned to walk away.

"Hey," he called out. She turned around. He was putting his helmet back on. "Do me a favor."

"What's that?"

"Let me pull off before you back up." He laughed. She put her hands on her hip and gave him an evil look as he climbed onto the bike. He started it and waved as he pulled out of the parking lot.

"So what are your plans for the tonight?"

"Nothing much. What's today, Thursday?"

"All day long," Nina told her, "Why don't we go hang out at State Street's for a little while? I hear their happy hour is off the chain."

"Girl, I'm not going to the club on a Thursday night and I gotta go to work on Friday morning."

"Come on, Paige. You said we were gonna start hanging out. We won't stay long, I promise."

She agreed and quickly called her mother, asking her to pick Myla up from day camp.

Whoever told Nina that happy hour at State Street's was off the chain was far from lying. There were wall to wall people and Paige could tell it was jumping from the moment they entered the door. They maneuvered their way through the crowd until they wound up at the bar.

"What are you drinking?" Nina yelled over Busta Rhymes' "Party Wit' Me."

"Ginger ale," Paige told her.

"What? Come on, you're having at least one drink." Nina began bouncing to the beat.

"I haven't been out to a club in so long, I don't even know." Paige shrugged.

"Well, I do." Nina leaned past them and ordered a Cosmotini.

They got their drinks and scoped out a table. Paige noticed a few attractive men as they passed the dance floor. The deejay went into a mix of DMX songs that she hadn't heard in a while, and by the time they found an empty spot, she was ready to hit the dance floor.

"Come on, drink up and let's go," she said. "I'm ready to party."

They quickly finished their drinks and Paige strutted near the dance floor, knowing that she would have a partner before she made it. She was right. Before she knew it, a cute guy wearing a grey linen suit had her by the hand and they were jamming. She was having such a good time that she almost didn't notice Nina dancing next her, trying to get her attention. She leaned over to see what her best friend was saying.

"Check out that couple over there. The chick in the silver dress. She looks like a runway model for aluminum foil."

Paige looked in the direction Nina was pointing her and sure enough, there was a thick woman wearing a tight-fitting silver dress along with silver shoes and silver accessories, right down to silver lipstick. The fact that the woman looked as shiny as she did didn't surprise Paige as much as whom the woman was dancing with. The man dancing right along with her was Eli.

"Okay, see the guy she's dancing with?" Paige said, still moving to the beat. Nina nodded and she told her, "That's Elijah."

Nina stopped moving. As if on cue, the deejay changed to a slow song. The two women walked off the floor, leaving their dance partners frowning.

"You're Elijah? From the mall?" Nina asked.

"Yep."

"Did you know he was going to be here?"

"No—I mean he mentioned that he comes here a lot, but he didn't say anything about being here tonight."

"Are you gonna go say something to him?"

"I don't think so. It's no big deal. He doesn't have to check in with me. I'm not his girlfriend."

"Okay. Well, the way you talk, I thought things were going pretty well for you two."

"They are, but it's not like we're committed or anything," Paige told her. She was kind of hurt to see Eli there with another woman, but they weren't committed, so there was nothing she could say.

Maybe I was reading more into it than was there anyway. I'm probably trying so hard to be over Marlon that I wanted it to be more than what it really is, she thought. She looked over to the dance floor and saw that Eli and his silver shadow were gone. She and Nina walked back to their table.

"See, isn't this fun?" Nina asked.

"Yes, it is. We should've come out and done this a long time ago," Paige told her.

"And look at all these fine men. Look at that one at the bar, in the cream."

"Where?" Paige looked to see who she was talking about.

"See him?"

She looked over at Nina, who was positioning her cleavage. "Come on, girlfriends, get ready. Mama ain't had a date in a while."

"Girl, you are crazy." Paige laughed.

"Good evening. How are you, Ms. Michaels?" Paige turned to see where the deep voice was coming from. She smiled when she saw who it was.

"I'm fine, Mr. Westbrooke. How are you?"

"Wonderful. This is my boy, Titus."

"Nice to meet you, Titus. I'm Paige.

"You remember Quincy, Nina?"

"Okay, good seeing you again, especially under better circumstances than the last time. Paige told me she ran into you the other day." Nina laughed. Paige gave her a look letting her know that she didn't find her joke funny.

"Yeah, she did. As a matter of fact, Titus owns the body shop I was telling you about," Quincy told Paige.

"Then maybe I should buy you a drink." Paige winked at Titus.

"Ha, that's okay. I gave Quincy the estimate. I think I should be buying you one. I can afford it."

"That's not funny," she told him.

"I know. I'm just kidding. But seriously, what are you ladies drinking?"

"Cosmotini for her." She looked over at Nina.

"All right then," Titus said. He looked at Paige and asked, "And for you?"

"Just a ginger ale. I already had my one drink limit. I'm the driver tonight."

"One drink? Oh no, that may be over your limit considering how you drive when you're sober," Quincy teased.

Paige pretended to be overwhelmed with laughter then abruptly stopped and rolled her eyes at him and said, "Whew, you're so funny. Psych!"

The men cracked up as they walked away.

"He is sexy as hell!" Nina gushed after the two men went to get the drinks. "And he likes you, too. You should holler at him."

"Girl, please. I don't think so."

"Why not?"

"First of all, he probably has a girlfriend."

"Not from the way he's looking at you," Nina suggested. "His attraction to you is quite obvious. Men who are already attached try to subdue their interest."

"And what makes you such an expert?"

"I've been with enough dogs to know." Nina laughed.

"Well, Titus has an obvious attraction for you, also," Paige pointed out.

"Oh, hell no. I don't do short men. You know that. Don't even play." Nina rolled her eyes playfully. "Now, if he has some taller friends, holler at me."

"You are so stupid. You know what they say, Cher was taller than Sonny, don't try to be funny." Paige laughed.

Once again, people began flowing to the dance floor as reggae music began playing. She looked over at the deejay booth and saw that it was Tobias, Isis' husband. *I should have known it was DJ Terror pumping the crowd up.* Leaning over the table, she told Nina about damn near putting her foot in her mouth the other night when she ran into him and Isis at Jasper's.

"I can't believe you!" Nina giggled. "What did Isis say?"

"She didn't say anything. They both acted like it was no big deal." Paige shrugged.

"That's because they're both secure in their relationship. Isis didn't have to say anything. She knows she got him now and that's all that matters. Not saying anything, says a hell of a lot."

"Yeah, that's true." Paige nodded.

"Paige?"

Paige turned at the sound of her name being called. It was Eli. She looked around for his little aluminum foil friend, but she was no where to be found.

"Hello, Elijah. How are you?"

"I'm good, I'm good. I didn't know you were gonna be here tonight."

I'll bet you didn't, she thought. Smiling, she told him, "I could say the same about you."

He was about to say something else, but Quincy and Titus returned to the table with their drinks. She could tell Eli was irritated, especially when Quincy told him, "Excuse me, bro," and sat down right beside her. It had to look suspicious, but she didn't care.

"It was nice seeing you again, Eli," she told him. "I'll talk to you later."

Elijah walked away without saying a word. Paige followed him with her eyes until he became lost in the midst of the crowd. She didn't mean to be cold, but the fact that he seemed to be questioning why she was here, when he was just dancing with another woman ten minutes ago, had her a bit perturbed.

She turned and watched Quincy stirring his drink. He took a swallow of the reddish liquid then closed his eyes, saying, "Ah, that's just what I needed."

Titus shook his head and began laughing.

"What is that, anyway?" Celeste asked.

"Cranberry juice with a dash of ginger ale. Don't even be fooled by him. He doesn't even drink," Titus told them.

"Man, you can't hold water, can you?" Quincy put his now empty glass on the table.

"Maybe not, but I can hold alcohol." He raised his glass.

"And what is that?" Nina smirked.

"Whiskey Sour. Wanna taste?" He winked, leaning in closer to her.

Paige couldn't help giggling. Titus was obviously interested in Nina, and she knew her girl wasn't having it. Not only did Nina like her men tall, but she liked them big.

"I don't think so," she told him, shrinking away. Sean Paul's "Get Busy" began playing, and she jumped up. "That's my cue to hit the floor."

"Do your thing, girl!" Paige called after her. Poor Titus looked disappointed.

"You wanna dance?" Quincy asked Paige.

Her eyes widened, but before she could answer, she heard his name being called by a female.

"Celeste?" Quincy spoke. Sure enough, her cousin was standing at their table.

"What's up?" Celeste's eyes widened when she saw Paige sitting with him. "Paige?"

"Hey, Celeste." Paige smiled.

"You know each other?" Quincy asked.

"Yeah, Celeste is my cousin."

"Damn, small world." Titus smiled.

"Sure is," Celeste replied. "Quincy is my ex-boyfriend."

Titus began laughing harder when Celeste said that. Quincy looked over at his friend and frowned. "Chill, Titus. We went out a couple of times, that's all."

"Wow, I had no idea," Paige told her. "Have a seat, join us." They all shifted around the table to make room for Celeste, who wasted no time sitting next to Quincy. Paige racked her brain trying to remember anyone mentioning Celeste dating someone named Quincy, but she couldn't recall.

"So, who are you here with, Celeste?" she asked, knowing there was no possible way Celeste came to a club alone. It was a shock that her cousin was even here at all.

"Some people from my job. We come over here from time to time for happy hour. Quincy, you are looking well. What are you doing these days?" Celeste asked. "How's Q-Master's? I heard you have three locations now."

"Yeah, I do. Life is good right about now."

"Q-Master's?" Paige asked.

"Yes, Quincy is the owner of a chain of barbershops," Celeste said, grabbing Quincy by the arm. Paige glanced over at Titus, who seemed amused by this entire scene.

"That's wonderful," Paige told him. "Titus, how about hitting the floor and leaving these two alone so they can catch up?"

"Yo, let's hit it!" Titus jumped-up and grabbed her by the hand. Quincy looked like he wanted to say something, but didn't. They walked to the floor and began dancing. Although he wasn't that tall, Titus had some moves and Paige was impressed. She looked around the floor for Nina and spotted her dancing with a guy that was built like a linebacker for the New York Giants.

"Why don't you go cut in?" Paige encouraged him.

"I don't think so. Don't worry, I'll make my move when the time is right," he told her. She smiled and they continued to move to the beat of Ludacris' "Throw Them Bows." She was slightly disappointed when the deejay changed the music to a slow song. Nina joined them, and they made their way back over to the table, where Quincy was now sitting alone.

"Celeste is gone?" Paige asked him.

"Celeste?" Nina balked.

"Girl, I was surprised to see her too," Paige informed her.

"Celeste Harper? Your cousin. Celeste?"

"Yeah, Celeste, Nina." Paige sat down. "Where'd she go?"

"Her peeps were ready to go, so she left," Quincy told them. "Yo, y'all ain't have to leave me like that with her. That wasn't even cool."

"What're you talking about, Q? We just left you two alone to catch up on old times," Titus teased him.

"You know Celeste?" Nina turned and asked Quincy.

"They used to date," Paige answered, smiling.

"Your cousin. Celeste? Wait a minute, are we talking about the same girl?" Nina was still in a state of disbelief.

"Stop playing, Nina. There's nothing wrong with Celeste," Paige snapped, not wanting to talk bad about her cousin in front of anyone.

"I ain't say nothing was wrong with her. I'm just surprised he used to date her. I definitely wouldn't think she was your type."

"Hold on, it's not like we were in a committed relationship. We went out two, maybe three times," Quincy told them. "And she's not my type. I tried to tell her that from the jump."

"She just didn't wanna hear it," Titus added. "She took the let-down really hard. You woulda thought they had been going out for years and planning a wedding the way she reacted. She came to my shop crying and carrying on."

"That's Celeste," Nina told them.

"Wait a minute, if you all think I'm gonna sit here while you talk about my family and not say nothing—"

"Hey, I'm back." Paige was interrupted by Celeste who had returned to their table wearing a big grin. "Oh, hey, Nina. I didn't know you were here too."

"Uh, hey, Celeste." Nina nodded.

"I thought your ride was ready to leave?" Quincy questioned.

"They are. I told them to go ahead and I would get you to take me home," Celeste answered. Noticing there was no longer an empty chair at the table, she didn't waste any time grabbing one from the table nearby and pulling it right next to Quincy. "So, Paige, how are you and Marlon these days?"

Paige's eyes widened and she looked at Celeste like she had lost her mind. She knew Celeste was trying to make a fool out of her in front of Quincy in an effort to make herself look good, but Paige wasn't about to let that happen.

"Celeste, you know Marlon and I aren't together anymore. But while you're asking, how's your fiancé, Cofie? Where has he been these past few weeks? I haven't seen him since I've moved back home."

Nina burst out laughing and Paige smiled innocently.

"I wouldn't know. We broke-up a while ago." Celeste turned her attention back to Quincy. "I'm very much available these days. What about you, Quincy?"

"What about me?" Quincy asked.

"Are you dating these days?"

"Uh, not really. A brother is too busy working these days." He looked over at Paige and added, "Uh, Celeste, I didn't drive here tonight Titus did."

"I'm sure Titus doesn't mind taking me home, do you, Titus?"

Titus looked over at Quincy then back to Celeste. "I guess not."

Paige was ready to leave. The adrenaline she had pumping moments earlier was now gone, and so was the buzz from her one drink, "Well, people, it's been real," she said, standing.

"You're leaving?" Quincy jumped up.

"Yeah, I have to be to work early in the morning," she told him.

Nina followed suit and added, "It was nice meeting you, Titus, and nice seeing you again, Quincy."

"I'll walk you guys out," Quincy volunteered.

"No, you stay here and enjoy the rest of your evening," Paige told him. "Celeste, I'll see later."

"Bye, Paige. Give my love to Myla for me, and I hope you and Marlon can work things out," Celeste sang out.

Paige didn't respond.

"You shoulda slapped that ho," Nina snapped as they got into the car.

"There was no need. You know how Celeste can be," Paige told her. "Always the drama queen."

Nina popped the glove compartment open and removed the cell phones they each placed there before going in the club. "Here, you have three missed calls."

Looking at her call log, Paige saw that all three calls came from the same person. "Oh no he didn't," she said aloud.

"Who is it? Marlon?"

"No, it's Eli. He's been calling me for the past hour."

"For what? He must've just dropped his silver shadow off." Nina laughed.

"And look, he's calling again."

"Answer, answer," Nina chanted like a cheering squad.

Paige clicked the talk button and sang into the phone, "Hello."

There was a pause and then finally, Eli spoke. "Hey."

"Hey, Elijah. What's up?"

"Nothing. I called your house and didn't get an answer. I was making sure you were okay," he said. Although she was still pissed about him being at the club with another woman, she knew not to let him know that she was bothered by that fact.

"That's so sweet of you. Actually, I haven't made it home yet. I'm still with some friends of mine. Thanks for checking, though," she said.

"I'm saying, I need to holler at you for a minute. What time do you think you'll be home?"

"I really can't say. Like I told you, I'm with some friends. Maybe we can chat some time tomorrow. Okay?"

Once again, there was a pause. She was hoping he thought she was with Quincy.

"Yeah, cool," he said then hung up.

"I know he wasn't trying to ask where you were," Nina said.

"No, he ain't that bold. He says he needs to holler at me."

"He was trying to come over? After he was in the club with a hoochie?"

"Girl, no. He doesn't even know where I live. He wanted to talk over the phone, I guess." She shrugged. "I'll talk to him tomorrow."

10

The following night, after taking a long, hot bath, Paige climbed into bed for some much needed rest. It had been an exhausting day. Staying out until after two in the morning and then dragging herself to work had given her a migraine. Luckily, her father was picking Myla up for the weekend. She promised herself that it would be the last weeknight she would hangout. Her exhaustion let her know that she definitely wasn't as young as she used to be.

As soon as she turned her nightlight off, the phone rang and she scolded herself for not turning the ringer off.

"Hello."

"Hey, it's me. Are you busy?" it was Eli.

"I'm in the bed."

"Already? It's only eight-fifteen."

"I'm still recuperating from last night."

"Oh, I forgot, you were with your friends after you left the club. My bad."

"Yeah, you were with your friends while you were at the club. Remember?" She laughed lightly.

"Come on, it wasn't like that. That was just a girl I'm cool with, that's all. She's a club regular. We dance together from time to time."

"You don't owe me any explanation. That's your business."

"If I would've known you were gonna be there. I would've been dancing with you. You know you're my baby."

"Oh, really?"

"Well, I thought you were until I saw you with those knuckleheads—oh, my bad. I mean your friends."

Paige couldn't help laughing, "They are my friends."

"And what am I? Am I your friend?"

"Yes, you're my friend."

"And what if I wanna be more than your friend?"

She didn't know how to answer that question. There was no denying the fact that she was attracted to Elijah, both physically and mentally, but there was something that wouldn't allow her to move on that attraction. Something held her back.

"You are more than my friend. You're my *special friend.*" Paige purred. She could hear him smiling through the phone. "Okay, at least I'm getting somewhere. And what privileges do I have as your *special friend*?" Elijah inquired.

"You get *special privileges.*"

"Now that's what I'm talking about!"

"Oh, don't get too happy. You don't even know what privileges they are yet."

"And what are they?"

"Hmmm, things like taking me to dinner and the movies, concerts, cutting my grass, washing my truck, things like that," she told him.

"I can handle all of that."

"Great, I'm glad to hear that." she tried to keep a yawn from escaping, but it was too strong.

"Well, I guess I'll talk to you tomorrow because you sound like you're about to fall asleep on me. You sleep tight, my *special friend*."

"You too," she told him and hung up the phone, this time remembering to turn the ringer off. She drifted to sleep and had a crazy dream that she and Elijah were buying a house, and when they went inside, Marlon was there waiting on them with a knife. Her heart began pounding and her eyes popped-open. Her room was pitch black, yet she could feel someone staring at her. She leaned up off the pillow and turned her head. There was a shadowy figure standing in the doorway. Reaching on the nightstand, she quickly clicked her light on.

"What the hell are you doing in my house?" She could not believe the nerve of him.

"Where is he?"

"Where is who? What are you doing? Get out before I call the police!" Paige yelled out.

Marlon opened the closet door and pushed her clothes back. When he didn't find who he was searching for, he looked under the bed and then went into her bathroom. Paige stood up, shocked by his behavior.

"Marlon, there's no one here. How did you get in here? How did you even find out where I live?"

He turned to face her, his eyes drifting down to her breasts, which were barely covered by her open pajama shirt. She snatched it closed.

"You know your daughter can't hold water. She's been bragging about you and her living in Meeko's townhouse."

112

Paige sat down on the side of the bed, "What the hell are you doing here? And who the hell were you looking for?"

"I'm looking for that negro you're fucking now. I figured he was here with you since Myla hasn't been staying here the last few nights. I've been calling your house and your cell phone and you haven't answered either one." He held up the extra key she kept hidden under the flower pot near the front door, the same place she kept it at their old house.

"Clearly you have lost your mind, Marlon Davis. How dare you come in here looking for someone? This ain't your house or your business. Whatever or whomever I do up in here is my business!"

"Don't fuck with me, Paige. I'm still pissed that you packed up lock, stock and barrel and left. And what the hell did you do to your hair?"

Paige touched her head and realized this was the first time Marlon had seen her new look. She decided not to even go there with him. "Please. What did you want me to do, Marlon? Tell me. You were playing house with the woman down the street and still begging me to come home. What? Were we all going to love together in one big house?"

"I keep telling you that woman meant nothing to me. I love you, Paige, and you know that." He grabbed her and pulled her to him, kissing her as if his life depended on it.

This is wrong. Stop it now before it goes too far. This is exactly what he wants you to do, and you're falling into this trap, the good girl in her thought. *He probably just got finished screwing that skank, Kasey.*

Forget that girl, the bad girl in her told her, *Get yours for once. It's been a while since you've had some good loving, and no point in starting nothing you ain't gonna finish.*

As her two inner beings fought it out in her head, she became caught up in the familiar taste and feel of his mouth. *Get yours, girl, get it.* Immediately, heat began to embrace her and she could sense that she was melting.

No, don't do it. You're going backwards instead of forwards.

His hands fumbled with the buttons of her shirt and found her nipples, anxiously awaiting his touch. They greeted him with hardness and he nibbled her collar playfully licking her neck, something he knew she loved.

Damn, this feels so good.

Her hands went under his shirt and caressed his back, her fingernails gently scratching the center. He inched her over to the bed and laid her down.

Get up now, before you do something you'll regret.

His mouth found its way to her breast, and she arched her back as he took each one into his mouth, sucking gently at first and then rougher. Her legs opened and she placed his hands in her center, letting him know that she was wet.

"Taste it," she moaned. He obliged and he let his tongue work its magic.

That's right, girl, get yours. Tell him what you want.

She missed Marlon so much that her heart ached. Here he was, satisfying her like he hadn't done in months. She bucked and held onto his head as she climaxed, her legs shaking uncontrollably. When she finished, he rose and lay on top of her, placing her hand on his thick, erect penis. She looked into his eyes and he smiled. It was sickening.

A'ight, you got yours, now put that nigga out! the good girl screamed in her head.

"Damn, I missed you. I can't wait to get inside you. You ready for me?" He whispered in her ear.

"I don't think so."

"What?" She could hear the confusion in his voice and see the frown on his face.

"Get up and get out."

"Now is not the time to be playing, Paige." He tried to kiss her, but she turned her head.

"I'm not playing. I want you to get up, pull your pants back up and get the hell out of my house."

Marlon's eyes widened in surprise and he looked to see if she was serious. She gave him a scowl that told him she was. She got out of the bed before she changed her mind and allowed her body to give in to its desires. The key that Marlon used to get in was lying on the floor, and she hastily snatched it up.

"Oh, I know your ass is tripping now," Marlon snapped. "You gon' just let me go down on you and then throw me out?"

"Yeah," Paige answered nonchalantly.

"That's some foul shit right there." He adjusted his pants and stood up.

"Call it what you will, Marlon. Just get the hell out. You said you broke in here trying to find a man, which you didn't. You basically disrespected me by even thinking I was going to sleep with you. But I was gracious enough to give you a taste of what you been missing. Now for the last time, get the hell out of my house and out of my life," she told him. For a moment, she saw the hurt in his eyes.

Marlon slowly walked past her. She followed behind him to make sure he indeed left. He said nothing as he walked down the hall and opened the front door. Just as he was about to walk out, he paused and looked at her.

"Lock the door behind me."

11

"Have you heard from your crazy baby daddy?" Meeko asked. They were unloading gifts from the trunk of her car and taking them into the restaurant which was already filled with members of their family. It was their Aunt Gayle's fiftieth birthday, and they were celebrating with a Labor Day brunch.

"No, I haven't talked to him. When he calls I give the phone straight to Myla, and when he picks her up, he picks her up and drops her off at Mama's, and I make sure I'm not there." Paige picked up a silver gift-wrapped box out of the trunk. "Where is Celeste? I thought she was coming out here to help. It *is* her mother's party."

"Girl, I don't know where she is. I wonder if she invited Quincy? You know that's all she ever talks about these days."

Paige was surprised. The way Quincy acted that night at the club, he definitely wasn't interested in rekindling his and Celeste's relationship. "Really? I didn't even know she had dated him before."

"Yeah, she was really into him a little while back, but then, she got with Cofie and we stopped hearing about Quincy," Meeko told her. Paige wanted to tell her that wasn't Quincy's side of the story, but decided not to.

"Did you ever pay for his broken mirror?"

"Actually, his friend Titus is letting me pay for it in installments. He has a big crush on Nina and I think this is his way of getting in with her."

"Is it working?" Meeko asked.

"Uh, no. You know Nina doesn't date anyone shorter than six feet. This brother is shorter than she is, so you know he doesn't have a chance. I have to give it to him, though. He's not giving up."

Stanley held the door for them as they entered. "You know I would have gotten those for you, sweetheart. You should have called me on my cell when you got to the parking lot."

Meeko looked lovingly at her husband, "That's okay, boo. Besides, you may need that strength later on tonight." She winked at him.

Paige couldn't help the twinge of jealousy she felt as she saw him take the boxes from his wife and kiss her on the cheek. She thought she heard her name being called. She turned to see Elijah walking up the sidewalk. He was dressed nicely in a green shirt and black pants. Paige smiled as she walked over to him.

"Hi there." He greeted her with a hug.

"Hi there, yourself. I didn't know you were coming. I thought you said you had to work."

"I got someone to take over my shift so I could make it. Are you surprised?"

"You know I am." She grinned. When she mentioned the dinner party to him a few weeks ago, he didn't really seem interested. She never mentioned it again. She invited him in an effort to become a little closer to him. He was a nice guy, and having him as her date seemed a lot better than having people continually ask about Marlon's absence, although she was sure by now they all knew of their breakup a few months ago.

They entered the restaurant arm in arm and she introduced him to her family as they sat down. Within moments, Eli's wit and outgoing personality had them all eating out of the palm of his hand. Paige looked over at her mother who gave her a simple nod of approval.

"Has anyone heard from Celeste?" Aunt Gayle asked Meeko and Paige.

"No, ma'am," Paige told her.

"She's probably running late as usual." Meeko shrugged. "You want me to call her for you, Aunt Gayle?"

"No, I guess she'll be here shortly. I guess we can go ahead and eat, though. No sense in just sitting here waiting. Jackie, you wanna lead us in prayer?" Aunt Gayle looked over at her.

"I would be honored. But are you sure you don't wanna wait for Celeste?"

"Chil', that buffet is over there calling my name. Now, will you go ahead and pray so I can eat." She nudged her sister's arm.

Paige looked at her mother standing between her two aunts. The three sisters were so different. Whereas her mother put you in mind of Patti LaBelle as far as looks and style, Aunt Gayle was more like Florida Evans: loving, yet homely. Meeko's mother, Aunt Connie was a firecracker. There was no denying where Meeko got her spunk from. They all stood and held hands as her mother led them in a prayer so powerful it brought tears to Paige's eyes.

"Amen," they all chorused when she finished.

"You go ahead and fix your plate. I'll be right back," she whispered to Eli.

"You want me to get your food too?" he offered. She smiled at his generosity.

"No, I'll get it when I get back. Thank you for offering, though." She motioned for Meeko to join her. The two women headed to the restroom.

"I like him. He has looks and personality," Meeko told her.

"Yeah, I like him too. I can't believe he actually came."

"Myla seems to like him, which says a lot."

"Yeah, it does," Paige agreed. "Where the hell is Celeste, though? I can't believe she's not here."

"Let me try to call her cell again. This doesn't make any sense. I bet she's somewhere laid up with Quincy. She's whipped already." Meeko took her cell phone out of her purse and called their cousin. "Celeste, where the hell are you? We're here at your mother's party and your ass ain't here. Your mother's about to be worried sick about you. I know you're with that nigga. You'd better get your tail down here and make it quick!"

"What did she say?" Paige ran her fingers through her hair and double-checked her makeup.

"I got her stupid voicemail. I'm going to cuss her out when she gets here, believe that," Meeko said as they walked out.

Paige noticed Eli helping Myla cut her food and was about to point it out to Meeko when she stopped in her tracks. She could not believe that coming though the door was Marlon Davis, looking fine as ever in a smoke-grey pinstriped suit. She rushed over to the lobby to stop him, not wanting to cause a scene.

"What are you doing here?"

"Hello to you too, Paige. What do you mean what am I doing here? I was invited."

"By who?" Meeko walked up.

"By Aunt Gayle. She invited me months ago and you know that, Paige," he told her. "Don't even try and say that you don't. You were right there when she told me about it."

Paige knew he was right. His aunt did specifically invite him to her big fiftieth birthday bash. But then again, she invited any and everyone she thought would come. What Paige didn't understand was how Marlon knew exactly when and where the party was being held, because she didn't recall her aunt giving him the specifics. The invitation Marlon took out of his breast pocket answered that for her.

"So, you got an invitation and felt obligated to come?" Paige asked, sucking her teeth.

"Well, actually, I forgot all about it until I ran into Celeste the other day while I was picking Myla up and she reminded me."

"Celeste," Paige said aloud. She knew her conniving cousin conveniently reminded Marlon in an effort to cause drama, as usual. There was no other reason for her doing it, and Paige was glad she hadn't shown up yet.

"Yeah, as a matter of fact, she assured me that my coming would be a welcome addition to her mother's event. It's not a problem, is it?" He smiled cynically at them. Paige wanted to stab him in his eye, but she didn't want to chance going to jail. She knew he was trying to get back at her for the other night, and she refused to play his little game.

"No, your being here is fine. As a matter of fact, we were just about to go and fix our plates. Come on," Paige told him. She looked over at Meeko, who gave her a look that said: *Go on, girl! Do your thing, and whatever happens, I got your back.*

All eyes were on them when they re-entered the private room where her family was eating. It was as if the entire party stopped to watch the three of them walk in.

"Daddy!" Myla jumped up and ran to her father.

Everyone was waiting to see exactly what reaction would be next. As if on cue, Paige's mother walked over and gave Marlon a big hug and marched him right over to the birthday girl herself, as if he was just another guest that showed up late. Paige looked over at Eli and shrugged. He smiled at her and she saw that instead of looking uncomfortable, he looked amused. Relieved, she fixed her plate and took a seat next to him.

"I'm going to kill Celeste," Paige whispered to Meeko.

"I'll help you bury the body," Meeko replied.

Paige made it a point not to look in Marlon's direction for the remainder of the meal. She didn't want to chance catching his eye and having him think she wanted to even talk to him.

When she tried to apologize to Eli, he interrupted her. "Don't go there. I ain't sweating him, and no one else is either."

Paige had already shared the story of her breakup with Marlon a little while ago, she had also assured Eli that she was no longer in love with Marlon, so there was no need for him to feel threatened. Now she was glad she had been open and honest with him because she could see that Marlon was infuriated by Elijah's presense. She was on her second trip to the buffet when he approached her about it.

"Who is that, Paige?" He asked through clenched teeth.

"That's my friend, Elijah. Not that it's any of your business," she answered him innocently.

"What's up with him being all in your face while I'm sitting at the table? You need to check him before I do," Marlon seethed.

"Marlon, please. Elijah is my guest and if you can't handle being at the same table, then I suggest you leave," she snapped.

"Is that who you're fucking now? Is that why I couldn't get none the other night?" He smiled cynically.

"No, you couldn't get any because as soon as I came, I came to my senses. But don't worry, you won't get the opportunity for me to have another lapse in judgment again." She walked off, leaving him to simmer in silence.

Hours later, the cake had been cut and the gifts had been opened, but there was still no Celeste. As they ventured out into the parking lot to leave, she finally called Meeko's phone.

"Celeste, where are you?" Meeko shouted, not caring that she was in public.

"Is that my baby? Let me talk to her." Aunt Gayle took the phone from Meeko. "Baby, are you all right? I've been worried sick. Again? Oh no, that's terrible.

Well, just stay there. I'll be home in a few minutes. I hate that you missed the party. I will. I won't forget. I love you." She gave the phone back to Meeko.

"Is she all right? Where is she?" Jackie asked, worried.

"She had one of those terrible migraines again. She tried to come, but she couldn't even drive because her head was hurting so bad. She took her medicine and was gonna lie down for a few minutes, and she just got up. She told me to be sure to bring her some cake, though," Aunt Gayle told them. Paige looked over at Meeko, who was just shaking her head. They both knew their cousin was lying.

"I don't see your car," Eli told her. "Where'd you park?"

"I rode with Meeko."

"Well, you want me to take you home?"

Paige thought about it then told him, "Sure. I'd like that. Let me tell my mother goodbye and get Myla."

After telling Meeko she had a ride home, she walked over to where her mother was talking to Marlon. Myla had her father by the hand and was leaning her head on his arm. As much as Paige was despising him, the sight of them was precious, and she wished she had a camera to capture the moment.

"Mama, I'm gone. I'll call you tomorrow." She walked over and gave her mother a kiss. Jackie said goodbye and left the three of them standing together.

"Mommy, can I go home with Daddy?" Myla pleaded.

"No, sweetheart. You can go home with him on Friday. You have to come home with me tonight."

"Well, can Daddy just bring me home in his car?"

"No, just come with Mommy now. Tell your daddy goodbye and come on. We need to go." She prayed that her daughter would cooperate and not put on a dramatic performance for her father. Paige looked to Marlon for support, but by the smug look on his face, she knew he was enjoying this.

"But—" Myla whined.

"Myla," Paige said in a warning voice.

"How about I give you a piggyback ride to the car?" Marlon leaned down and asked Myla, who now had tears in her eyes.

She nodded and wiped her face as she climbed on her father's back. "Okay."

"Where'd you park?" he asked, looking at Paige.

"I didn't drive. We're riding with Elijah," she told him.

"Oh, so that's the shoe guy," he said sarcastically. "Come on, Myla, let's take you to your ride. Where is it?"

Paige led them to the black Neon that Eli was standing next to.

"How are you?" Marlon asked, placing Myla on the ground next to her mother. He walked over to Eli and extended his hand. "Marlon Davis, nice to meet you."

"Elijah Green, same here."

"Well, thanks for taking my two ladies here home for me. I certainly appreciate it," Marlon told him.

"Hmph." Eli laughed as he walked over to open the door for Paige and Myla. "It's not a problem. I'm the one that should be thanking you."

At that comment, Marlon stiffened. He cut his eyes at Eli. "Myla, you be good for Mommy. I'll call you later."

"Yes, Dad." Myla blew her father a kiss.

"Nice meeting you, Elijah. Paige, remember to lock that door. We wouldn't want anyone coming in on you and Myla in the middle of the night," he smirked. Then started to walk off. He turned back around and told her, "Oh, I meant to tell you that new hair is sexy as hell. I likes that. Keep it that way."

Paige suppressed the urge to flip the bird at him. She climbed in the car and Eli closed the door. He was quiet when he got in and started the engine. After a few moments, he finally said, "So, that's Marlon."

"That's Marlon." she sighed. Hoping he wouldn't make any negative comments, especially while Myla was sitting in the backseat.

"That was a nice suit he was rocking."

Paige smiled. "Thanks. I gave it to him for Father's Day year before last."

"Somehow I knew you would take credit." Eli laughed.

She gave him directions to her house. He was familiar with the area, commenting that his best friend's mother lived right down the street when they pulled in front of her townhouse. The two little girls who just moved next door were outside playing with a jump rope. Myla ran over to talk to them.

"So, would you like to come in for a few minutes?" she asked.

"Yeah, that sounds cool," he answered and he followed her inside.

"Myla, come on and change clothes. You can come back outside," Paige called out. The little girl skipped-over to the house.

"You can come in and see my room, Mr. Eli. I have a canopy over my bed," Myla suggested.

"Really? Yeah, I gotta see that. It sounds like its fit for a princess," he said.

"It is, Mr. Eli. It's a princess bed. Next year when I turn eight, I'm going to get one fit for a queen," Myla told him.

Paige allowed Myla to give Eli a tour of the house as she changed out of the dress and heels she was wearing, into a pair of sweats and a T-shirt. When she came out of her room, Myla was talking Elijah's head off, yet he still gave her his full attention. You would've thought she was E. F. Hutton the way he was listening. Paige couldn't help laughing.

"Myla, it's time for *That's So Raven*. You'd better go change clothes before you miss the beginning," Paige told her. In a flash, Myla was down the hall, leaving Paige and Marlon alone. "Sorry about that."

"No need to apologize. She's a funny kid. I think I can name all the Bratz: Chloe, Jazmin—" Elijah counted on his fingers. "Oh, and then there are the Go to Tokyo ones."

"Go Go Tokyo," Paige corrected him. "You want something to drink? Tea, soda, water?"

"I'm fine right here." He reached over and touched her hair. "I hate to say it, but Marlon was right."

"Right about what?"

"You are sexy."

"He said my haircut was sexy and he was trying to be facetious. Marlon hates my hair short. That was one reason why I cut it all off. Why are we talking about him anyway?"

"We're not talking about him, we're talking about you and how beautiful you are."

"I thought I was sexy?" She smiled and leaned back onto his shoulder.

"You are. You're sexy, beautiful, gorgeous, attractive—"

"All that in these sweats?"

"I wouldn't care if you had on a hazmat suit. You would still be all-that and then-some," he responded.

"What's a hazmat suit?"

"You know those hazardous materials suits that Homer Simpson wears to work?"

Paige cracked up laughing. "Never in a million years has anyone compared me to Homer Simpson."

She turned and faced Elijah. He leaned in and kissed her, nibbling on her bottom lip. She could feel his arms around her waist, pulling her to him. She closed her eyes and enjoyed the feeling of being held. The kiss ended and she placed her head on his shoulder.

"Paige," he said.

"Yeah." She looked up at him.

"I love you."

Hearing him say those words stunned her. She enjoyed talking to and being with Elijah, but she was far from being in love with him. She didn't know how to respond. It was the first time someone had said those words to her that she didn't feel the same way.

"Elijah, you know I just got out of a long-term relationship. I don't think—no, I know I'm not ready—"

"I understand that, Paige. I just wanted you to know up front that I'm not trying to play games with you or mess with your head. I love you, and I love

Myla, too. This may sound sudden, but I do. I love you."

"I hear what you're saying, Eli, and I respect it, too. I'm just saying that I want to take things slow. I'm not ready to jump head first into another relationship. I'm not playing games with you, either. So, if a commitment is what you're asking me for right now, I can't make one. And that's just me being honest."

Elijah shrugged and looked into her eyes. "Then I guess we'll take it slow. I don't care about that. I just wanted you to know where I am in this."

"I appreciate that." Paige smiled. It was Paige that kissed him this time. She tried to see if maybe there was something there that she didn't realize she was feeling, but there wasn't. She wanted it to feel like it was when she was with Marlon, but it didn't happen. There was no doubt, she definitely wasn't in love with Elijah, at least not for now.

12

Before Paige knew it, September had come and gone. She barely had time to see Elijah. Now that school had begun, her days were much busier at work and at home. The library stayed busy and Myla had homework nearly every night, and Paige made it a point to help her with it.

One evening, she was helping Myla study words for a class the school had introduced on character Development. The point of the class was to help the students develop positive characteristics and citizenship skills that they would use in everyday life. Paige thought the class was a wonderful idea.

"Okay, Ms. Myla, what are your words for today?" she asked, sitting across from her at the kitchen table.

"Trustworthiness and honesty," Myla announced.

"Ohhh, those are two good words. What do they mean?" Paige sat back in her chair and waited for Myla's answer. Myla picked up a note card bearing the word "trustworthiness."

"Trustworthiness means to be able to be trusted. Like to have faith in that you'll do the right thing, no matter what and you won't let people down when they need you," Myla told her.

"Very good answer. I like that." Paige nodded. "And honesty?"

Myla picked the card up and said, "Honesty means to tell the truth and be for real, even when you don't want to."

"You are so smart, Myla. You know that?"

"Yes, Mom. I—"

The sound of the phone ringing interrupted her. She jumped-up and ran over to the cordless phone and said, "It's Dad."

"Don't answer it, Myla. Come on let's finish your homework first. You can call him later," Paige told her.

"I will only talk for a minute, Mommy, I promise," Myla picked up the phone before Paige could even protest. "Hi, Daddy. Doing my homework. Yes, uh-huh. Okay. I know. Yeah, hold on." She covered the mouthpiece of the phone and whispered, "He wants to talk to you."

Paige shook her head. "Tell him I'm in the bathroom. I'll call him back later."

"But you're not in the bathroom," Myla hissed.

"He doesn't know that. Just tell him."

"You want me to lie?" Myla frowned at her mother. She paused then said into the phone, "She's right here. Love you too."

Paige was shocked that Myla had blatantly disobeyed her. She snatched the phone from her, rolling her eyes in the process.

Myla walked back to the table and smiled at her mother as she held up the two note-cards, bearing the words "honesty" and "trustworthiness." In that moment, Paige felt like the worst mother ever. Here she was supposed to be setting a good example for her daughter, and instead she was teaching and encouraging the child to lie. She mouthed the word "sorry" to her and said, "Hello."

"Hey, Paige. I know you're busy helping Myla with her homework, but I just wanted to know if you've

131

talked to Camille. I've been trying to call her the past two days and I can't get in touch with her. Have you talked to her?"

From the sound of his voice, Paige knew Marlon was worried. Since Camille had left this summer, he and his sister communicated daily, even if it was through e-mail. "No, I haven't heard from her, Marlon. Have you tried calling the dorm?"

"Yeah, I left messages on her cell, in her room, with the dorm R. A., I can't find her."

"Calm down, Marlon. When is the last time you talked to her?"

"Saturday morning."

"Marlon, today is just Tuesday. I know you're used to talking to her all the time, but she's a freshman in college. She has classes and extra-curricular activities. Come on now. Don't act like you don't know how it was when you went off to school."

"I know. But, Paige, I'm beginning to get worried. Listen, can you call her and if you talk to her, tell her to call me?"

"I will, Marlon."

"Promise me, Paige."

"I will, Marlon."

"Thank you."

Paige hung up the phone and told Myla to go and get her cell phone. When Myla returned, she dialed Camille's number. Camille answered on the first ring.

"I was about to call you."

"What's going on, Camille? Your brother is worried sick. Are you all right?"

"Hi, Aunt Camille," Myla sang in the background.

"Finish your homework," Paige warned her. She got up and walked into the living room where she would have some privacy. "Okay, what's up? Why are you MIA?"

"I'm not, but I just can't talk to Marlon right now. Not yet, anyway." Camille sighed.

"Why not? What's wrong, Camille? Are you pregnant?" Paige's heart began beating. She knew that if Camille was pregnant, both Marlon and her mother would take turns trying to kick the fetus out of her belly.

"Nooooo!" Camille yelled.

Paige was relieved, but she knew there was something going on. "Okay, then what is it?"

"I can't talk about it over the phone. I need to tell you this face-to-face. I found a cheap flight on the Internet and I can fly there tomorrow night. Can you pick me up?"

"Sure, that's no problem. What time?"

Camille gave her the flight information and Paige agreed to pick her up.

"Thanks, Paige. And please don't say a word of this to Marlon. Don't even tell him I'm coming home."

Paige hesitated, but finally agreed. As she hung up, something told her that she was about to be in the middle of something she really didn't want to be in.

Camille looked fine as she walked through the airport terminal. Paige tossed and turned all night thinking that maybe Camille had been diagnosed with some terminal illness and didn't want Marlon or her mother to know. Paige ran over and gave her a big hug, telling herself that she had to be strong for Camille's sake.

"Hey there, Pajamas!" Camille giggled, calling Paige by the nickname she gave her years ago.

"Hey, Cami Cam! You look beautiful. I see you've lost some weight. Don't go getting anorexic on me!" Paige teased her.

"Please, try partying and still trying to go to class. Being tired as hell definitely works as an appetite suppressant."

"You don't have to tell me. Girl, my freshman year, you would've thought my major was Spades!"

"Where is Ms. Myla?"

"You did tell me you didn't want Marlon to know you were coming this weekend, right?"

"Yeah, I did."

"Then you didn't want Myla to know either. There are no secrets between those two. She's with Nina and Jade for the weekend."

"So, it's just you and me?"

"Just you and me."

Paige looked over at Camille. She didn't want to press her for information, knowing that Camille would tell her when the time was right. But she was ready to know now. Obviously, Camille wasn't ready to tell her because she suggested they go to Smokey Bones and grab a bite to eat. *Maybe she'll confide over dinner*, Paige thought as she they loaded the car and headed to the restaurant.

As they feasted on ribs, chicken and the best cornbread Paige had ever tasted, Camille told her all about school and living in Atlanta. Her roommate was a girl named Miriam, whose nickname was Magic.

"She just moved back from New York, and I'm telling you, the girl is crazy. She keeps me laughing and I couldn't ask for a better roommate. She's off the chain."

"I'm glad things are going well for you, Camille," Paige commented. "Which is why I don't understand why you can't talk to your brother."

Camille took a sip of her tea and then said, "I'm afraid."

"Afraid of what?" Paige was totally confused.

"Afraid to tell him."

"Tell him what? Did something happen to you, Camille? Did someone do something to you?"

"No, it's nothing like that. It's just crazy."

"Camille, you're talking in riddles and I'm about to get frustrated. Now tell me what's going on and start from the beginning."

"Okay, when I was growing up, we had this neighbor named Ms. Franklin that lived across the street. She moved away a few years ago. Well, Magic and I were in the grocery store the other night and I ran into her. I couldn't believe it. Well, we talked for a few minutes and she was filling me in on her kids and other people in the neighborhood, and she told me that she came home a few weeks this past summer and ran into my father."

Paige nearly dropped her fork. "What was she talking about? Your father has been dead for years."

Camille nodded her head. "That's what I told her. Ms. Franklin told me that was a lie Mama told us so we would stop asking questions about him. She says she felt bad that Mama would tell Marlon and I something as mean as that, but felt it wasn't her place to say anything while we were children. She was glad to see that I was an adult and doing well with my life, so she felt moved enough to tell me. She even took my phone number and said she would get in contact with him for me."

Paige didn't know what to say. She just sat staring at Camille, trying to absorb everything she had just told her. Marlon's father was alive. His mother had been lying all these years. It was all too much.

"He called me Sunday night." Camille sighed.

"Whoa, this is crazy."

"I know it is. I talked to him for a long time. From what he says, he really is our father, Paige. That was one reason I had to come home, so I can go and meet him. That's also why I can't talk to Marlon until after I do that. I don't know how he's going to take this."

Paige had to agree with her. The memories of his father weren't all that great. He mostly talked of his mother and father arguing, but there were some he had of his father teaching him to ride his bike and coming to his pee wee football games, each time, being drunk. Paige thought it was funny how he often ridiculed his father's alcoholism but accepted his mother's.

"Wow, so when is this meeting going to take place?" Paige asked.

"Saturday morning. We're meeting for breakfast. Then, after we check him out, we can tell Marlon."

"Wait a minute. *We*? I don't think so. I'm not getting involved with this, Camille."

"You're already involved, Paige. I'm staying at your house and you haven't told Marlon, and he's worried to death about me. You're already covering for me.

Please, I need you to help us get through this," Camille pleaded. "I don't have anyone else to help me tell him. You know I can't be there by myself. I need you, Pajamas."

Paige saw the tears forming in Camille's eyes and her heart melted. She knew that she was the only one Camille had to help her, and she would do anything for her. "So, what's your game plan for telling him?"

Camille smiled with relief. The two women continued talking until the waitress informed them the restaurant was closing.

"I don't know about this," Paige said when they got to her house.

"Just tell him you want to meet him for dinner Saturday night. You know what to say. You were with him for ten years."

"I was with him for seven years. And we only lived together for five."

"Close enough. My point is you know you can get him to meet you at the restaurant," Camille yawned. "Man, I'm tired. I've been keeping that in for so long that it's been keeping me up at night."

"I guess partying with Magic had nothing to do with it, huh?" Paige led her to the guestroom, which she had already prepared with an air mattress.

"Hey, what happened to the furniture I used to sleep in at the other house?"

"I sleep in that now," Paige informed her.

"Oh, sorry." Camille shrugged. "Thanks again, Paige. I know that you're hating Marlon right about now, but I'm glad you care enough about him to be there for him."

"I'm doing this for you, not him. Now, get some rest." Paige hugged her and closed the door behind her as she walked out. She went into the kitchen and saw Myla's character cards lying on the table. She picked up "trustworthiness" and thought about her daughter's definition.

She grabbed the phone and dialed Marlon's cell number.

"Hello." He sounded as if he was asleep.

"Hey Marlon, it's me."

"What's going on? Something wrong with Myla?" he asked. She could hear him sitting up and wondered if he was in bed with Kasey. She told herself to focus and not think about that.

"No, nothing's wrong."

"You talked to Camille? Did she call you?"

Instead of lying, Paige avoided the question. "Marlon, I need to talk to you. You think we can meet for dinner Saturday night?"

"Huh?"

"Can we meet for dinner Saturday night or do you have plans?" She knew she had thrown him for a loop by asking him to dinner.

"Naw, I don't have any plans. Where do you wanna meet? What time? I'm playing golf until five, but I can come straight from there. It shouldn't be any traffic."

"I can drive up there, Marlon. We can meet at Fat Tuesdays." She picked a restaurant that was their favorite and held a lot of good memories for them.

"Cool. I'm looking forward to it, Paige. I'm glad you called. Are you gonna stay the night?"

"No, fool! Didn't I say I needed to talk to you? That does not mean I wanna sleep with you!"

"I'm just playing." He laughed, but Paige knew he was serious.

"Bye, Marlon."

"Bye, Paige."

She hung up, wanting to be mad. But she knew there was no denying the grin she wore on her face.

13

"So, I guess this means we won't be going out this weekend," Elijah said. She knew he was disappointed because she had promised they would spend time together Saturday. Now that Camille had enlisted her help, that wouldn't be happening.

"I'm sorry, Eli. This definitely isn't something I thought that I'd be doing this weekend. You know I was looking forward to hanging out with you."

"I hear you."

"Look, I promise I'll make it up to you next weekend."

"I have to work next weekend. That's why I was looking forward to spending the entire day with you. I have to work the next two weekends as a matter of fact." He paused and asked, "Are you sure you don't still have feelings for Marlon? I mean, you're getting all involved with this situation."

"No, Eli, I don't. I'm doing this for Camille, not Marlon. Believe me, if she had anyone else to be there for her, I wouldn't have to do it, but, she doesn't. This has nothing to do with me and Marlon."

Paige felt bad. She knew Elijah was feeling neglected and she wanted to spend time with him. There was no way it was going to happen this weekend, though. She tried to think of a compromise, but couldn't. It was already late Friday afternoon, and she and Camille were headed to meet Roni at her mother's shop to get their hair done. She looked over at the clock and saw that if she didn't leave now, they would be late.

"Let me see what I can work out for Sunday evening, is that cool?" she asked, hoping he would accept that.

"Yeah, just call me and let me know what's up."

"I will," she promised. She hoped he wasn't too angry, but was more worried about making it to her hair appointment on time.

"So, how's the new man in your life?" Roni asked as she washed Paige's hair.

"Hard to say, Roni. I mean, he's a nice guy and I like him, but I'm just not rushing into anything right now," Paige told her. "He's really attentive and gets along great with Myla, but— I don't know. I'm not ready to take it any further, I guess."

"That's understandable. Take your time, girl. There's no reason to rush anything, anyway. If it don't fit, don't force it, that's what I always say." Roni walked her from the shampoo bowl to the chair.

"But I'm not trying to hurt his feelings, either." Paige sighed.

"Hurt whose feelings?" Meeko's voice came out of nowhere.

"What are you doing here?" Paige grinned, happy to see her cousin.

"I saw your truck outside. Hey, Camille." Meeko walked over and gave Camille a hug, "You look good, girl. You see Paige has turned into a diva since moving back, huh? Getting her hair done and stuff!"

"Shut up, Meeko. Shouldn't you be home hanging curtains or something?" Paige tossed at her.

"Divas don't do such tedious household tasks," Meeko replied.

"I heard that." Camille gave Meeko a high-five and said, "I wanna be like you when I grow up."

"Honey, that's impossible," Roni said. "When God created Meeko, he definitely broke the mold. There was no-way he was gonna make that same mistake twice."

The shop erupted in laughter. The door opened again and Celeste walked through the door. "Meeko, I thought you were only gonna be in here a minute. Oh, hello everyone."

"Hey, Celeste," Roni said.

Paige gave her an unenthusiastic hello and waved. She had yet to cuss her out about inviting Marlon to the birthday party, but now was not the time nor the place to do so.

"I think I'm going to stay for a few minutes, Celeste. Come on in and sit down. You sure you don't wanna jump in Roni's chair and get primed and proper?"

"My man likes me just the way I am, thank you." Celeste half-heartedly came in and sat beside Camille and Meeko in the waiting area. "Are you sure you need to be around here with all these chemicals in your condition?"

Meeko gave Celeste an angry look. "Shut up, Celeste."

"What condition?" Roni asked.

Paige looked over at her cousin who looked like she had something to say but was afraid to say it. "Meeko, what's going on?"

"Damn, Celeste, why didn't you stay your ass in the car and wait?" Meeko sighed.

"Sorry, I didn't know your pregnancy was a big secret. My bad." Celeste rolled her eyes.

Meeko was having a baby! As happy as Paige was for her cousin, she still couldn't stop the feeling of sadness that overwhelmed her. She got up out of the chair and walked into the restroom. Camille followed behind her. Everyone else was so caught up in congratulating Meeko that they didn't notice her sudden departure.

"Are you okay?" Camille asked, rubbing her back.

"Yeah, I'm fine." Paige tried to smile as she grabbed some tissue and wiped the tears from her eyes.

"It's okay if you're not. I mean, I know this has to be hard for you," Camille said softly.

Paige looked up and saw that Camille was also crying. She embraced the pretty girl and they hugged and cried together. It was one of the few times Paige had actually grieved for her son.

"Paige, I'm so sorry. I wanted to tell you myself," Meeko's voice came from behind them.

"It's okay. I'm happy for you, Meeko. It's just so shocking, that's all," Paige sniffed.

"I know, baby, I know." Meeko nodded.

"You're gonna be a mom." Paige smiled and added, "You're gonna be fat. I can get all your clothes now!"

Paige heard Camille up at the crack-of-dawn on Saturday morning. She knew Camille must be nervous, and hoped that she wouldn't throw up in the two-hour drive they had ahead of them. She packed a change of clothes, wondering what they would do during the hours between meeting Mr. Davis for breakfast and Marlon for dinner. The only solution she came up with was to hang out at the mall, of course.

There was a knock at her bedroom door.

"Come in," she called out.

"Are you up?" Camille opened the door. Paige laughed when she saw that the girl was already fully dressed and ready to go.

"Uh, no. It's only six-fifteen. What time are we meeting him?"

"At ten." Camille sat on the side of her bed. "How do I look? Do these jeans look okay?"

"I take it you're nervous. There's no need to be, Camille."

"I know, but I can't help it. I mean, I want to look nice for him."

"You do look nice. You're beautiful, inside and out, and he doesn't care what you look like."

"I have so many questions I wanna ask him. It's been hard not to call and just ask him over the phone."

"I can imagine. But can you do me a favor? Can you please call your brother and let him know you're okay? He's going to drive all the way to Atlanta looking for you if you don't. I'm surprised he hasn't already done so."

"Okay, I will."

"Why don't you do it now? You know he's asleep and you can leave him a voicemail," Paige suggested.

"Good idea. I'll go and do that right now, while you get up and get dressed." Camille smiled and stood up. "Are you sure these jeans aren't too tight? I don't want him to think his daughter is a hoochie."

"It's not the jeans that make you look hoochie, it's the tight sweater! Now, get out of my room," Paige teased.

You would've thought that Camille and Marlon came from two totally different households. Whereas Marlon almost worshipped the ground his mother walked on, Camille seemed to hate every single step she took. Lucille Davis was probably too drunk to see the difference in the way she raised her two children. She made sure Marlon had the best of everything. He was her son, the only child she wanted. Her unplanned daughter, Camille, on the other hand, didn't seem to matter to her one way or the other. Marlon was always the responsible older brother, and it was he who made sure Camille had the things she needed in life. He helped her with her homework, made sure she ate three meals a day and had clean clothes to wear to school. It was Marlon who taught her about the life changes her body was going through and taught her about sex. Whereas Lucille was his mother, Marlon became mother and father to Camille.

When he went off to college, he made Camille promise to take care of their mother. Although she hated to do it, she didn't want to let her brother down. So, for over four years, she became head of household because their mother was too drunk to do so. The care of the house and their mother became her responsibility, but no matter how hard she worked at school, no matter how clean she kept the house, no matter how good a meal she cooked, she could never be as good as Marlon. It was for that reason that Camille vowed that the day she walked across that stage to receive her diploma would be the last day she would live in her mother's house. Paige now realized that Camille meant what she said, and she agreed whole heartedly. Camille had a poor excuse for a mother growing up, and now she had found her father. Paige prayed that he didn't turn-out to be as big a disappointment to Camille as Ms. Lucille had.

You would've thought Paige was meeting her own father for the first time the way the butterflies were fluttering in her stomach. The waitress escorted them to the table where Mr. Davis was waiting. He smiled as he stood up and greeted them. He stared at Camille and Paige stared at him. There was no denying he was their father. Both Marlon and Camille were the spitting image of him. The cocoa-brown skin, the thick eyebrows and long lashes that even Myla possessed. It was uncanny. Tears flowed from Camille's eyes as she embraced her father. Paige dabbed at her own eyes, catching the tears before they fell.

"Um, this is Paige, I told you about her. She's Marlon's—uh, she's . . ." Camille tried to think of Paige's correct title.

"Hi, I'm Marlon's ex-girlfriend and Camille's friend." Paige extended her hand.

Mr. Davis shook it. "Vernon Davis. Wonderful to meet you. You're Myla's mother."

"Yes, sir."

"Well, ladies, let's have a seat," he told them.

Paige couldn't help but look from Camille to her father, still amazed at how much they looked alike.

They ordered, and there was a nervous quietness at the table. Paige knew Camille wanted to talk, but

146

didn't know where to begin. She decided to start the conversation for her. "So, how long have you been living here?"

"I just returned in April. I'm a long-distance truck driver, so I've pretty much been all over. I retired and decided to just move back and settle here."

"Do you have any other children?" Camille asked.

"No. Just you and your brother."

"So, you've just been driving trucks all these years? That's all?"

"Pretty much. Well, for at least the last fifteen."

"And before that?"

"I was out on the streets, pretty much, doing nothing. I had a substance abuse problem. I was deep into heroin. That's pretty much why your mama put me out. I don't blame her for that. I do blame her for not being honest and telling you all that I had a problem and telling you I was dead, instead.

"Her telling you that was one of the things that inspired me to get clean. I came to visit one night when I was in my right mind. It was late and I came knocking on the door. She opened it and she was drunk, of course. I told her I was sorry and I wanted both of us to get help. She told me she didn't need help. Told me I was nothing and she had told you I was dead and to stay out of your lives. Said that you all were better off without me.

"I walked away that night a broken man, but I was determined. Determined to get clean and determined that one day, somehow, someway, you all would find out the truth. And when you did, I was going to be a better man, a clean and sober man.

"I finished rehab, got my CDL and started driving trucks. I sent money every month, and she would send it right back to my P.O. box. I kept up with all of your accomplishments though. I was right there for your brother's high school and college graduations. I was at your graduation too. I'm proud of you."

Paige didn't stop the tears from falling this time; there were too many. She could not believe the damage that Ms. Lucille had caused within her children—for no reason. She looked over at Camille, who as also crying. She thought about her own father, who had always been there for them and she became angry at her mother for her unforgiving spirit.

"And now the truth is out," Camille sniffed.

"All I want to know is if you can forgive me. I know that I should've been a better father. Sometimes I thought about going to the courts and asking them to give me some sort of visitation, but then I would think about them knowing about my drug abuse and thought I wouldn't have a chance in hell. The courts aren't like they are now. They wasn't trying to give men a chance back then," he told them. "I'm sorry, and I want us to start healing and making amends. I want to have a relationship with my children."

"I forgive you, Daddy. I'm just glad you're alive and you can be honest with me." Camille hugged her father.

The waitress came and placed their food on the table. "Can I get you all anything?"

"Hot sauce," Camille and her father said at the same time.

Shoulda, Woulda, Coulda

Fat Tuesday's was Paige's favorite restaurant, and she was looking forward to throwing down on some gumbo, jambalaya and shrimp etouffee. She hoped Marlon knew he was paying.

"How many will be joining you?" The waiter asked.

"Two—I mean three, but just leave these two place settings and then we can add more after they arrive," Paige told him, hoping their plan would work.

"Can I get you an appetizer?"

"Yeah, a Hurricane," she said, knowing she would need a drink to get through this, "and some stuffed mushrooms. Better yet, make it a Bourbon Street Sampler and an Incredible Hulk for my guest when he arrives."

She had started on her drink when Marlon arrived at the table. She looked up to find him smiling.

"Damn, this must be serious as hell. You already got a Hurricane?" The waitress brought the platter of appetizers and placed it in front of them. "Aw hell, I must be paying."

Paige laughed while trying not to spit out her drink. Marlon knew her better than anyone she had ever known.

"So, have you already ordered?" He picked up the menu and scanned it. She couldn't help admiring how handsome he looked. He had grown a full beard and it was trimmed to perfection, something he had never done before.

"I like the beard. It looks nice."

"Thank you. I decided to try something different with my look too." He rubbed his chin. "I think it makes me look suave, debonair."

"You sound like JJ on *Good Times*."

149

"I thought it was more like Sweet Daddy." He smiled. The waitress returned with his Incredible Hulk, taking him by surprise. "Oh, who knows whom, now?"

"Well, you know, what can I say?" She impersonated JJ to the best of her ability. He laughed and then looked at her strangely.

"What the hell is going on, Paige?" he asked, suddenly sounding serious. "We've had more fun in the past five minutes than we've had in the last two years. You said you needed to talk to me. What's up?"

"Well," Paige began, "I talked to Camille."

"When? Did you tell her I was worried about her? Where the hell has she been?" Marlon raised his voice and people began looking at their table.

"Calm down, Marlon," she hissed at him. She gave him a moment to regain his composure. "She's fine. She needs to talk to you, but decided it was better to do it in person."

"Fine. I'll fly out there tomorrow." He picked up his drink and took a swig.

"No, you don't have to do that."

"Why not?" He frowned.

"Because she's standing right behind you."

Marlon turned to see his sister and grabbed her into his arms. She didn't know if it was because he had been so worried about her the past few days, or that she had been gone these past few months, but from his reaction, she knew he truly missed her.

"Cam, I'm so glad to see you! I was 'bout to lose my damn mind when I couldn't get up with you these past few days. When did you get here?"

"I've been staying with Paige the past few days."

"Why didn't you call me? You could've stayed at the house." He turned toward Paige, "I asked you if you talked to her. You knew I was about to lose my mind because I hadn't heard from her. Why didn't you say something?"

"She asked me not to," was Paige's response.

Camille sat at the table with them, "I know, Marlon, and I'm sorry you were worried. I just needed to talk to you face-to-face. I have something to tell you."

"What is it?" he asked. His eyes widened and his voice jumped up an octave as he questioned, "Are you pregnant?"

Once again, all eyes were on their table.

"God, no! Why does everyone keep asking me that?" Camille looked over at Paige who shrugged.

Marlon took another swig of his drink, this time a much bigger one. Paige knew he was going to need a refill soon, especially after Camille broke the news about their father.

"Are you calm now?" Paige asked him. He nodded and she said, "Good. Now, I need for you to listen to what Camille is about to tell you. Don't interrupt, okay? And Marlon, you've got to promise me you'll remain calm."

"Okay," he mumbled.

Camille told him the same story she told Paige at Smoky Bones, two nights ago. As Paige predicted, his glass was empty by the time she finished.

"I couldn't tell you all of this over the phone, Marlon. I knew I had to tell you in person."

"So, now what?" Marlon asked.

"He wants to meet you, Marlon. He seems nice and sincere in wanting to develop some sort of relationship with us."

"Why now? After all these years? What does he want, money?"

"No, he doesn't want anything but to tell you his side of the story and make amends with you—that's all. He's not looking for a handout or sympathy. He just wants to talk."

Paige reached over and touched Marlon's hand. She knew this was hard for him.

"Where is he at now?" Marlon looked Camille in the eyes, still trying to understand what was going on.

"He's sitting at that table over there." Camille stood and motioned for her father to join them.

"I need a refill," Marlon whispered to Paige.

Me too, Paige thought as she watched the Davis family reunite.

All in all, dinner was a success. At first, Marlon was very introverted, not saying much. But, after hearing his father's story and realizing that there was no secret motive behind this reunion, by the time dessert arrived, he was talking to his father as if he were an old friend. The two men had a lot in common. They both loved golf and the Detroit Pistons, and even made plans to play a round the following week. Camille promised to call her father as soon as she got back to school. He hugged all of them before he left the table.

"So, that was Vernon Davis. Never in a million years would I have thought I would be having dinner with him," Marlon commented.

"Me either," Paige said. "But I'm glad you got the opportunity to. He's a nice man."

"Good ol' Vern, that's what Ms. Franklin called him. Can you believe Mama has been lying all these years? I just don't even know what to say about her," Camille sighed. For some reason, Paige still sensed nervousness from her.

Marlon defended his mother. "Well, he did say that he was on heroin. She was only trying to protect us, Camille. She didn't do it to be vindictive."

"Marlon, I don't know why you continue to stand up for her after all she's done. You are always taking up for her and making excuses. Mama is a mean and hateful woman with a drinking problem, and for some reason, you just don't see that."

Finally, someone to talk some sense into him, Paige thought. She had been waiting a long time for Marlon to see his mother for what she was. Now, after everything his father had told him and with what Camille was saying, he would get her some help. Marlon looked over at Paige, but she knew better than to comment.

"Camille, I'm not going to sit here and let you talk about my mother like she's some drunk on the street. She's worked hard all her life to take care of us and from what I see, she's done a damn good job," he huffed.

"What job did she do, Marlon? Fuss, cuss and complain all the time? Hell, you were the one who's always taken care of us. You've worked hard since you were fourteen and helped Mama pay bills, and now we find out Daddy was willing to take care of us the entire time. She took that away from us. She took away your

childhood and she even cost you the love of your life."
Camille pointed to Paige who was sitting across from
her. She was crying. "Marlon, she's taken so much
from you and you don't even know about it."

"Cam, what are you talking about?" Paige
questioned.

"Ms. Franklin told me something else that Mama
kept from you. Do you remember a girl named Rachel
Simpson?"

"Rachel Simpson? I don't know her." Marlon shook
his head.

"A girl named Rachel would come every summer
and visit her grandmother, who lived around the
corner. She was a really pretty girl from New Jersey."

"Oh, yeah, I remember her. Dark-skinned chick,
real pretty. We kicked it a few times back in the day."

"Well, you kicked it enough to knock her up,
Marlon."

"Huh?" He and Paige said at the same time.

"Marlon, you have a fourteen-year-old daughter."

"Are you going to be all right? You need me to
drive?" Paige asked Marlon as they left the restaurant.

"You've had just as much to drink as I have."

"But I haven't received as many life-altering
revelations tonight as you have. I know you have a lot
on your mind. Come on, let me drive you home."

Marlon reluctantly gave her his keys and she told
Camille to follow them in her truck.

"Is he going to be all right?" the young girl asked
when they walked into Marlon's house. Her face was
swollen from all the crying she had done. Marlon had
gone upstairs without saying a word.

"He'll be fine. I think he's in a little bit of shock. Why didn't you tell me about his daughter?"

"I don't know. I only found out about Rachel Simpson this afternoon. Maybe I should've waited until later to tell him. But when he started defending Mama, I just couldn't take it. Is he mad at me?"

Paige put her arms around Camille and assured her she did nothing for her brother to be angry at. "Camille, you did the right thing. You laid everything out there for Marlon to see. What he does with the information you gave him is up to him. I'm proud of you. I know this was hard for you to do."

"Thank you for being there. I know I couldn't have done any of this without you. I hope you and my brother find a way to work things out because you are truly my sister-in-law and I love you."

"Even if things don't work out between Marlon and I, I will still be your sister-in-law, Camille, and you know that." The two women hugged.

"Don't you think we should stay here tonight?" Camille raised her eyebrow. "It's late, and I know you don't feel like driving back home."

Paige knew she was right. She really didn't feel up to the drive, and she was worried about Marlon, "Yeah, we can camp out down here. Which one do you want? The chaise or the sofa?"

"The sofa," Camille said quickly.

"It figures," Paige laughed. "I'll get us some blankets and let Marlon know we're down here."

She climbed the stairs and tapped on the bedroom door which was closed. There was no answer. She quietly turned the knob and peeked inside. Marlon was laid back on the bed, his arms folded across his

155

face. She walked over to him and softly called his name.

He sat up and she saw the tears. He pulled her close to him, burying his head into her chest as he held her. She could feel him crying and rubbed his back, not saying anything. It was the fourth time she had seen him cry. The first two times had been at their children's births and the last time had been at their son's memorial, but this time was different. This time it was as if he was letting out years of tears that had built up. She stood comforting him for what seemed like hours. When he finished, he lay back on the bed. She took off her shoes and climbed in beside him and held him until they both were asleep.

The next morning, her eyes opened and she found him staring at her. "I love you."

"I love you, too," she smiled.

14

"Wow, I can't believe all of that happened in a weekend," Nina said. "So, now what? Are you and Marlon back together?"

"No, we're not back together."

"Well, I figured after all of that, you would be back together. You did tell each other you love one another."

"And I do love Marlon. I always will."

"You did sleep with him."

"Yeah, technically we were asleep in the same bed. But we didn't make love. We didn't even kiss."

"But you stayed by his side, Paige. When he needed you the most, you didn't just leave him and come home. You stayed all night and comforted him. You still love him." Nina sat back and folded her arms.

"I already admitted that I love him, Nina. But that doesn't mean I'm in love with him. Marlon and I still have issues, and the fact that I was there for him doesn't make those issues disappear," Paige replied.

"Yeah, that's true. But does this make you look at things differently? Does it make you wonder that if you can be there for him after all you all have been through—good and bad—can't you work through those issues?"

Paige had to think about what her best friend was asking. She did have to wonder. She thought about it all last night as she wrapped her arms around Marlon and held him to her. She thought about it as she told him goodbye and promised to call him. She thought about it as she dropped Camille off at the airport. And now, here she was picking up their daughter, created out of their love, thinking about it again.

"Yes, I wonder. I can't even lie. Nina, one thing I can say about Marlon is that good or bad, as much as I say I love or even hate him, we will always be friends. We were friends before we became lovers, and that's the most important thing we have: our friendship. My being there for him had nothing to do with my still loving him or trying to get back together. I was there for him because he's my friend."

"Mommy!" Myla gave her mother a big hug. As she looked at he daughter, Paige noticed the features she had seen in Vernon, Marlon and Camille. Then, another thought struck her. Something she hadn't done in a while. She wondered if her son would have had the features as they did.

"Hey, Ms. Myla, did you have a good time?"

"Oh, yes. Aunt Nina took us to Chuck E. Cheese and the movies."

"Wow, you did have a good time. Tell her thank you and give her a big hug."

Myla ran over and hugged Nina, "Thanks, Aunt Nina. And I hope the next guy that hollers at you won't be a bug-a-boo."

Paige looked over at her best friend who shrugged and smiled innocently. "It's a long story. I'll tell you later."

Paige was helping a med-student look up some information when she was told that she had a phone call. She began to panic because no one ever called her on the library phone except Myla's school when it was an emergency. Everyone else used her cell.

"Hello."

"Hey, it's me."

"Elijah?"

"Yeah, I know you're at work, but it's sort of an emergency."

"What's wrong?" she asked.

"My car has been stolen. My cell phone was in it. That's why I called your job, because I don't know your cell by heart. It's just programmed into my phone."

"Wow, where was your car at?"

"Parked outside the mall. I can't believe this."

"Did you call the police?"

"Yeah, I filed a police report and everything. But listen, do you think I can get a ride home?"

"Yeah, that's no problem," Paige told him. She felt kind of obligated since she had blown him off the previous weekend, anyway. "What time do you get off?"

"I leave at six tonight."

"That's fine. I'll pick you up out front at six."

"Thanks, Paige. I appreciate it."

At six o'clock, Paige and Myla pulled in front of the mall where Elijah was waiting. He looked somber as he climbed in.

"Hi, Mr. Eli, sorry to hear someone took your car," Myla told him.

"Thanks, Myla. Hey, Paige, thanks again for giving me a ride."

"It's no problem. We were gonna go and get some dinner. Would you like to join us?" Paige asked, hoping it would lift his spirits.

"No thanks. I just wanna go home and chill for the night," he said.

"Are you sure?"

"Yeah, just take me to the crib."

"Uh, where do you live?" she asked. He gave her the directions and they headed to his house. When they got there, another guy was standing out front playing with a puppy.

"Who's that?" Myla asked.

"That's my roommate, Henry."

"Is that your dog?"

"Yeah, that's Egypt."

"Can I pet her?"

"Sure, if it's okay with your mom." He looked over at Paige.

"I don't mind. Just be careful," Paige warned.

"I will," Myla promised and got out of the backseat, running toward Henry and the dog. Paige cut the engine off and waited.

"You're not getting out?" Eli asked.

"It's cold out there."

"You can come inside." He laughed. Paige got out and locked her truck. Myla was talking Henry to death about the dog.

"Henry, this is Paige."

"Nice to meet you. I've heard so much about you," Henry told her.

"Thanks," Paige said and followed Eli inside. The house was nicely furnished and very neat. "This is nice."

"No, it's not, but thanks for saying that. You want something to drink?"

"I'm fine."

"Yes, you are definitely fine. But are you thirsty?"

Paige laughed. "No, I'm not thirsty. So, what are you going to do about a car?"

"I don' know. Hopefully they'll find it. I know I have to wait thirty days before I file an insurance claim. This is so damn messed up."

"It's not that bad. It's just an inconvenience. What about a rental?"

"I don't have that kind of loot. I mean, getting to work is no problem. For the most part, Henry can take me. But I know he's going out of town this weekend and I'm gonna have to find a ride for Saturday."

"I can take you and pick you up Saturday. That's not a problem," she told him.

"I'm not trying to interrupt your schedule or anything. I know you have things to do."

"Elijah, it's not a problem. I can take you," she assured him. He walked over and gave her a kiss.

"You are so special. I don't know what I would do without you."

"Catch the bus," she teased.

"What time do you get off?" Paige asked as she dropped Elijah in front of the mall. She had to hurry because Marlon was picking Myla up from her mother's in thirty minutes.

"Ten. Is that too late?"

"No, I'll be here," she told him. "You wanna check out a movie or something later on tonight?"

"How about you rent some movies and we can watch them at your place?" he suggested.

"Sounds like a winner to me," she said. He got out and walked over to the driver's side of her truck. She

161

rolled down the window and he gave her a brief kiss on the lips. She looked in the rearview mirror to see if Myla was looking, but she was too busy playing her Game boy.

"I'll call you on my break."

"Okay, have a good day," she told him and waved as she pulled off.

She made it to her mother's just before Marlon pulled in front of the house. He looked nice in a black sweat-suit and a pair of Jordans. Myla ran and jumped into her father's arms.

"Hey there, sweetheart. Hi, Paige."

"Hi, Marlon. What do you all have planned for the weekend?"

"Nothing really. I have some errands I have to run and that's about it," he told her, taking Myla's bag from her hand.

"Everything going okay?" she asked.

"Yeah, everything's fine."

"Then I'll see you all tomorrow then. Be good, Myla."

"I will, Mom. Love you."

"Love you too," she said. She walked into her mother's house and plopped down on the couch. Her mother came in and sat beside her.

"Ms. Myla's gone?" she asked.

"Yep, her dad just picked her up."

"How's he doing?"

"He seems to be doing fine. Every time I've talked to him he says he's great. I asked him if he's talked to his mother yet about his dad, and he keeps saying it's not the right time."

"He's probably scared." Jackie shrugged.

"Scared of Ms. Lucille? He has a reason to be. The woman is crazy." Paige laughed.

"Not scared physically. Scared emotionally. He's probably afraid that maybe his mother really did keep their father away from them for no reason, and that would shatter his entire outlook on her. Marlon's love for his mother has been unconditional, and this may be the one thing that he just can't get over. So, instead of confronting her with the truth, he's avoiding it."

"Mama, not only did she keep his father away from him, she kept the fact that he had fathered a child from him. You're telling me he's gonna just pretend like it never happened? Like she never did those things?"

"If that's his way of dealing with it. How are you dealing with it?"

"What do you mean? I'm fine. I'm just there as a support system for him and Camille, that's all."

"No, the fact that Marlon has another child."

"It's not that big of an issue considering she's half-grown. This isn't the result of some fling he had while we were together. This happened a long time ago when they were kids," Paige told her.

"I know that you're still dealing with the loss of your own child, and now you've found out that he has another one."

"I'm fine, Mama." Paige leaned over and gave her mother a kiss.

"What's that for?"

"For loving me enough to always tell me the truth and allowing Daddy to be a part of my life. You could've turned him away just like Ms. Lucille, but you didn't."

"That's because no matter how I felt about him, he was still your daddy. I was so angry when I found out about him and Lovey Brown. He broke my heart, I swear. But broken heart or not, he was your father and nothing would ever change that. I had to learn how to put all that anger aside and get past all the emotions and do what was best for you. Always remember that no matter how you feel about Marlon, that's still Myla's daddy."

"I will, Mama." Paige kissed her again.

Paige was cleaning up and doing laundry when she heard the doorbell ringing. She peeked out the window and saw Elijah's car parked behind hers. She opened the door expecting to see him standing there, but instead, found two women. One standing at least five-ten and weighing a good 120 pounds. She had buck-teeth and brown skin with acne and looked like she was about to have a nervous breakdown. The other woman was only about five-six, but she clearly weighed 220 pounds. She was fair in complexion and had long hair. It was obvious she was the dominant of the two because in her hands she carried a wooden bat. Paige was taken aback and prepared herself to deal with whatever was about to go down.

"Can I help you?" she asked.

"Yes, my name is Lori, Lori Waden. I saw you dropping Elijah off at the mall today," she said, her voice quivering.

"Yes, I gave him a ride because he said someone stole his car."

"His car? I don't think so. That's Lori's car and as you can see, it ain't stolen!" The big girl spoke loudly.

"How long have you been with Elijah?" Lori asked.

"I'm not with Elijah. We're just friends," Paige informed her.

"Whatever, just friends. You looked like more than friends when he was kissing your ass goodbye this morning!" big girl yelled.

"First of all, you need to calm down. I live in a respectable neighborhood and I don't need for my neighbors to be disturbed by your yelling in front of my house," Paige said.

"Then invite us in and we can get to the bottom of this," the big girl demanded.

"You're standing outside my doorstep, yelling, with a bat, and you want me to invite you in? I don't think so."

"Darla, just be quiet. I don't know why you brought that bat anyway," Lori said. "Look, I didn't come here to start any trouble. I just wanted to know who you were and what was up with you and Eli. I know he's been creeping for a while. That's why I finally took my car back."

Paige looked at the girl and felt sorry for her. She was right, Elijah had been trying to get with her for a while. They met in June, and now it was almost November. She couldn't believe him.

"Come inside and we can talk," she told Lori. "But if you come in here trying to start some shit, I will regulate your ass! And you can leave that bat outside," she looked back and warned Darla. The two women came in and sat in the living room. Paige could see them admiring her place.

"I hope you believe that I'm not with Elijah. We've gone out a few times and he comes over sometimes, but that's about it," Paige said.

"Is that your little girl?" Lori asked, pointing to pictures of Myla that lined the mantle.

"Yes," Paige answered.

"She's beautiful." Lori began to cry. "I have a little boy. He's six months old. He's sick right now."

"I'm sorry to hear that."

"Did Eli tell you he even had a son?" Darla snapped. "Did you know that while he was creeping over here to be with you and your daughter, his son was laid up in the hospital?"

"No, I didn't know that," was Paige's response. She wasn't about to feel guilty about something she didn't even know about. The doorbell rang again and Paige went to answer it.

"Hey, Paige, is Eli here? I saw his car parked out front," Henry greeted her. Paige opened the door wide enough for him to come inside.

"No, Henry, he's not here," she told him.

He saw the two women sitting on the sofa and a panicked look came across his face. He did a double-take then smiled. "How are you all doing? I'm Henry."

"You don't know these women, Henry?" Paige asked.

"Nope, never seen them before in my life," he said.

In a flash, Darla jumped up, snatched the door open then came back in yielding the bat. "Oh, you don't know us, Huck? Let me see if this bat can help you with your memory."

"Hold on, now! You need to sit down. I told you that won't be happening up in here!" Paige yelled.

Darla stared at Henry who wasted no time running out the door. Lori was crying as she watched them. Suddenly, she jumped. She reached in her pocket and took out her cell phone.

"It's Elijah!" she exclaimed.

"Please, let me answer it." Paige reached for the phone. "Hello."

"Who is this?" he asked. "Where the hell is Lo-Lo?"

"This is Paige, Elijah. She's sitting right here. I want to talk to you first, though."

"Who is this?" He asked again.

"Paige, Paige Davis, the woman you claim to be in love with. I gave you a ride to work this morning."

"I must have the wrong number," he said and hung up the phone.

"That punk hung up." Paige gave her the phone back.

"He's calling back," Lori whimpered. "Hello. Yes. Because I—no. I didn't. Why? But, I . . ."

"What the hell are you crying for? Cuss his ass out!" Darla hissed at Lori. Paige had to agree with her. Here she was whimpering and explaining herself to a man that was cold busted. Paige reached and took the phone from her.

"Elijah, this is Paige again. I don't know what's going on with you and Lo-Lo here, but I guess it's safe to say that I won't be picking you up tonight. As a matter of fact, I won't be talking to you ever again. I don't know if you realize this, but I don't do drama. I didn't approach you, you approached me. And now I have two ghetto queens showing up at my door with a bat. So, goodbye and God bless and you can keep all that mess. Don't call me again!"

167

"But Paige," was the last thing she heard before she ended the call.

"Well, ladies, thank you for coming over and sharing, but it's time for you to leave," she told them. They both shuffled out the door and Paige slammed it behind them. She noticed Darla's bat still sitting near the sofa.

She had been played, something she was determined wouldn't happen to her. Just as she allowed herself to begin to care for Elijah, he turned out to be full of lies. She was furious. It was all such a waste, the same as with Marlon. Time she could have been doing other things, focusing on other goals, but instead, once again, she had been dealing with a liar.

It won't be happening again, she thought as she grabbed her cell phone and went to Elijah's entry. She changed his name to "ignore" and went back to cleaning.

15

Two weeks before Thanksgiving, Paige's truck decided it no longer wanted to start. Not knowing why, she called the only mechanic she knew. He had his tow-truck driver get her truck and tow it to his shop. Thinking it would be to her advantage, she called Nina and asked her to take her to check on it.

"Paige, you have a problem," Titus told her, smiling at Nina who pretended to be engrossed in her *Essence* magazine.

"What's that?" she asked.

"You need a new transmission."

"What? Come on, Titus, can't you just fix it?" she pleaded.

"There wouldn't be any point. You would have to have it towed right back in here next month. Just let me put the new transmission in and you won't have to deal with this problem again," he advised.

"But it's too close to Christmas, Titus, and you know money is tight."

"Don't worry about it. We can work something out like last time. You just pay me every month. I'll have the truck ready in about two weeks."

"Two weeks? Why so long? I can't bum a ride for two weeks." She was beginning to stress out.

"Get a rental car," he suggested.

"What part of *I am broke* don't you understand?" Paige whined.

Nina walked over to the counter, "Come on, Titus, can't you have it fixed in a few days? Please, *for me?*"

Titus grinned and licked his lips, "You know I would do *anything* for you, Nina. Look, wait right here and let me check on something right quick. I may be able to do something for you."

Nina smiled at Paige. "See what I do for you? I used my power of persuasion and he's about to fix that truck today."

"Yeah, right." Paige rolled her eyes at Nina. They could hear Titus on the phone talking to someone. After a few minutes, he came back, still grinning at Nina, who was smiling back.

"Okay, I got a solution for you," he announced.

"I knew you would be able to get it fixed for me today, Titus." Nina winked at him.

"Ha, there's no way I can have that truck fixed in less than two weeks. I'm sorry. But follow me." They walked outside and across the parking lot, stopping at a Maxima with a FOR SALE sign on it. "Here you go."

"Titus, are you crazy or just slow? If I can't afford to get my car *fixed,* what makes you think I can *buy* another one?" Paige snapped. She was beyond frustrated and he was making it worse.

"Lord have mercy, Titus. I thought you had a solution." Nina sighed.

"No, you don't understand. You can *use* this car until yours gets fixed. Just keep the sign in the back window, though, so people can see the number," he told them.

"Oh," they both said at the same time.

"It's a really nice car. It's a ninety-nine, power everything, sunroof, CD player, rims."

"You don't have to go through all that, Titus. She's not buying it. I don't think it would matter if it was an eighty-five Chevette? As long as it can get her around." Nina laughed.

"Well, here are the keys." He handed them to her.

"Thanks, Titus. You're a good man, and I know good men are hard to find. One day somebody is gonna come and scoop you up, and Nina is gonna be disappointed because she had first dibs and didn't take it," Paige told him.

"Yeah, I am." Nina nodded. "But thanks for everything, Titus. We'll see you later."

Marlon said he had something for Paige to see, so he was picking Myla up at the house. She said there was no problem with that.

"You bought a new car?" He asked when they arrived.

"No, I'm getting a new transmission in my truck so it's a loaner. What's up?"

"I have someone for you to meet. This is Savannah." He ushered a pretty young lady through the door. Paige knew instantly that this was his daughter. She looked exactly like a younger version of Camille and an older version of Myla.

"Well, hello, Savannah. It's so nice to finally meet you." Paige took her by the hand. "You are so beautiful, just like your Aunt Camille."

"Thank you," Savannah said shyly.

"I guess her father had nothing to do with that, huh?" Marlon teased.

"Myla is going to freak out when she finds out she has an older sister," Paige whispered.

"Where is she?" Marlon asked.

"In my room on the computer. She's probably on Barbie.com e-mailing items to me that she wants for Christmas. I got fourteen e-mails from her this week."

"Fourteen, that's all? I got like twenty. At first I was flattered because she sent them, until I realized they were all Christmas wish items," he replied.

"She sounds like she's funny."

"Believe me, Savannah, funny is an understatement. Marlon, call her."

"Midget, are you ready to go?" Marlon called out.

"Daddy, will you stop calling me that? I'm not coming out until you call my right name!" Myla yelled. Paige and Savannah cracked up.

"I'm sorry, Midget, I mean, Ms. Myla. Come on, I have a surprise for you."

They could hear Myla's footsteps as she ran down the steps. She was headed straight for her father then stopped when she saw Savannah standing there. "Is she Aunt Camille's sister?"

Marlon took his daughter by the hand. "No, honey, this is *your* sister. This is Savannah."

"Hi, Myla, nice to meet you." Savannah smiled.

"I have a big sister?" Myla looked at her mother. Paige knew that the questions were about to start flowing.

"Yes, she's your big sister."

"For real? Well, where has she been? Did she come out of your stomach, Mommy?"

"Myla, go get your bag. Your dad is ready to go."

"Is Savannah going with us?"

172

"Yes, now come on," Marlon told her.

"I'll be right back." Myla turned and then asked, "Can Savannah come and see my room?"

"Go ahead," Marlon told the girls. Myla grabbed her sister's hand and led her down the hall.

"Are you sure you're ready for this? You can barely handle Myla," Paige teased.

"I'm ready. You should come with us." He looked into her eyes and she felt herself drawn to him.

"No, you need some time with them alone. When did you finally get in contact with her?" she asked.

"Her mom called me last week. Camille has been keeping constant contact with her. I talked to Savannah a few times over the phone and she asked if she could come and visit. I was surprised that she was so ready. You know what I mean?"

"She's your daughter, Marlon. She's probably been waiting for you to call for years. Look at how excited Camille was when she met your father. It's the same thing. Hey, this is an important moment for you, her and Myla."

"Yeah, I know. And you should be a part of that moment. I miss you so much, and I want us to be a family again."

"Marlon, I don't know. We've found a place where we can talk and be friends again. Let's just enjoy that for right now. Besides, what would Kasey think? You know you all flow together perfectly. Weren't those her words?"

"Paige, will you stop bringing her up? There was nothing between Kasey and me." He walked over and kissed her. She felt herself wanting to lie on the floor and have him make love to her right then and there.

173

That was the one thing Elijah was never able to do. His kisses never made her swoon.

"So what was it like seeing Rachel, your ex?" She teased him, raising her eyebrow. It was something she had thought about ever since she found out about him and Rachel having a child.

"Don't even try it. I haven't seen that girl since we were in the ninth grade. She's hardly my ex." He laughed. "You sound a little jealous. Don't worry, you don't have anything to worry about." He pulled her to him and kissed her again. They heard the footsteps coming back and regained their composure.

"Will you think about it?" he asked.

"Yes, I'll think about it," she promised.

"Mom, can Savannah have Thanksgiving with us?" Myla asked on the way to school the following Monday. Her big sister was all Myla talked about. Paige was glad that the girls had accepted each other and gotten along well.

"I'm sure she is going to have Thanksgiving with her own family, Myla. Her mother probably already has plans," Paige answered.

"What about the week after Thanksgiving? Can she come and stay then?"

"I don't mind. Sure, she can come. But I have to talk to her mother first and make sure it's okay," she said. "Come on. Get out, you're going to be late."

Myla hopped out of the car and ran to the school building. Paige's cell phone began to ring and she checked the caller ID. It read IGNORE and she did. In order to distract herself, she called Meeko.

174

"How are you feeling, Prego?"

"Better than yesterday, worse than last week."

"Great. Have you decided what you're bringing to Mama's on Thursday?"

"Rolls." Meeko groaned. "I may not even be able to get out of bed on Thursday, you know that?"

"Girl, please. You'd better be at dinner. You know I can't deal with Celeste by myself."

"Don't worry. She won't even be there. Aunt Gayle told my mother that Quincy invited Celeste to dinner with his family."

"Whoa, go ahead, Celeste. When did all this come about? Hold on." She checked the phone again and once again read IGNORE. "Why the hell is he calling me? Some guys just don't get it."

"Who is that, Batman again?"

Paige laughed at the nickname they had devised for Eli because of Lori, Darla and the bat. "Girl, yes. I just don't get it."

"How's your other man doing?"

"What other man?"

"Marlon, who else?"

"He's fine. He brought Savannah over for me to meet her. She's nice and looks just like him. She and Myla talk on the phone all the time now. Her mother has just moved back from Jersey along with her grandmother and they're living in the same house Savannah was conceived in."

"Ew, T.M.I. That was definitely too much information. How do you know that's where she was conceived?"

"Marlon told me." Paige laughed.

"I guess he's still trying to get back with you?"

"Yeah, he is," Paige admitted. "But I'm not even thinking about getting back with Marlon. I like things the way they are now."

"Smart girl, I taught you well," Meeko replied. "Now I guess you understand how your parents relationship works, huh?"

Paige thought about what Meeko just pointed out. It did seem as if she and Marlon had turned into her parents. "I guess so. I'll call and check on you later. And I will see you on Thursday."

"Okay, hopefully I'll still be alive," Meeko groaned.

The smell of sweet potato pie, collard greens, ham and chocolate cake all hit Paige at the same time as she opened her mother's door. Her stomach immediately began growling and she regretted not indulging in a bowl of Honey Nut Cheerios along with Myla. She told herself that dinner would be served in a little while and she would survive until then. The rumbling in her stomach told her otherwise.

"Mama, where are you?" She called out as carried the bags of soda inside the kitchen and placed them on the table, which was already full of food.

"I'm setting the table. Did you bring the ice?" Her mother called from the dining room.

I knew I forgot something, she thought.

"No, she forgot," Myla answered for her. Sometimes her daughter was too smart for her own good.

"I'll run out and get some. It'll only take a minute."

"Paige Michaels, was that not the last thing we talked about before you hung up the phone this morning? How could you forget it that quick?" Her mother walked over and gave her a kiss on the cheek.

"I don't know."

"Hi, Darling, Happy Thanksgiving." Myla hugged her grandmother. "Is PawPaw coming?"

"He probably is, Sweetie."

"Did you know I have a new big sister? Her name is Savannah."

"I heard all about her."

"She's gonna visit me next weekend. I'll make sure we stop by so you can meet her. Does that mean you'll have two granddaughters now?"

Paige shook her head at her mother, who leaned over and kissed the top of Myla's head. "I guess it does."

"But I'm still your little princess?" Myla asked just to make sure.

"Of course, you'll always be my little princess. Now come and help me set the table." she grabbed Myla's hand and they set-off for the dining room.

Paige grabbed her keys and went to get the ice. She drove to the convenience store and pulled into the parking lot. Memories of the robbery filled her head and her heart began pounding in her chest. There was a tapping on her window and she nearly jumped out of her skin. She rolled the window down halfway to hear what he was saying.

"Excuse me, I didn't mean to scare you." The young guy looked embarrassed. "I was just wondering how much you wanted for the car."

"Huh?" she asked, confused.

"The car, it is for sale, right?" He pointed to the sign in the rear window.

"Oh, yeah, it is. You have to call the number and get the details. I'm just borrowing it for a minute," she told him.

"Oh, cool. Well, thanks anyway." He sauntered off. She put the car in reverse and drove back to her mothers. She thought for a minute and called Meeko.

"Where are you?" she asked.

"Almost there," Meeko answered.

"I need you to stop and get some ice for me."

"All you had to bring was ice and sodas. How the hell did you forget ice?" Meeko teased.

"I can stop and get some ice for her," Stanley said in the background. Good ol' Stanley, you can always count on him.

"Tell Stan I said thanks so much," Paige said and hung up the phone. When she got back to the house, she noticed a few other people had arrived and Celeste and her mother were pulling up. "Happy Thanksgiving, Aunt Gayle."

"Happy Thanksgiving to you, Paige," Aunt Gayle called out. She opened her trunk and began taking items out while Celeste headed toward the house empty-handed.

"Let me help you, Aunt Gayle." Paige walked over and helped her aunt with the pies she had brought.

"Thank you, chil', I appreciate that. Is your young man coming this afternoon? The one that was at my birthday party? He told me he liked lemon meringue, and I made a pie just for him."

"No, I'm not seeing him anymore, Aunt Gayle. But I'm sure the pie won't go to waste." Paige laughed.

"With all these greedy folk, I'm sure it won't either," Aunt Gayle whispered. They carried the pies into the kitchen and placed them on the table. Soon Meeko walked in carrying bags of rolls. Stan was right behind her with two bags of ice.

"It's about time," Paige yelled, her hands on her hip. "What took you guys so long?"

"Girl, do not play with me. You know my hormones are raging and I have no problem cussing you out in your mother's house," Meeko snarled.

"Your hormones never had anything to do with it before, and you've done that plenty of times," Paige continued teasing Meeko. It was so funny to see her become upset so easily. It was payback for the times Meeko irritated the hell out of her when she was pregnant.

"We probably would've been here if we didn't have to stop at three different stores looking for ice that you were supposed to bring."

"Don't even try it, Meeko. We were looking for barbeque pork rinds," Stan corrected her.

"Oh, so now the truth comes out. Thanks Stan, I knew I liked you for some reason." Paige put her hand on his shoulder.

Meeko noticed Celeste sitting on the sofa and spoke to her. "Hey, Celeste, I thought you were going to Quincy's parents' house for Thanksgiving."

Paige was still surprised by this. From the way Quincy was acting, he had no interest in Paige whatsoever. But from the look on Celeste's face, things obviously had changed.

"His family is eating later on this evening. He's picking me up later."

"So, I finally get to meet Quincy?" Meeko asked.

"Well, no. He's picking me up from home," she said then quickly added, "Our house is closer to his parents than here. Don't worry. You'll meet him."

"From what Paige tells me, he's quite a catch." Meeko sat beside her.

Celeste frowned and turned to Paige. "Why have you been discussing Quincy?"

"Uh, calm down. I haven't been discussing him. I just told her he was a nice guy, that's about it." Paige folded her arms.

"I saw the way you were flirting with him at the club, Paige." Celeste sat up. Everyone else in the room looked over at them.

"You have clearly lost your mind. We were sitting at the table talking. Don't even try it," Paige told her. She was about to give Celeste a piece of her mind when the door opened again. "I'll finish this with you later."

"Happy Thanksgiving," her father bellowed as he walked inside. Paige walked over and gave him a big hug, relieved to see him.

"Daddy!"

"PawPaw," Myla called out and ran into her grandfather's arms. Being with her family brought so much joy to Paige's life and she thanked God for each and every opportunity they spent together. She looked around the room and her heart swelled with love. Her mother walked in and even gave her father a kiss on the cheek. "All right, time to eat," her mother announced and they began filing into the dining room. Paige was about to follow the rest of the family when Meeko touched her on the arm.

"Wait a minute, Paige."

"What's wrong?" she asked, seeing the serious look on Meeko's face.

"I know Celeste was a little out of line, but from what Mama tells me, she's really into this guy Quincy. So you know that means she's really defensive about him."

"But she's acting like I want him," Paige hissed, "Which is far from the truth."

"Just let it go." Meeko smiled. "After all, it's Thanksgiving."

Paige took a deep breath and agreed. "Fine, only because you asked me. You know I owe her about two or three cursing outs. But, since it's Thanksgiving . . ."

"Thank you." Meeko hugged her and they went inside to join the rest of the family. Everything was beautiful. There was a turkey, a ham and all the fixings. They even had a bowl of pork rinds for Meeko.

"Wendell, can you lead us in prayer?" Aunt Gayle asked.

Paige's father beamed with pride at her mother. He cleared his throat and then said, "I would be honored." They all bowed their heads as he began to pray. "Most merciful and graceful Father, we come today with our hearts full of thanks. Thanks for bringing us here together and letting us share, once again, another meal as a family. Lord, we thank You for the bountiful blessings You've bestowed upon us and given us. We bless those that we have lost this past year and we thank You for those that You have blessed us with. We take no one and nothing for granted. Bless the food that was prepared for us, and bless the hands that prepared it. In Jesus' name we pray, Amen."

"Amen," everyone chorused.

"All right now, Wendell. Don't let me find out you been called to the ministry," Aunt Gayle remarked.

"Believe me, that hasn't happened." Paige's mother laughed.

They fixed their plates and began eating. This was the first Thanksgiving Paige and Myla had spent without Marlon and she missed him. He was usually the first one finished eating and the first-one asleep on the couch. She had called him that morning and he told her that he would be spending the day with his mother, of course. Camille had already told her that she would be having dinner with her father and his side of the family. It would also be Marlon's first Thanksgiving without his sister.

"Marlon, why don't you at least go to your father's family gathering a little later? Just to spend time," Paige suggested.

"And leave my mother alone on Thanksgiving?" He sounded like she offended him by even making the suggestion.

"I was thinking maybe later on in the evening after you've spent the day with her." she sighed.

"No, it's bad enough that Camille is abandoning her," he replied.

"Aren't you the least bit curious about them?"

"Were they curious about me all these years? They had to know about my father and his drug issues. They knew he had some kids somewhere. Were they worried about if we were taken care of all these years? Did they ever reach out and invite us to Thanksgiving dinner before now?" Marlon snapped.

Maybe they did and your spiteful Mama turned them away like she did everyone else, Paige thought but didn't dare say. She knew that there was no point in even getting into the discussion, so she left it alone. She was just grateful that she had her own family to spend the holiday with.

"Well, Happy Thanksgiving, Marlon."

"Yeah, same to you."

16

"Hi, Ms. Paige, it's me, Savannah."

"Hi, Savannah, did you have a good Thanksgiving?"

"Yes, ma'am. Is Myla there?"

"Yes, she's here. Let me get her for you. Myla, telephone."

Myla came skipping in her mother's room. "Who is it? Daddy?"

Paige passed her the phone. "Just answer it and find out."

"Hello. Hi, Savannah. Yes. Did you ask your mom? What did she say?" Myla turned to Paige and said, "Her mother said she can stay. Can you go pick her up Friday?"

"I need to talk to her mother," Paige told her.

"Mommy needs to talk to your mom. She's right here." Myla passed the phone to Paige.

"Hello," Paige said.

"Hi, how are you? This is Rachel, Savannah's mom."

"How are you? I'm Paige."

"I've heard so much about you. Savannah has been talking nonstop about you and her sister," Rachel said. Paige detected a strong New Jersey accent.

"Myla's been talking nonstop as well, so I know the feeling. I'm just happy for the both of them."

"Me too. It's been a long time coming for Savannah."

"Well, I really want the girls to get to know one another and spend some time together, and I'm sure you already know that we've invited her to spend the weekend with us, if it's okay with you."

"I think that's a wonderful idea. The problem is that I have to work this weekend, and I'm not going to be able to bring her."

"That's not a problem at all. I can pick her up Saturday morning."

"That's perfect. She'll be ready. I look forward to meeting both you and Myla."

"Same here," Paige said. She knew that she liked Rachel instantly and she, indeed, did look forward to meeting her.

Saturday morning came faster than she anticipated. She was just as excited as Myla by the time they pulled in front of the brick home Rachel directed her to. It was not far from Ms. Lucille's house. She could see Savannah peeking out of a window upstairs and before she could even ring the doorbell, the door was open.

"Hi, Ms. Paige," Savannah greeted her with a smile.

"Hi, Savannah. I see you're all ready to go."

"Don't be rude, Savannah. Invite them in," a voice Paige recognized as Rachel's came from inside.

"I am, Mom. Come in." Savannah grinned. They followed her inside. The home reminded her of her mother's, it welcomed you from the moment you entered. A neatly dressed woman was standing in the living room. She was beautiful. Her skin was the color of dark coffee, and her jet-black hair hung to her shoulders. She smiled not only with her mouth, but her eyes.

"Hello, you must be Rachel." Paige shook her hand.

"Hey, Paige, I'm glad you found the house."

"Your directions were great."

"Would you like some coffee? I have a few minutes before I have to leave."

"I figured I would get here kind of early so we could talk," Paige told her.

"Savannah, why don't you take Myla upstairs and show her your room?" Rachel said. "We can talk in here."

Paige followed Rachel into the living area. An older woman was seated in a recliner, reading the newspaper. She looked up and smiled and Paige recognized Rachel's smile.

"Hello," Paige greeted her.

"Paige, this is my mother, Eloise. Mom, this is Paige."

"So nice to meet you. Please sit down." The woman gestured toward the sofa.

"I'll be right back with the coffee. You like cream and sugar?" Rachel asked.

"Yes, please." Paige nodded. "You have a beautiful home."

"It was my mother's. I grew up in this house, as a matter of fact, until I married Rachel's father and we moved to Jersey. My mother passed away last year and left the house to Rachel. When she moved back here, so did I, since I no longer had my husband either. Kind of makes me feel like my life has come full circle."

"I bet it felt good to return home," Paige told her.

"Yes, it did. This house holds some good memories, and there are a few not so good ones too," Eloise commented.

"Sounds a lot like life," Paige said.

"Indeed. It's nice of you to drive all the way here and pick Savannah up."

"It's no problem at all. I'm happy to do so. I used to live not far from here in a neighborhood called Silver Spring."

"Oh, I know where that is. That's not far from where Lucille lives. It's taken me years of restraint not to go and burn her house down. Every time we would come and visit throughout the years, I thought about it."

"Mama, you need to stop." Rachel arrived with steaming mugs of coffee. She carefully gave one to Paige.

"Stop what? Telling it like it is? That's the reason those girls upstairs are just now meeting one another, because of Lucille Davis."

"That's not all true, Mama. You and Daddy had a part in that too. All in all, Marlon and I were young and dumb."

"You got that right," Eloise mumbled.

"Just how did all of this happen?" Paige couldn't help asking. She wanted to find out the same night Camille told them about Savannah, but emotions were already running high, so she didn't ask.

Camille later told her how she came to Rachel's house and once she laid eyes on Savannah, there was no doubt in her mind that she was her brother's child. Unlike her brother, she did ask her mother about

187

Marlon having a baby. Lucille cursed her out and told her she had no idea what Camille was talking about.

"Every summer, I would come and visit my grandmother, and the summer I was fourteen, I fell in love with Marlon. I thought he was so fine, and I just knew he was the man of my dreams. I went back home that August with a smile on my face, until I found out I had a baby in my stomach. I didn't even really know until I was about five months. My parents were upset, but they were supportive. I didn't even tell them who the father was."

"Yeah, we were pissed," Eloise interrupted. "But she was almost six months, and being mad wasn't gonna stop us from being grandparents, so we just accepted it and helped her along the way."

"A lot of parents wouldn't be that understanding," Paige said. "I know my parents wouldn't. They were upset when I was pregnant with Myla, and I was grown."

"So you can imagine how we felt about our fourteen-year-old daughter. But the more we demanded for her to tell us who the father was, the more she refused to tell us," Eloise replied.

"I didn't want to get Marlon in trouble—believe it or not." Rachel shrugged. "I may have been pregnant, but I still had the mind of a fourteen-year-old. The next summer, I came back and brought the baby with me. The first chance I got, I went to Marlon's house. I knocked on the door and his mother came out. I knew she was drunk and I should've left then, but I didn't. I asked if Marlon was home and she said he wasn't. He was gone to some basketball camp. She saw that I had a stroller with me and asked who I was, and what did I want with Marlon. I picked Savannah up and told her she was Marlon's baby. Girl, what did I do that for? That woman went off on me! She started cussing and screaming so bad that it upset my baby. She told me I was trying to trap her son with this tar-black pick-a-ninny of a child and told me to take my bastard baby and get off her property or she was gonna call the police. What could I do? I grabbed the stroller and went back to my grandma's house. I called my mother and told her what happened, and she drove straight down here."

"In record time, too. Believe that," Eloise added. "Honey, I marched straight to that woman's house and told her that my daughter and granddaughter didn't need her liquored-up behind or her son, and they would be just fine without them. Honey, then she tried to call my child a slut, and that's when things got real ugly. I put one good cussing on her and then we left. I told Rachel she'd better not ever step foot on that street again. She had us, and that's all she needed."

"And until a few weeks ago, I had never heard from Marlon. I thought someone was playing a joke when I answered the phone, so I hung up." Rachel laughed.

"Wow, Ms. Lucille is one sick woman." Paige shook her head.

"And I've already told Marlon that I don't have a problem with him getting to know Savannah, but his mother is to have *no* contact with her," Rachel snapped.

"Well, that's one problem I don't have. Ms. Lucille doesn't care for Myla, so he rarely, if ever, takes her over there. I figure that's her loss if she doesn't have sense enough to enjoy her grandchild."

"So you mean to tell me that woman is still being mean and hateful after all these years?" Eloise asked.

"Probably even more so." Paige sighed, thinking about the fight they had months before.

"Oh, shoot, look at the time. I'm gonna be late sitting around here talking to you two." Rachel jumped up. "Paige, I'm so glad I got the chance to meet you. I know my child will be in good hands."

"Yes, she will be. You don't have to worry about that," Paige assured her. "And it was so nice meeting you, Ms. Eloise. You have to come and visit so you can meet my mother. I know you all would get along great."

"We can probably swap horror stories about Lucille," Eloise said.

"Mama, let it go," Rachel warned.

"I'm just playing. You get outta here and get to work."

Rachel called Myla and Savannah downstairs and they all left together.

"Can we stop and get my skates?" Myla asked as they drove down the street.

"Myla, why don't you just ask your dad to bring them to you next weekend?"

"I've been asking him and he keeps forgetting. Please, Mom? And I need my jean jacket too," Myla pleaded. "It's right on the way."

Paige gave into her pleas and headed toward Marlon's house. She knew he wasn't home because it was the last football game for their alma mater and he always went to tailgate with his fraternity brothers.

She turned onto his street and saw that Kasey's house was still for sale after all this time. It must be a dump, she thought, just like the owner, as she pulled into her former driveway, she hoped Marlon hadn't changed the locks and her key still worked. Luckily, it did.

"Hurry up and go get your stuff," she said, looking around. Things still looked the same. For some reason, she was relieved.

"Daddy must've left the TV on because I hear talking," Myla said.

Paige listened closer and heard voices coming from the family room. She walked toward them. Myla brushed past her and entered the room with Savannah right on her heels.

"What are you doing here?" The voice sent chills down Paige's spine.

"Oh, hi, Ms. Lucille. We thought you were the TV," Myla said, her voice barely audible.

"And who the hell is *we?*"

Paige sped to her daughter's rescue. "That would be me. I didn't know you'd be here, otherwise I wouldn't have stopped by."

"That's okay." Another voice came from across the room. Paige saw Kasey struggling to get off the chaise lounge. Her blood began to boil.

"And who are you?" Kasey walked over and stood before them. Her big teeth and thick lips took up most of her face. About the only thing that was attractive were her green eyes.

"This is my sister, Savannah," Myla answered before Paige could stop her. She noticed a strange look cross Ms. Lucille's face, but it definitely wasn't one of surprise.

"I didn't know you had a daughter this old, Paige." Kasey looked Savannah up and down.

"You don't know anything about me, anyway," Paige snapped. "Come on, girls. Let's go."

"You need to tell Marlon to change these damn locks," she heard Ms. Lucille say as they walked out. "That bitch still thinks she owns the place."

It took everything Paige could muster to stop herself from going back inside and smacking the hell out of both women. She knew one thing: Marlon Davis had lied to her for the last time.

17

Paige and the girls were on their way to dinner when Titus called and told her she could pick up her car if she got there in the next twenty minutes. She made a quick U-turn and hurried to get to his shop before he closed. Although the Maxima he loaned her was nice, she missed the feeling of power she had when she was driving her Jeep Cherokee. She could look down into nearby cars and be nosy if she wanted, not that she ever did.

"Where are we going, Mom? I thought you said we could go to Jillian's," Myla whined.

"Stop whining, girl. I'm going to pick up the truck. It's fixed." Paige checked the clock and prayed she would make it in time. She was relieved to see the garage door up as she pulled into the parking lot of the shop.

"Wow, look at that cool motorcycle," Savannah said. "That's the bomb. And look at the truck it's on."

"See Mom, you should get a truck like that!" Myla told her.

Paige turned and saw the shiny black Denali with the trailer on the back, carrying the familiar purple-and-silver motorcycle. Fascinated, the girls opted to wait outside and admire the bike. Sure enough, when she got inside, Quincy was at the counter talking with Titus.

"Oh, you was about to be short," Titus said, looking at his watch.

"Don't even try it. You said twenty minutes," she snapped at him.

"That was thirty minutes ago. You'd better be glad Quincy was in here talking me to death."

"Hold on, hold on, hold on." Quincy raised his hands in disagreement. "I was talking you to death? I guess your going on and on about how you were hoping Paige brought Nina with her and how fine she is didn't take that much time, huh? How you doing, Paige?"

Paige couldn't help laughing at Titus, who had been completely embarrassed by his friend. "Now, you know you're wrong for that, Quincy. I'm fine."

"I ain't lying. See, he was trying to be funny, and I turned the tables on him. Oh, he had a plan and everything. Since it was closing time, he was going to ask her out to dinner and—"

"Shut up, Quincy. Don't start tripping," Titus replied. "You play too much."

Quincy began laughing so hard that tears came to his eyes. "My bad, my bad."

"He's just jealous, Titus. Don't let him fool you. Celeste has him whipped too."

"What?" Quincy's eyes grew wide and his deep voice squealed so high that Paige nearly snorted.

"Oh, see, he ain't tell me about that." Titus laughed. "You been creeping, huh?"

"Hold on, hold on, hold on, now she's tripping."

"You don't have to play it off, Quincy." She nudged his arm. "I'm happy for you. I think you make a nice couple."

"You think wrong. We're not a couple," he told her.

Paige became heated. Here he was dating her cousin for the past few weeks and now he was trying to front for his boy. "I don't know why you're trying to be funny, Quincy. My cousin is a nice girl."

"I ain't say that she wasn't, but she ain't *my* girl."

"That's not what I heard." Paige folded her arms.

Quincy shook his head. "I'm sorry, but you heard wrong. I mean, Celeste and I are cool and everything, but that's about it."

Paige was confused. She wondered if Celeste had been lying this entire time or if Quincy was lying since Titus was there. "Celeste says that she went to your family's house for dinner Thanksgiving night. Are you saying she's lying?"

"Considering I didn't have dinner with my own family, yeah, she's lying. And I'm calling her right now." He reached for his cell phone.

"That's not necessary," Paige told him. "I believe you."

"I can't believe she lied like that. I told you that night at State Streets that I wasn't feeling her like that."

"Things could've changed." She shrugged.

"They haven't," Quincy said matter-of-factly and leaned back on the counter.

"So, my ride is ready?" She turned her attention to Titus.

"Yeah, it is. Uh, when is the last time you had an oil change? A tune-up?" Titus passed her the keys.

She thought about it. She really didn't know since those were things that Marlon usually took care of. All she did was put gas in it and got it washed every now and then. "Okay, I have been slacking a little on the maintenance. But now I've got a wonderful mechanic, so that'll change."

"See, that's how women are, Titus. Now you're wonderful. Remember the other week when she brought it in and you told her it would take two weeks to fix? She was ready to cuss you out and tear your head off." Quincy winked at her.

"Titus! I can't believe you would tell someone something like that about me. You know that's not true." Paige pretended to be offended. "Now you see how I felt."

"You know what, Quincy? You're an instigator, you know that?" Titus put his jacket on and they walked out the door.

"Wow, it's got TVs in the seats!" The girls were looking in the windows of the truck. They saw Paige and ran over.

"Who are these beautiful rugrats loitering near my truck?" Quincy asked.

Savannah blushed, but Myla quickly informed him, "I'm Myla, and this is Savannah, my sister."

"These are your daughters?" he asked Paige.

Paige looked at both girls, who were waiting for her answer. "Uh, yeah. This is Myla and Savannah," she said, smiling at them. She saw Savannah's eyes light up, and was glad she gave the answer that she did.

"Is that your motorcycle?" Myla asked, pointing to the helmet Quincy was holding.

"Yep, it is. It's a Suzuki GSX1300R. A Hyabusa," Quincy said as if he would be giving a test later.

"Can I sit on it?" Myla asked. Paige opened her mouth to object.

"Sure you can." Quincy beamed with pride, passing her the helmet. They followed him to the trailer and watched as he unhooked the bike and rolled it onto the pavement. He lifted Myla up and sat her on the seat of the bike. She put her hands on the helmet and pretended like she was really riding.

"Go on, girl. You look like a pro. I ain't lying." Quincy grinned.

"Can you take me for a ride?" Myla batted her eyes. If Paige didn't know any better, she would've thought her daughter was flirting.

"Now *that* you have to ask your mother." Quincy looked at Paige. "Is it okay if I take her around the block?"

"Please, Mom. We'll be right back, I promise."

"You're not the one driving, so how can you promise anything?" Paige questioned. "Besides, you don't have a helmet."

"I got an extra one," Quincy replied as he opened the back door of his truck. He took out a silver helmet and put it on. "It's a little big, but it'll work."

The large helmet wobbled on Myla's head and she grinned. "This is so cool!"

He shifted Myla to the back of the bike and he climbed on. "We'll be back in ten minutes. I'll give you a ride next, Savannah."

The motor roared as they sped out of the parking lot. Paige prayed that her daughter would be safe and nothing would happen in the short time they would be gone.

"She'll be all right. It's just around the corner," Titus told her.

"Huh?" Paige asked him.

"You look kind of nervous."

"Oh, you got me. It's the first time she's ever been on a bike," Paige confessed. "Heck, I've never even been on the back of one."

"You've gotta be kidding me. For real?" Titus seemed shocked. "Never?"

"Wow, Ms. Paige, even I've ridden on the back of a bike before," Savannah said.

"Oh, really?" Paige looked over at the pretty girl who was beaming with pride.

"Yes, my godfather has one," she answered. "He takes me on rides all the time."

Savannah was in the midst of telling them all about her godfather, his bike, his house with the pool in the back, and started telling them about the time his wife tossed all his clothes in the front lawn, when the roar of the motorcycle interrupted her.

Perfect timing, Paige thought as Quincy pulled right beside them. Myla slid off the back of the bike and removed her helmet. She wore the biggest grin Paige had ever seen.

"That was da bomb! Oh, it was so much fun. Whew!" Myla gushed.

"I take it you had fun?" Paige asked.

"It was the best! Thanks, Mr. Quincy."

Quincy removed his helmet and Paige saw that his grin was just as big as Myla's. He looked over at Savannah. "You ready?"

"You go, Ms. Paige. You've never been on a bike before. I have." Savannah said.

"Oh, I don't think so." Paige shook her head in disagreement.

"Yeah, Mom. You go! Its fun," Myla squealed and passed her the helmet.

"You've really never been on a bike?" Quincy asked.

"No, never. And I won't be getting on one today," Paige replied.

"If you're scared, say you're scared," Quincy said, challenging her.

"Awww, she ain't scared," Myla told him. "Show him, Mom. Get on!"

Paige looked at Titus, who was thoroughly enjoying this entire spectacle. "I'm not scared. I just don't feel like riding. It's cold out here. And will you stop laughing?"

"Why are you looking at me? I didn't say you were scared." Titus shrugged. He was right.

She tried to turn her attention away from Quincy, who was looking attractive as hell straddled on the bike. She had been fighting the urge to stare at him since they had arrived. She tried to think of a way to play it off.

"I'm looking at you because I'm trying to give you the keys to the car." She reached in her pocket and pulled out the keys to the Maxima.

"Oh, I almost forgot about those," Titus told her. "But you may wanna give those to him."

She was confused. "You bought the car?"

"No, I'm selling it," Quincy told her, taking the keys from her hand. "You like it? It's a nice car, huh?"

"Yeah, it is. It drives really nice. I thought it was Titus' car, though. He didn't even mention that it was your car." She looked at Titus, who was whistling and looking around like he was an innocent bystander.

"Did it matter?" Titus asked.

"Mr. Quincy, you wanna go have dinner with us?" Myla asked, causing all of them to stare at her. Paige was bowled over by Myla's suggestion.

Savannah joined her little sister. "Oh yeah, Mr. Quincy. Come and go with us."

"And what about me?" Titus pretended to be offended that the girls didn't extend an invitation to him.

"You can come too." Savannah smiled.

"That's okay," Titus told them. "I have a date with my bed."

"Girls, I'm sure Mr. Quincy has plans for the evening also." Paige motioned for them to go to the truck, but they remained by her side. "Sorry about that."

"Well, actually, I don't have any plans. Where are you all going?" He looked past Paige and asked the girls.

"To Jillian's," Myla answered. "We're gonna eat and play video games."

"Now, that sounds like fun," he told them. "I tell you what, why don't we leave your truck here and we can ride in my truck? I've seen your mother drive."

"You're so funny." She rolled her eyes at him. Titus snickered.

"Yes, yes!" The girls didn't try to hide their excitement as they ran over to Quincy's truck and waited.

Paige wasn't so sure. "I don't think that's a good idea."

"What's the problem?" Quincy asked. "You don't want me to go?"

"That's not it at all," she told him. It was so confusing. Part of her wanted him to go just as much as the girls did. The other part of her felt like calling Celeste and asking if it was okay.

It's just hanging out with the girls at Jillian's. It's not like it's a date or anything.

"Damn, Paige, it's the least you can do. You have been rolling in that man's car for two weeks," Titus told her. Looking over at him, she somehow had the feeling she was being set up. "Whatever y'all gon' do, you'd better hurry up. It's getting dark, and I ain't trying to be out here all night."

"I think we're being asked to leave," Quincy leaned over and whispered loudly. "What's it gonna be?"

Paige looked over at Myla and Savannah and then at Titus, who had the nerve to be standing with his arms folded. "I bet we wouldn't be rushed off if Nina was with us. That's okay. I'll be sure to let her know about how you treated me. Let's go."

"Oh, so it's like that?" Titus called behind her as Quincy walked her to the truck and opened the door.

"Peace out, Titus. Don't hurt nobody!" Quincy smiled at his boy as he got in the truck.

18

Paige had never laughed so much in her life. Inviting Quincy to Jillian's with them was the best thing the girls could have done. Throughout the evening, he told so many jokes and talked about unsuspecting strangers so bad, that by the time they left the arcade, Paige's face hurt.

"You know you're going to hell for talking about people, right?" she told him.

"Hold on, hold on. I'm going to hell? If that's the case, then you know you're going to be right there with me for laughing. Because you know you're wrong for laughing at that girl with that red dress on," Quincy said as he drove.

"What? Don't even try it. You were the one that yelled 'Hey, Kool-Aid' when she walked by the table." She hit him on the arm. Just the memory caused her to start laughing all over again. She was having so much fun that she was disappointed when they pulled into the parking lot of Titus' shop so she could get her truck.

"They are knocked out." He pointed to Myla and Savannah fast asleep in the backseat. He pulled beside her Cherokee and cut the engine off.

"Yeah, you wore them out," Paige told him. He had turned his body in her direction, and now they faced each other. It had been a long day, and she really didn't want the evening to end, which surprised her.

"I can't front, a brother did have a good time with them. I'm glad they thought enough about me to invite me. Unlike some people," he commented.

"Oh, it wasn't even like that. I mean, it's not every day that you go hang out with your cousin's boyfriend."

"Will you stop saying that? I'm not your cousin's boyfriend."

"If you say so." She sighed, looking back at the sleeping girls. "This is going to be a challenge."

"Listen, why don't I trail you home and I can help you get them out?" he suggested.

She gave him a suspicious look. "Yeah, right. Nice try."

"What? You're the one that said it's gonna be a challenge. I'm just trying to help you out."

"Myla, Savannah, come on. Wake up," she said loudly. She reached back and tapped her daughter on the leg. Myla began whining and shifted, but she didn't wake up. Savannah didn't even move.

Quincy sat smugly. "You don't have to do this alone. I can follow you. Just leave them alone. What's the big deal?"

"There is no big deal," Paige told him. She tried to wake the girls once again, to no avail. Frustrated, she looked at him and said, "Fine. Follow me."

"Wait." He stopped her. "Where are your keys?"

She reached into her purse and took out her keys. "Right here."

He took them from her and got out. She wondered what he was doing as she watched him unlock her doors and climb in. He started the engine of her truck, waited a few moments, then walked over and opened her door.

"What are you doing?" she asked. The coolness of the wind hit her as she stepped out. "Whew, the temperature dropped just that quick."

"That's why I went to warm your truck up," he told her, as he walked her over to her truck. "Okay, now don't forget I'm trailing you. I know your driving skills."

"Still trying to be funny about that, huh?" She closed the door. "What the hell are you doing?" she asked herself as she admired him in the rearview mirror, walking back to his truck. "We're just hanging out. It's not that serious. There's nothing to worry about."

Quincy flashed his lights, letting her know that he was ready, and they set off for her house. Her cell phone began ringing, and she checked to see who it was.

"Nina, girl, what's up?" she asked.

"Nothing much. I was calling to see how things went tonight. How was Savannah?"

"She's fine. We're heading home now," she told her. "I took them to Jillian's and we hung out for a while." She conveniently left out any mention of Quincy going with them.

"That sounds like fun. So, tell me, how was her mother? Was she cool?"

"She was beyond cool. I like Rachel a lot, and her mother too. I'll have to tell you about that later," Paige said.

"Okay, I know you have little ears there with you, so I'll let you go. Call me tomorrow."

"I will," Paige promised.

Closing her phone and placing it back in her purse, she realized how much better her car was driving. She turned her radio up. Her Maroon Five CD was still in the player and mellowed her out. She checked her mirror to make sure Quincy was behind her, and saw that he was right on her tail. Seeing that she was only going fifty miles an hour on the Interstate, she thought, *Oh, he is going to dog me out for sure.* She sped up and made sure she maintained a steady speed all the way home.

Paige pulled into her driveway. Quincy pulled in front of the house. She unlocked the front door and turned to see he was headed up the walkway with a sleeping Myla in his arms. She held the door open for him and led him up the steps to Myla's bedroom. Once Myla was in bed, he went to get Savannah. She was too big to be carried, so he just navigated her to the room.

"Whew, now that was a challenge," he said when they made it back downstairs.

"Thank you so much," she told him. Her cell phone rang again from her purse. She saw that it was Marlon. Against her better judgment, she answered it.

"What the hell did you say to my mother?" Marlon screamed as soon as she said hello.

"I didn't say anything to your mother. You'd better come again and this time, check your tone," she told him. After all of the excitement of hanging with Quincy, she had forgotten the drama with Ms. Lucille and Kasey.

"She said you came busting in the house telling her and Kasey to get out. She also said you had some smart-mouth little girl saying she was Myla's sister with you. Kasey said the little girl cussed her out. What kind of games are you trying to play, Paige?" Marlon continued to go off. The more he talked, the angrier Paige became. "Why did you take them to my house anyway?"

"Let me tell you something, Marlon Davis, I don't give a damn about your mama or what she says. She doesn't scare me. You should know that by now. I kicked her ass one time, and I have no problem doing it again. So, please give me a reason. I am a grown woman, and unlike her and your whore of a neighbor, I don't have to play games. I went to your house to get *your* child's skates. I didn't even know they'd be there," she snapped at him.

"Paige, what you did was cause a whole bunch of nonsense by taking them to my house while I wasn't there. Now my mother—"

"You know what, Marlon? I don't have time for you or your drama, so from this point on, don't bring me into it because I'm not the one. Goodbye." She hung the phone up. She couldn't believe the nerve of him. He was such a punk, and she refused to be bothered by him, his mama, Kasey or any other drama that came along with him. It was too much.

"Uh, I can show myself out." A voice came from behind her, and she squealed with fright. "Whoa, hold on there. You need to start living right," he teased. Her mood lightened a little.

"My bad. I forgot you were even here. I am so sorry," she apologized.

"It's all good. Is everything okay?" he asked. The way he looked at her was so sincere and his eyes were so warm that she felt compelled to talk to him.

"My ex, but I guess you know that already."

"Yeah, I figured that out as you yelled at him about *his* children."

Paige smiled. "You want a glass of wine?"

"A glass of wine?" Quincy imitated in a fake British voice, then asked in a thuggish manner, "What? You ain't got no Courvoisier around this joint?"

"You'd better hope I got some wine up in here," she answered. "Oh, where are my manners? You can have a seat."

"Don't even front. I already know you don't have any manners," he said, sitting on the sofa. She clicked the television on and turned to ESPN. "Whoa, I'm impressed."

"Whatever," she said and went into the kitchen. She prayed that the bottle of wine Meeko gave her as a housewarming gift was still in the back of the fridge. It was. She reached into the cabinet and grabbed two glasses and carried everything into the living room.

"No Courvoisier?"

"Nope, won't be passing any of that up in here." She gave him the bottle of wine to open. He popped the cork and poured them each a glass. She picked hers up and he said, "To old flames."

"Oh no, I won't be drinking to that." She put her glass down.

"Okay," he pretended to be deep in thought. "Oh, I got it, I got it. To driving school."

"Oh, hell naw." She smirked.

"Just playing, just playing." He had a beautiful smile and his laugh was infectious. She felt comfortable with him.

"How about you let me toast?" she asked.

"Fine then, since you insist." He slid closer to her.

"Hmmmm, let's see. To . . . Kool-Aid!"

"To Kool-Aid." He clinked his glass to hers and then sat back. "So, you really kicked your ex-mother-in-law's ass?"

She corrected him quickly. "She was never my mother-in-law and never will be, believe that."

Paige took a swallow of her wine and began telling Quincy all about Marlon. She told him all about how they met and gave him a quick history up to what just happened over the phone. It felt like she was in therapy. All the feelings she had bottled up inside came gushing out. The only thing she didn't tell him about was the birth and death of her son. That was something she couldn't bring herself to talk about.

"Wow," was all he said when she finished.

"Drama, huh?"

"No, that's more like dysfunction," he told her. "So, this cat hasn't even mentioned to his mother that he found his father?"

"Nope."

"And he's not even going to bring up the fact to her that he's caught her in this big lie?"

"Nope."

"Yeah, that's definitely dysfunction."

He looked down at his watch. "Aw damn, I gotta be at work in three hours."

Paige had been so caught up in talking that she hadn't even noticed the time. She now saw that it was after three in the morning, "I can't believe it's that late. I've been talking you to death."

"Yeah, you have been," he said. "It's been cool though. I get the feeling that you needed to share some things."

"You always have to try to be funny," she said, picking up the glasses and the now empty bottle of wine and taking them into the kitchen. When she returned, he was putting his black leather coat on.

"I really had a nice time tonight," he told her.

"I did too." She smiled at him.

"I'd really like to do this again. Can I call you?" He stepped toward her.

"Quincy, I don't—"

"So you just use a brother to vent, and I can't even call you?"

Paige reluctantly gave him her numbers, telling herself that they would just be friends. He promised to call later on in the week. He leaned in close and she gave him a quick hug, fighting the urge to kiss him. As soon as the door closed behind him, she was consumed with guilt.

What have I done? Not only did I go out with the man Celeste says is hers, but I damn near spent the night with him.

As she took a shower and got into bed, she was still trying to convince herself that nothing was wrong.

Will you chill? All you did was talk. There's nothing wrong with that. This man not only saved your life, but loaned you his car for two weeks. He is your friend.

As she closed her eyes, Quincy was still on her mind, and friend or not, there was no denying the chemistry between them.

It wasn't later in the week when he called, it was the very next day. She had just taken Savannah home, taking the time to explain to Rachel and Eloise everything that had transpired at Marlon's house and hoping they wouldn't be upset. She was relieved when they understood and invited Myla to come and stay the following weekend.

"So, do you and Myla have plans for the evening?" Quincy asked.

"Yeah, prepare for this week," she told him.

"You wanna go grab a bite to eat before or after you do that?"

Yes, I would love to, she wanted to say, but after thinking all night about the situation, she decided that she'd better quit while she was ahead. "No. Thanks for inviting me, though."

"Does this mean that you'll be turning me down every time I ask you out? Cuz a brotha is not down for begging."

"I'm not asking you to beg, Quincy. And I already know that begging is definitely not your style. I'm just saying that I don't think we should be hanging out. At this point in my life, I'm trying to resolve some issues I have in my life and become drama-free. Knowing how much I like you, and the fact that you used to date my cousin, hanging out with you definitely wouldn't be helping my situation. I wish things were different, but for right now, it just can't happen," she half-heartedly told him. She thought that by saying it, it would make her feel less disappointed, but it didn't. She liked him and wanted to get to know him better.

"I refuse to go there with you anymore about Celeste. This is crazy. I ain't lying. Well, I guess I'll holler at you later then," he said. She could hear the frustration in his voice.

"All right. Bye, Quincy," she said.

"Don't hurt nobody, Paige. And for you, I mean that literally."

"Always trying to be funny," she said with a laugh and hung up the phone.

19

Before she knew it, Christmas had come and gone and the New Year was upon them. Meeko called and invited her over to ring it in with her, Stan and a few friends, but Paige declined. She was sitting in the food court of the mall, doing some after-Christmas shopping while talking to Meeko on the cell phone.

"What's your problem? You haven't even been in the holiday spirit lately. I feel like you're turning into Celeste," Meeko told her.

"Don't even try it. I'm not that bad." Paige dipped a fry into some ketchup and popped it into her mouth. "I don't know. I mean, nothing's wrong. I'm just enjoying some me time, that's all."

"Is it Marlon? Do you miss him because of the holidays?"

"Hell no," Paige said quickly. "It doesn't have anything to do with him. Can't I enjoy being by myself?"

She wasn't lying. Her new attitude had nothing to do with Marlon. She wasn't even thinking about him. She refused to talk to him when he called, and wouldn't talk about him when Camille called.

Because of all the drama that had transpired the day she and the girls went to his house and ran into his mother, neither Myla nor Savannah had spent any time with their father over the holidays. Myla had been calling and leaving messages for him, but Marlon still hadn't contacted them. Although Myla tried to act as if it was no big deal, Paige knew her daughter was disappointed by her father's sudden lack of involvement in her life. She wanted to tell Myla that Marlon wasn't worth worrying about, but she thought about her mother's advice. *He'll always be her father, no matter what.*

Paige no longer had the strength to be involved in all of their dysfunction, as Quincy called it. Quincy, her new buddy. They talked on the phone once or twice a week, and he constantly made her laugh. She refused to go out with him, though, not wanting to cross that line, and he stopped asking. She didn't even tell anyone she talked to him, not her mother or her cousin. Not even Nina knew about him.

"So, you are turning into Celeste? You're being *anti* now?"

"Meeko, you are crazy." Paige laughed. "No, I'm not being *anti*. I'm just chilling, by myself, that's it. I'm enjoying solitude."

"Whatever you say. I think you're lonely, but that's just me," Meeko told her. "Well, I have to go to Aunt Gayle's and get my tablecloth back that she borrowed at Christmas and never returned. If you change your mind, you know where we live."

"Okay," Paige told her. She continued eating her food and watching the crowd of people. She heard angry voices and turned to get a better view. A couple was arguing near the fountain in the center of the food court. She laughed when she realized it was Elijah and Lori. A mall security guard walked over to them and said something, but Lori continued to get louder and louder. Paige looked around, wondering if batgirl Darla was somewhere lurking, waiting to pounce, but she

213

didn't see her. The security guard began escorting Lori out of the court, Elijah walking behind them. As if he felt her staring, he suddenly looked up and caught Paige's eye. She smiled at him and he looked down, as if to say "Busted again." Paige cleared her table and went to finish her shopping.

"Looking for that perfect New Year's outfit?"

Paige grinned when she saw Titus standing near her. "Yeah right, for what?"

"Aw, come on, don't even try it. I know you probably have big plans for the evening."

"Not me," she told him.

"You don't have to lie to me. I won't tell." He winked.

"First of all, there's nothing to tell. Second of all, there's no one to tell." She folded her arms.

"If you say so, but I think Q would say differently."

"Titus, now you know he and I are just cool. Don't even play."

"Yeah, I also know that he wants to be more than cool. You got his nose so wide open that I can damn near see his tonsils when he sneezes."

Paige laughed so hard that her sides began to hurt. "Titus, that's not even funny. How you gon' play your boy like that?"

"I call 'em like I see 'em. But I can't help but ask, what's up? Are you feeling him out or you just don't like him like that?"

"Titus, come on now. You know he dated my cousin. How would that look if I started dating him? That's wrong. Truth be told, he's wrong for even trying to go there with me."

"Paige, I wouldn't lie to you. He never dated that girl seriously. It was just a couple casual dates. She was blowing his cell phone up and that's about it. She still does. He ain't lyin' on that one. He never wanted anything with her. He does, however, want to date you. And Paige, he's serious. He ain't about no drama and no games. He really likes you."

Paige didn't know what to say. "I feel what you're saying, Titus. But you have to understand, Celeste really liked him. I know that for a fact. And that reason alone makes him off limits."

"But just because she liked him does not mean he liked her. Look, just give him a chance and see where it goes. He is feeling you, and I'm tired of seeing him walk around here moping like he lost his best friend."

She thought of how Meeko just talked about her somber attitude lately, and she wondered if it was because she denied herself the chance to go out with Quincy.

"Titus, you're a good friend to Quincy, and I hope he appreciates it," she told him.

"And I hope you'll be just as good a friend when you talk to Nina. Does she have plans for tonight?"

Once again, Paige laughed at Titus' feeble attempt to get with Nina. "Titus, you are one determined brother. And to answer your question, yes, she has plans," she told him. Nina was going to some posh party with a lawyer she met a few weeks ago.

"I'm still gonna keep on trying, too," he told her. She gave him a hug and wished him a happy new year.

On the way home, she thought about stopping at the store and buying some champagne, but she didn't have anyone to toast with. Even Myla was going to a

215

party being held at her grandmother's church. It would be Paige's first New Year's Eve alone.

That night, she was fast asleep when she heard someone banging on her door. She looked over at the clock and saw that it was one-fifteen. She pulled a robe on over the T-shirt and flannel pants she wore and went to see just who it was. Marlon was standing on her doorstep.

"What the hell do you want?" she asked without opening the door.

"Paige, I want to see Myla," he called out to her. "I wanna wish her a happy new year."

"She's not here," she said.

"Open the door. It's cold out here!" He banged and yelled.

"I'm not opening nothing. Myla's not here, so you can leave."

"I need to talk to you, Paige. Please open the door. It'll only take a minute. Let me say what I need to say to you face-to-face."

From the way he was talking, she knew he was drunk. Paige snatched the door open in frustration. "What? Say it and leave!"

He waved to the parked cab sitting outside her house and it pulled away. "Can I come in? You know it's cold as a beast out here."

She didn't have the chance to protest before he stumbled in the door and tripped his way to the couch.

"Marlon, get your drunk ass out of my house."

"Wait, Paige. Please let me talk to you. I know you're mad at me and I don't blame you. I fucked up."

"Yeah, so what's new, Marlon? I know that and you know that, so get the hell out of my house.!"

"Nooooo, you don't understand. I really fucked up. I'm so sorry. I need for you to know how sorry I am and how bad I feel. I love you and I love Myla. You all are my life. I don't wanna lose you." He began to cry.

"Marlon, it's too late for all this. You lost me and now you're on the verge of losing your daughter. You didn't even come and see her for Christmas."

"I sent her presents. Camille brought them."

"She didn't want any presents. She wanted her father, you asshole."

As she yelled at him, Marlon cried harder. He rolled off the sofa and onto the floor, crawling toward Paige. "I know, I know. Please forgive me. I'm sooooo sorry. I love you so much. Paaaaiiige, I love you."

Paige stared wide-eyed at Marlon, astonished at his drunken theatrics. She wished more than anything she had a video camera so she could get all this on film. "Marlon, get your drunk ass up."

"Paaaaiiige," he continued bawling. The next thing she knew, he stopped and got a funny look on his face. He began vomiting all over the floor.

"Marlon, get up! Oh God, Marlon, go to the bathroom. Ewwww! Damn it!" She screamed, running into the kitchen and grabbing a garbage sack. When she returned, he was leaning against the sofa, his face and shirt covered in vomit. There was a pile of liquor-smelling grossness in front of him. He looked over at her and she put the bag in front of him just in time. The stench made her want to vomit right along with him.

Paige rushed upstairs to the linen closet and grabbed a handful of towels. She came back down and began cleaning the mess, gagging as she did so. She paused long enough to grab a can of Lysol out of the bathroom cabinet. Calling Marlon every awful name she could think of and then some, she cleaned up his mess.

Paige stared at him and kicked him on the leg. He didn't respond because he was now passed out. She was livid. Not only did she know what she had to do next, she knew she had no choice. She removed the chocolate-brown leather coat he was wearing and took it outside to air. Paige then took off his soiled clothes and put them in the washer. There was no way she could pick him up, so she sponged him down with warm, soapy water and then helped him onto the sofa, which she fixed up with clean linen. As she put the blanket over his body, she thought about smacking him in the face, but she didn't.

"Happy New Year, you bastard!" she said then went upstairs and climbed into bed.

What the hell did you just do? she thought as she lay in bed. *Why did you clean him up? Why didn't you just call him another cab and drag his drunk ass out the house? Why didn't you let him lay in his own vomit, so that when he came to, he could see what a mess he really is? Marlon isn't your responsibility. What makes you so obligated to continue to clean up his mess?*

Paige began to cry because she had no real answers why she continued to clean up after Marlon. Why she continued to feel like she had to be there for him when he was never there for her, even when she needed him the most. It was as if she continually gave and gave and gave, and got nothing in return. It was like he had some kind of hold on her that he wouldn't release. For the longest time, she thought it was love, because love was natural and it was unconditional. Catering and caring for Marlon had always come easily to her. But now, she honestly felt like Marlon had placed a curse on her that wouldn't allow her to heal and move on. She was determined to make a change, though, no matter how hard it was.

"What's wrong with me, Nina? Am I crazy?" Paige cried into the phone. She called Nina the next day immediately after Marlon left her house. She had surprised both herself and Marlon by refusing to even take him home, forcing him to call a cab as soon as he woke up.

"No, Paige, you're not crazy," Nina assured her.

"Am I that much in love with him that I'm gonna keep allowing him to walk over me? If that's the case, then not only am I crazy, then I'm pathetic," she whined.

"You're not pathetic either, Paige. You're just suffering from a little co-dependency, that's all."

"Co-dependency?"

"Yeah, you need Marlon to need you. It makes you feel justified and secure. And you know what, Paige? I think Marlon knows this. That's why he keeps running back to you. I have no doubt that you love him, but you haven't been in love with him for a long time, have you? There's a big difference." Paige didn't answer, and Nina kept talking. "You and Marlon were together for so many years and he's the father of your children and because you all built this fairytale life together, you feel obligated to him, even though he wouldn't even consider marrying you."

The more Nina talked, the more Paige was amazed at how she was putting her feelings into words.

"It got to the point where he took more and more from you, Paige, and you kept on giving. You gave so much until you had nothing more to give, and when he realized that, he even went looking somewhere else— as close as the neighborhood slut. He wasn't there for you after Myles died, and you stayed with him. It took his mother physically assaulting you in order for you to finally leave him. You've taken a step in the right direction, Paige. You just gotta keep walking."

"A lot of good it's doing me, Nina," Paige sniffed. "Every time he needs me, I'm right there for him. I can't keep doing this."

"Then don't. You realize now what the method to his madness is, and I ain't saying it's gonna be easy, but you can do it. If that's what you really want to do."

"When did you get to be so insightful?" Paige asked her.

"Girl, you know I got Dr. Phil on TIVO. I watch him every night." Nina said with a laugh.

20

"Hey, sweetness, how was your day?" Paige greeted her daughter as she climbed into the truck.

"It was good, Mommy. How was yours?" She leaned over and kissed her mother on the cheek.

"Mine was good too," Paige told her.

"I figured out what I want to do for my birthday," Myla said. It was already February, and her birthday was the first day of March.

"And what's that?" Paige asked. Myla's birthday party plans changed daily. First it was a slumber party, then skating, then a painting party, then a tea party. Paige listened to her daughter's latest idea.

"I wanna have a pool party," Myla announced.

"Uh, Myla, in case you didn't know this, your birthday falls in the dead of winter. It's going to be too cold."

"Not if it's an indoor pool," Myla told her.

"And who do we know with an indoor pool, sweetie?"

"The Hilton!"

Paige looked over at her daughter to see if she was as serious as she sounded and saw that she was. "Myla, you've got to be kidding. Your name is not Paris or Nicole."

"Aw, Mommy, please. It'll be fun."

"Aw, Myla, think of something else." Paige smiled.

"I don't want anything else. I want a pool party."

"Not happening," she said.

"Can we stop at Darling's for a minute or that can't happen either?"

"You and your smart mouth better pray that you make it these next two weeks because you may find yourself toothless on your birthday."

"Yes, ma'am," Myla muttered and focused her attention out the window.

Paige drove to her mother's house and pulled into the driveway. Myla jumped out and ran in before Paige could even stop the engine. Myla was sitting at the table, explaining to her grandmother how wonderful a pool party at the Hilton would be when Paige got inside.

"Hey, Ma." She walked over and gave her mother a kiss.

"How are you doing? Myla is telling me her latest birthday brainstorm." Her mother laughed.

"Which won't be happening." Paige shook her head. "I don't understand her."

"And I didn't understand yours when you wanted me to let you have ponies all up in my backyard for your party in the dead of winter, but you had a pony party in the backyard, didn't you?"

"That's different," Paige said.

"No, it's not," her mother said. "I told you, it always comes back on you."

Paige's cell phone began ringing. She went into the other room to take the call.

"I need a favor," Quincy told her.

"What?" Paige asked. He normally didn't call her until after ten, and they would talk sometimes until two in the morning.

"I need you to ask your mom to watch Myla tonight."

"Why?"

"I have somewhere to take you. And I'm not taking no for an answer. This is too important for you to turn me down. Don't ask any questions. Just trust me on this one."

Paige wondered what he was up to. He had stopped asking her out a long time ago, so she knew something was up. "Hold on. We're at her house now. Ma, can you watch Myla for a little while for me tonight?"

"What's a little while?" Jackie asked.

"Where are you going?" Myla questioned.

She thought about it, not knowing where she was going or how long she would be. "Can she spend the night? I'll pick her up for school from here in the morning. She still has an extra uniform in the closet, right?"

"Yeah, that's fine," Jackie answered.

"Thanks, Ma," she said and walked back into the other room. "Okay, now, where are we going?"

"Just be ready by seven, and I mean ready to walk out the door, too," he told her.

"I don't know where we're going. How am I supposed to know what to wear?"

"Just be you: fly but casual." He hung up the phone. *What the heck does that mean? Fly but casual.* She was tempted to call Meeko and get some fashion advice, but knew she would have to explain where she was going and who she was going with. She kissed her mother and Myla goodbye and rushed home.

Going through her closet, she opted for her black leather pants and a grey sweater and her black leather stiletto boots. She prayed that wherever they were going, she wouldn't be standing for too long. She made her face up and moussed her still-short hair, and by the time seven o'clock arrived she was ready. Her doorbell rang two minutes later.

"You're late," she said as she opened the door. Quincy whistled as he stared at her from head to toe.

"Damn, you look fine!"

"That line is sooooo overused. But thanks. Am I fly but casual?" She turned and modeled for him.

"You're perfect. Conceited as hell, but you have the right to be."

She took the time to notice he was also dressed in black and grey. He sported a pair of grey pants and a black sweater under his black leather coat. He helped her put her jacket on and she locked the door as they left. Parked out front was a silver Acura with chrome rims.

"Is this your car too?" she asked as he held the door open for her.

"Yeah, this is what I got after I sold the Maxima."

"Do you sell drugs?"

"What?" He seemed offended and she was mad at herself for asking.

"I mean, why do you have so many cars?"

"Hold on, hold on, hold on. Let me explain something to you. First of all, I only have one car, this one. I also own an SUV, the black one which I bought to pull my bike—"

"The Habusa," she said.

"*Hya*busa," he corrected her. "And those are the only vehicles I have. I can't believe you. Here I am, a hardworking brother, single, no kids, no drama, own my own crib, and it just so happens that I love cars, so that's what I choose to spend my money on, and I gotta be selling drugs."

"I'm sorry, Quincy, really I am. But you know a sistah gotta ask." She shrugged.

"Oh, and just in case you're wondering, a brother ain't on the down-low either!" He rolled his eyes at her and pretended to be angry.

"I said I was sorry, dang! Now can you tell me where we're going?" she asked.

"Just chill and relax. Enjoy the evening. We'll be there shortly," he said.

She sat back and settled into the comfort of the car. He turned the music up and she enjoyed the sounds of Lyfe. They talked as he drove and she tried to figure out exactly where they were headed. Soon, he pulled into a crowded parking lot. The sign over the building read MCDOUGAL'S. She saw that there was a pretty long line to get in, and it was a mixed crowd of both Blacks and Whites. Quincy walked past the line and straight to the door, where a huge bouncer was standing.

"What's up, Frankie!" He greeted the big man.

"Yo, Q, you made it. I see you talked her into coming. Come on in." He gestured for them to enter.

"Frankie, this is Paige. Paige, this is my boy, Frankie. We work together," he told her. She reached out and shook Frankie's hand, which he was holding out to her.

"Nice to meet you. Enjoy the show," he told them, and they walked inside the nearly packed club.

"What show?" she asked.

Quincy didn't answer her. He just took her by the hand and led her to two empty seats at a table near the stage. There was a rock band playing, and she was totally confused.

"You want a drink?" he asked over the loud guitar.

"I think I'm going to need one," she told him. He ordered her a Cosmotini and a ginger ale for himself from the passing waitress.

"Will you relax? You look like you're ready to punch me in the face." He smiled at her.

She didn't answer but turned back towards the band. By the time the waitress returned with the drinks, Paige was all into the lead singer, who was performing a flawless rendition of "First Cut is the Deepest." Paige thought of how fitting that song was at that very moment, she glanced over at Quincy, who eased his chair closer to her and put his arm around her shoulder. When the band finished, she was on her feet along with the rest of the crowd.

"See, this isn't so bad now, is it?" he whispered into her ear and a chill went up her spine.

"No, I'm having fun," she told him.

A man that looked very much like Frankie took center stage. "Everybody having a good time?" The crowd yelled and clapped, letting him know that they were. "Then that means you're ready for who you all really came to see. Put your hands together for Maroon Five!"

Paige began jumping up and down as the curtain opened and she saw that indeed it was Maroon Five. The crowd went wild and Paige felt Quincy's arms around her waist. She began singing "Sunday Morning" right along with the band and the crowd. She heard Quincy singing as well and she began rocking. It was awesome. By the time the concert was over, she was hoarse. It had to be one of the greatest concerts of her life. She was still smiling when they pulled in front of her house.

"Aren't you glad you trusted me?" he asked, getting out and walking to her side of the car.

"That was the best," she said, barely above a whisper. "Thank you so much, Quincy."

He walked her to the door. "I'm glad you had fun."

"How come they didn't advertise the show? You woulda thought it would be on a big marquee or something."

"Naw, sometimes bands like that play clubs like McDougal's rather than the big venues, because it gets them a better feel for the crowd."

She unlocked the door and asked, "You wanna come in for a few minutes?"

He looked into her eyes and said, "Naw, I don't think that's a good idea."

"What?" She saw he was teasing by giving her the line she had given him so many times before. "Being a comedian again."

They walked into the living room and she hung up their coats. He sat on the sofa and she flopped on the opposite end, putting her legs across his lap. "Next time you take me to a concert, tell me not to wear stilettos."

He reached down and unzipped her boots, taking them off. She closed her eyes and was grateful for the relief. She felt his hands caressing her stocking covered feet and then he began massaging the arches of her feet. "Feel good?"

"God, yes. Feels wonderful," she moaned, but it came out as a squeak since her voice was still strained. "How did you know I like Maroon Five?"

"That night we picked your truck up from the shop, it was playing when I cut the car on. I knew Titus ain't leave it in there. So when Frankie told me they were performing at the club, I thought you'd like it."

"You are so thoughtful," Paige told him, still enjoying the foot massage.

"I try to be, anyway," he told her.

Paige was so relaxed that she didn't feel herself falling asleep. She heard the door creak open and her eyes popped open. She saw Quincy creeping out. "You're leaving?"

"Uh, yeah, you're 'sleep." He smiled.

"I am such a loser. Let me walk you out." She stood up.

"That's okay. I'll talk to you tomorrow," he said.

She walked over to him, and suddenly she was nervous. Her feelings for Quincy had grown past that of friendship, and she was torn. She wanted to be with him, but she knew that because of her cousin, it would be wrong.

If Celeste started dating Black Mike or worse yet, Marlon, how would you feel?

But there was no denying her attraction for Quincy, and the way he was looking at her made her feel like there were a million butterflies in her stomach. He reached out and pulled her to him, hugging her close. She leaned back and stared into his eyes, then pulled his head down to hers and kissed him. And for the first time in a long time, Paige felt something. As her mouth met Quincy's and his tongue met hers, as she savored the taste of him and enjoyed the feel of his mouth, Paige swooned.

After kissing for what seemed like hours, they finally broke away. She whispered to him, "I'll walk you to the car."

"Then I'll have to walk you to the door again and get another good night kiss," he told her.

She smiled and winked. "I'll walk you to the car."

21

"Happy birthday, Mommy!"

"Happy birthday, Myla!" Paige tickled her daughter and she squealed in delight. She loved the fact that they shared the same birthday. It was another one of the special bonds they shared. "I love you."

"I love you too, Mommy. Do I have to go to school?"

"Yes, you do. I'm going to work." Paige said with a laugh.

"I think we should both stay home. We can go to breakfast." Myla hopped out of bed.

"Darling has already made breakfast. She's downstairs now. Hurry and get dressed." Paige stood up and stared at Myla. She couldn't believe her daughter was eight years old already. Time flew by.

"I knew I smelled waffles. I thought I was dreaming." Myla ran into the bathroom so she could get dressed.

Paige walked downstairs and joined her mother, who had arrived at her house promptly at five-thirty with bags of breakfast items and ready to cook. She couldn't do anything but laugh when she opened the door and let her in.

"Did you wake Ms. Myla up? Is she coming down to eat?" Her mother asked in one breath.

"Yes, Ma, she's washing up and getting dressed right now. Look at all this food. You ought to be ashamed of yourself," Paige said, picking up a piece of bacon. Her mother had fixed enough food to feed an army. There were eggs, grits, waffles, bacon, sausage, fried apples and homemade cinnamon rolls. Looking at the massive breakfast, she picked up the phone and dialed Nina's number. Her best friend sounded like she had just rolled over and hit the snooze button.

"Hello," she grumbled into the phone.

"Rise and shine, Nina Seymone!" Paige sang in a cheery voice that she knew would irritate her.

"What the—who is—Paige? What time is it?"

"It's six-thirty and time to wake up."

"Six-thirty? Oh, no, call me back in thirty minutes."

"No, Nina. Mama made this huge breakfast—"

"It's your birthday! Happy birthday, Paige!" Nina was wide awake now.

"Thanks, Nina. You and Jade get up and get dressed, so you can come and have breakfast with us."

"Awwww," Nina groaned.

"Don't even try it. Get up." Paige wasn't trying to hear any excuses.

"What is your mother doing over there cooking breakfast this early, anyway?" Nina asked. Paige heard Nina's alarm going off in the background.

"See, it's time for you to get up anyway."

"No, that's the alarm telling me it's almost time to get up."

"I'll see you in thirty minutes," Paige said and hung up the phone.

Myla entered the kitchen and hugged her grandmother. "Darling, thank you so much. You made all my favorites."

"Happy birthday, baby. You know I had to do something special for both my sweet babies on their

231

birthday." Paige's mother put her arm around both of them and squeezed tight.

"Ma, I can't breathe!" Paige laughed.

"Darling, you don't have to go to work today?" Myla sat at the kitchen table.

"I'm going in late this morning," she answered.

"Don't eat yet, Myla. We have guests coming over this morning," Paige told her. The phone rang and Paige answered it.

"Happy birthday, Paige," Marlon greeted her. She was expecting his call, but not this early.

"Thanks," she told him. She still hadn't held a conversation with him since his drunken escapade at her house on New Year's Eve. He must've known she was still pissed at him, because he had been keeping a low profile.

"How does it feel to be the big three-one?" He tried to make small talk.

"The same as it did to be the big three-o," she told him.

"Well, last year you weren't feeling all that great, remember? You were eight months pregnant and miserable. But we made the best of it, didn't we?" He laughed.

Paige thought about her birthday last year. She was very much pregnant and mad because she wanted to celebrate her thirtieth birthday with a bang. Marlon originally planned a festive soiree at a hotel with all of her family and friends. Instead, Paige, Marlon and Myla had pizza and cake and rented movies from Blockbuster because she became frustrated when she couldn't fit into anything decent.

"Yeah, we did," she said with a sigh.

"Is Myla having a party?" he asked.

If you called more often, you'd know. Thanks to Uncle Stan and Aunt Meeko helping, Myla's party was being hosted at the indoor pool at the Hilton. Meeko said it was practice for her own child's parties.

"Yeah, she's having a pool party at the downtown Hilton tomorrow at three. No, we pretty much have everything taken care of. Are you coming?"

"What kind of question is that? Of course I'm coming."

"I'm just asking because you haven't been all that visible these days," she commented.

"That's because I've been swamped at work. I give you more than enough money to take care of her and make sure she has everything she needs. Don't even try to make me look like a deadbeat dad," he huffed.

"I'm not trying to make you look like anything, Marlon. It's you that don't come and get her and spend time like you used to. It's not about her financial well-being, it's about her emotional and psychological well-being also." She turned around and saw Myla staring at her from across the table, and realized that this was not the time to be having this conversation. "Hold on, Marlon."

Myla reached for the phone. "Hi, Daddy. Darling came over and made Mommy and me breakfast."

Paige shook her head at her daughter whose enthusiasm for her father was apparent, even though he hadn't been spending as much time with her as usual. She prayed that Marlon realized how much he meant to Myla and didn't take it for granted. She had no doubt that he would be there for her financially, but from his recent distant behavior, she began to worry if he was slowly pulling away from Myla in his own way. She didn't want that to happen. The fact that she maintained a wonderful and loving father-daughter relationship, even though her parents were no longer together, let her know that such a relationship was possible, even with Marlon and Myla.

"Is Marlon coming to the party?" her mother asked, interrupting her thoughts.

"He says he is." Paige shrugged, taking plates down from the cabinet and putting them on the table.

"You say that like you don't believe him."

"I mean, I wouldn't be surprised if he didn't," Paige answered.

"Don't do that, Paige."

Paige stopped and stared at her mother. "Do what? Be realistic?"

"You're not being realistic, Paige. You're being pessimistic, and that's not fair to Marlon or Myla."

"Why do you always take his side, Mama?"

"I'm not taking anyone's side. I'm just wondering why you're around here slamming dishes on the table while Myla is trying to hold a conversation on the phone with her father. You need to check the attitude."

"Mama, I did not slam any dishes down."

"Yes, you did, Mommy," Myla said as she hung up the phone.

Paige started to defend herself, but was saved by the doorbell. She left her two accusers standing in the kitchen and went to let Nina and Jade in.

The remainder of the day went by quickly. Paige was pleased as punch to receive a beautiful bouquet of lilies and tulips at the library from Quincy. He sent her a text message precisely at midnight to wish her a happy birthday. She leaned over and smelled the flowers which were sitting on her desk at work. She was talking to Meeko on her cell.

"So, what are you doing tonight to celebrate?" Meeko asked.

Paige was looking in her closet for something to wear and wondered if she should tell her about the plans she had with Quincy later on that night. Nina was the only one she told about seeing him the past couple of weeks. It wasn't like she was hiding it, she just wanted to wait and see how things went before saying anything to anyone in her family. She was enjoying getting to know him without having everyone else's opinion affecting how she felt. They saw each other once or twice a week, often meeting for lunch. He would sometimes come by the house before he went to work the midnight to seven shifts, after Myla was in bed. Tonight he was taking her to dinner and then a comedy show, and she was looking forward to it. Their physical relationship hadn't moved past heated kisses, and he never pressured her for anything more. This was another fact that she liked about him, He was indeed a gentleman.

"Getting things ready for tomorrow," she said. It wasn't a lie. She did have some last minute items to pick up before going out.

"What's there to get ready? The hotel staff is taking care of all the food and decorations. The cake is being delivered."

"And who is bringing the gifts?"

"Oh, yeah, gifts. What are you getting her?"

"Bratz, of course."

"Gats what I got 'er," Meeko answered, her mouth obviously full.

"What are you eating?" Paige asked.

"Popcorn."

"You are pitiful, you know that? By the time these next two months are up, you're gonna weigh a million pounds. You'd better slow down."

"I know you're not talking. If I recall, we had to cancel your party last year because we couldn't roll your fat tail through the hotel door."

"Oh, now you know that ain't even funny. But it's all good because on your birthday, you'll be too busy breastfeeding to do anything. Too bad, so sad!" Her home phone began ringing and she saw that Quincy was calling. She hadn't talked to him all day because he was at work. "I'll call you in the morning."

"Not too early," Meeko warned before she hung up.

Paige took a deep breath and answered the phone, trying to cover her excitement.

"Hey there, birthday girl. How was your day?"

"It was wonderful. I got flowers from this guy I've been checking out for a minute," she told him.

"Oh, really? And who is this special dude?"

"My cousin's boyfriend," she teased.

"Oh, hell naw! I ain't even trying to hear that tonight."

Paige knew it irritated Quincy every time she joked him about being Celeste's man. "Come on, it's my birthday. I'm entitled to laugh a little."

"Yeah, you are. But you need to find something a little more comical than that to laugh about. I ain't lyin'."

"So, what time are we meeting?"

"You don't want me to pick you up?"

"No, I have to drop Myla off at Nina's, so I may as well meet you at the restaurant. Where are we going anyway?"

"I thought we'd chill at Jasper's before the comedy show," he said. "Is that cool?"

"That's fine," Paige agreed, hoping she wouldn't run into Isis at the club. She knew that if she did, Meeko would find out she lied to her. "What time?"

"Eight o'clock."

"I'll be there. Fly but casual?"

"You know what to wear." He laughed.

She smiled as she got off the phone. She was so looking forward to going out with Quincy. It was as if she was in a comfort zone whenever she was with him. She felt at ease, as if she could talk about any and everything. Although befriending him was nothing she planned, he had become someone she trusted. She knew that her feelings for him were growing, and she didn't even stop them from doing so.

Celeste exaggerated from the beginning, about her and Quincy's relationship, and there is no way I can be responsible for her feelings, anyway, if the relationship was just in her head. I'm tired of taking everyone else's feelings into account before my own. I like Quincy and he likes me.

She liked the secure feeling she had when he held her in his arms, the way the hairs on the back of her neck stood up when she would hear his voice over the phone. She would save his voicemails and replay them sometimes, just to hear him. She knew tonight would be special. She wanted to be with Quincy in more ways than one.

She looked at the Victoria's Secret bag lying on the bed when she got home and felt the butterflies begin creeping in her stomach. *No point in getting nervous now. You said you were ready to move on, and you've finally found someone you enjoy, someone that makes you laugh, someone to talk to, someone who understands you. Face it, Paige, you're in love.*

"I just hope he feels the same way. I guess we'll find out tonight, won't we?" she said aloud and hurried to shower and get dressed.

Jasper's wasn't as crowded as it usually was on a Friday night. Paige had to wonder if this was a good or a bad thing. It was good because they didn't have to wait to be seated and served, yet bad because she felt like all eyes were on them as the hostess led them to their table.

"Why are you acting so nervous?" Quincy asked, holding her chair for her as she sat down.

"I don't know, it just feels like people are staring at us." Paige looked around.

"Okay, did you not get your fix before I picked you up or something? Because you're acting straight Whitney Houston on me," he told her.

She chuckled and said, "Hell-to-the-naw, Quincy!"

His laughter caused her to ease up some. He ordered a bottle of champagne to celebrate the occasion and toasted to her birthday.

"So, tell me the real reason why you're so uptight," he said after taking a sip.

"I don't know. I just feel like someone is gonna see us, that's all."

He frowned. "So what if they do? Are you embarrassed to be seen with me?"

"No, I'm not embarrassed." She shook her head.

"Then what? Is there someone else I need to know about? Are we out here creeping or something?"

"No, there's no one else and you know that. It's just that no one knows that I'm out with you . . ."

"Oh, so I'm some big secret that you've been keeping from your peeps? I mean, not that it matters, but I still don't get why."

"I don't know. Part of it is because of the whole Celeste situation and my not wanting to explain why I'm dating my cousin's ex. And before you even go there, I know what you're gonna say. She was never your girl to begin with."

"Good, then I ain't gotta say it. Now, go on with the other part of why I have to be your *closet man.*" He stared at her and she was almost too embarrassed to tell him.

"I know this is going to sound crazy, but I wanted to keep you all to myself. I didn't want anyone to give me their opinion or what they thought, or do anything that might change the way I feel about you." She looked over at him.

A grin spread across his face and he asked, "And how do you feel about me?"

"Wouldn't you like to know?" She smiled back.

"I already know." He leaned over and kissed her so tenderly that she thought she would melt.

The jazz band on stage began playing and he took her by the hand, leading her to the center of the dance floor. They were the only couple dancing, and it didn't matter to Paige that now, all eyes really were on them.

He held her body close to his and she swayed to some Brian McKnight tune that she couldn't name. As the music faded, he looked down at her and said, "We'd better hurry up and eat or we're gonna miss the comedy."

"If we miss it, we miss it." She shrugged.

"You don't want to go the comedy club?"

"We don't have to if it means we have to rush. Let's chill here for a little while," she said as they walked back to the table. As soon as they sat down, the waitress was there to take their order.

Quincy looked down at his watch. "Now, when we first walked up in this joint, you were all paranoid. Now you wanna chill here for a little while. So, what do you wanna do when we leave here, Whitney?"

Paige gave him a seductive smile. "Go home."

She knew she had shocked him from the way he looked at her and said, "Home?"

"Home." She leaned over to him and licked her lips.

"Check, please." He raised his hand in the air.

"You are so crazy." She laughed.

"I ain't lying. You know you really ain't even that hungry. As a matter of fact, we can stop at Burger King on the way home. It's your birthday; you can have it your way."

Paige's face was beginning to hurt from smiling so much. Every time she tried to regain her composure, Quincy would begin making jokes. By the time their food arrived, she could hardly breathe from laughing. He became serious for a moment as they bowed their heads and he prayed over their food. When she looked up, he was staring at her.

"What?" she asked as she began cutting her steak.

"Are you happy?"

"What do you mean? Of course I'm happy. I'm having a great time."

"No, not just for the moment. I mean overall. Every year on my birthday, I ask myself if I'm happy. I reflect on everything that's happened in the past twelve months and the effect it's had on my life."

She thought about the question. "So, you're happy every year?"

"No, I wouldn't say that. But if I do find that I'm not happy, I try and figure out why I'm not. If there's someone or something that's causing the drama or negativity, I make a point to remove myself from the situation by my next birthday—believe that. Life's too short to be unhappy," Quincy told her.

Am I happy? That's a deep question. Paige thought about everything that had gone on in her life for the past year. It had been one hell of a year. She had experienced the birth and death of her son, a gain and loss all in 24 hours time. She had summoned up enough strength to leave Marlon, knowing their relationship was at a dead end. That in itself showed how much she had stepped into a new level of maturity. She had been robbed at gunpoint, but lived to tell about it. She also met Quincy because of it, so that was good thing. She now had a new home, a new job, renewed relationships with Nina and Meeko, and she was experiencing new love.

"Yeah, I'm happy. It's been rough, but by God's grace, I'm happy," she said, fighting the tears that were forming. "I know that God's ways aren't our ways, and there was a purpose for everything that happened, good and bad, this year. I didn't realize that until now." She felt ready to open up to Quincy and was about to share the loss of her baby, but the pain was too much and she couldn't—not yet.

Quincy reached for her hand. "I didn't mean to make you cry. I'm sorry. That's what a brother gets for trying to be deep."

"No, you made me realize how thankful I should be," she replied.

He made sure the remainder of the meal was light-hearted. As soon as the table was cleared, the waitress came over carrying a huge piece of chocolate cake with a candle on top. The entire wait-staff surrounded her table and the band began playing "Happy Birthday." Paige was elated. She closed her eyes and made a wish, blowing out the candle. They all applauded. She thanked them and stood up, taking Quincy by the hand. They once again made their way to the center of the dance floor.

"Paige Nicole Davis!"

Paige turned around and nearly fainted. As perfect as this evening had been, she knew that it was about to turn awful.

Just breathe, breathe Paige.

She closed her eyes, hoping that this was a nightmare and not reality, but when she opened them, her aunt was still standing in front of her.

"Hi, Aunt Gayle." Paige walked over and reached out to hug her, but her aunt took a step back and glared at her.

"Hey, Ms. Friedman, how are you?" Quincy asked.

"I was doing fine until a few moments ago," she spat. "I don't believe you. I just can't believe you."

"Aunt Gayle, I know this must look really bad . . ."

"This looks worse than bad. How could either of you do this to Celeste? Especially you, Paige. She's your family. You know how much she's been through and how much she cares about Quincy." Aunt Gayle shook her head at them.

"Ms. Friedman, I don't know what Celeste has been telling you about our relationship, but she and I are just friends—nothing more. As a matter of fact, I've been telling Paige this for weeks now," Quincy replied.

"Weeks? So, this has been going on for weeks?" Aunt Gayle continued to rant.

"Aunt Gayle, no! Quincy and I are just friends. He just took me to dinner for my birthday. It's nothing like that, I swear," Paige told her. She refused to look over at Quincy because she knew he probably didn't like her answer.

"You two look like more than friends to me. I just don't know what to say. Celeste is going to be devastated when I tell her this. I would've never thought you would do this to her." Aunt Gayle threw her hands in the air in a gesture of exasperation. "And does your mother know that you and Quincy have become friends behind Celeste's back?"

Once again, Paige closed her eyes, trying to think of what to say to get her aunt to understand.

"We're not doing anything behind Celeste's back, Ms. Friedman. What we do is our business, not Celeste's. Again, you need to realize that Celeste is not my woman, therefore, not my concern." Quincy's words made Aunt Gayle even more upset.

"And now all of a sudden Celeste is not your girlfriend. I guess you haven't called my house and talked to me about being my son-in-law, huh?" Aunt Gayle glared.

Paige's neck snapped as she turned to face him.

"Hold on, hold on, hold on. Now, I will admit I called and you said you couldn't wait for me to become your son-in-law and I agreed, but you and I both know it was all in fun. I ain't lyin'." Quincy frowned. "Paige, I swear, it was never like that."

Paige looked back at her aunt, who was fidgeting with her hands, and didn't know what to do. "Aunt Gayle, I'm sorry."

"Why are you apologizing?" Quincy asked. "We haven't done anything wrong."

"She's apologizing because she knows that's the right thing to do. I am so disappointed in you, Paige. If nothing else, Celeste is family," Aunt Gayle said as she turned and left. Paige watched her as she snatched her takeout bag off the table and stormed out of the restaurant.

"Paige," Quincy called her name softly.

"Quincy, you said that you went out with Celeste a few times and it meant nothing. How did Aunt Gayle know who you were?"

"The one time I picked Celeste up from her house, I met your aunt. She talked me to death for about thirty minutes before we left," he told her. "I guess she remembered me."

Paige looked at him like she was waiting for him to say more to convince her that his side of the story was the truth.

"Come on, Paige," Marlon continued. "After getting to know me, do you really think I would try and holler at you if Celeste and I had a real relationship?"

244

"Just take me home," she told him. Her mind was heavy with confusion and her heart was heavy with grief. She knew from her aunt's reaction that even if Celeste had been exaggerating about being with Quincy, Paige had crossed a line that she should have never crossed.

Celeste is family. Aunt Gayle's voice echoed in her head. She looked at the un-eaten cake sitting on the table. She knew that her happy birthday definitely wasn't happy anymore.

22

Paige felt like a train had run over her the next morning when she woke up. She got out of bed and looked in the mirror. Her reflection looked worse than she felt. Her face was swollen from crying and she had dark circles under her eyes.

As bad as she felt, she knew that she had to get herself together. She looked over at the clock and saw that she only had a few hours to get ready for Myla's party. The doorbell rang and Paige quickly splashed water on her face. She knew that it could only be Nina and the girls.

"Hi, Mommy. Did you have a good birthday night with Aunt Meeko?" Myla walked through the door and gave her a big hug. Nina and Jade came in behind her.

"I sure did. Did you have a good birthday sleepover with Aunt Nina?" Paige asked.

"Yep. Jade and I stayed up until one o'clock in the morning."

"Then you and Jade should be too tired to go to the party," she said.

"I don't think so, Mom. Come on, Jade," Myla called to her best friend.

"Whew, girl, you must've had a good time last night. You look tore up. I'm surprised Meeko had enough energy to party like that. The way she's been complaining about being tired lately, I'm surprised she went anywhere." Nina flopped down on the sofa.

Paige didn't even feel like telling her what happened the night before. She just shrugged and went upstairs to get dressed. When she walked into her room, her cell phone was ringing. She looked on the caller ID and saw that it was Quincy. She didn't say anything to him on the way home last night and had gotten out of the car before he could even put it in park when they got to her house. She walked in and shut the door without even looking back. He called several times on both her home and cell phone, but she ignored his calls.

She picked up her phone and quickly changed his name to "IGNORE" as she would any other bug-a-boo. It broke her heart to do so. She dressed and went downstairs, still trying to muster up energy to make her daughter's day special.

Myla and her friends were jumping and splashing in the pool as the parents watched from a safe, dry distance. Sounds of Li'l Bow Wow poured from the CD player nearby. So far, the party was a success. Quincy had mentioned that he had gotten Myla something special, and she wondered if he would show up.

"What's up, Paige?"

She turned to see Marlon standing behind her. She really didn't feel like even talking to him, so she just said, "Marlon."

"Everything really looks nice," he said as he admired the room, decorated in all shades of pink and purple. There were streamers and balloons all over and a large banner that read "Happy Birthday Myla."

"Thanks," she said. Normally, she would have tried to make small talk with him, but instead, she noticed the gifts he was carrying and said, "Oh, let me get those. The gift table is right over here."

They walked over to the table already overflowing with gifts and placed his alongside all the others.

"Daddy!" Myla climbed out of the pool and ran over to her father. He held his arms out before she soaked him.

"Myla, get a towel and dry off before you get your daddy all wet," Paige told her.

"Sorry, Daddy," Myla said and ran over to get her towel.

Paige walked Marlon to where the other adults were seated. She looked over at her mother, who hadn't mentioned talking to Aunt Gayle, so Paige figured her aunt had yet to call her. She knew that once her mother found out, she would be upset.

"Hey, Marlon. It's so nice to see you," Jackie greeted him.

"Nice to see you, too, Ms. Jackie." Marlon smiled. "You're looking beautiful as always."

"She looks exactly how Paige will look when she gets her age," Paige's father commented. "Whomever she marries will be a blessed man, I'll tell you that."

The smile Marlon was wearing quickly left his face. "Mr. Wendell, good to see you again, too. You haven't changed a bit."

"Neither have you," Wendell replied. Paige gave him a look that told him to sit down.

"Food's over there, Marlon," Paige told him. She directed him to the table and watched him as he piled his plate with cold cuts and pizza then she walked back into the hotel lobby. The kitchen manager came out carrying Myla's cake, which looked large enough to feed a small army. Paige peeked at it, smiling at how pretty it was.

"You want me to carry it?" the nice woman with a British accent asked after she lit the candles.

"No, I think I can manage," Paige said.

"You sure?"

"Yeah, I got it." Paige was just about to lift it when Meeko, Stanley and Isis arrived. "You all are just in time."

"Whoa, you want me to get that?" Stan offered.

"Nope," she answered.

"It's so pretty," Meeko squealed. "She's going to be so excited."

"You guys go ahead in."

"Yeah, it should be a big entrance," Stanley said. "We don't want Meeko's belly to be a distraction."

"Oh, that ain't even funny." Paige said. "Hurry up, this thing is heavy." Paige waited until she saw them enter the pool area. She had made it halfway to her destination when she heard Celeste.

"Paige!"

She turned and saw Celeste walking toward her. She began to panic, seeing the anger in her cousin's eyes.

"Celeste, let me take this cake in and then we can talk," she told her.

Celeste ignored her and continued walking. Her chest was rising and falling with each breath she took. She looked straight into Paige's eyes and slammed her fists into the cake so hard that it fell straight to the floor, splattering at their feet. Paige screamed and scrambled to salvage the thick, sugary mess.

"Celeste, what the hell is wrong with you? That was Myla's birthday cake!" Paige yelled. Celeste turned to leave without answering.

Everyone had gathered to see what happened. Paige stood, too shocked to move. She couldn't believe Celeste had knocked the cake out of her hands and run off like a mad woman.

"Mommy, what happened to the cake?" Myla asked with tears in her eyes.

"It fell, sweetheart. I'm sorry. I'll run to the store and get you another one." Paige rubbed her daughter's back.

"Don't worry about it. We can get one from the restaurant. It won't be as pretty, but I'm sure it'll taste just as good," the manager said.

"Everyone back into the pool until the other cake comes out," Marlon announced. Hearing that, the kids all ran and jumped in the water. Seeing that they were gone, he asked, "What the hell happened?"

"Nothing, Marlon. The cake fell, that's all," Paige told him. "I'll handle it."

Paige found a secluded seating area behind some large green plants. She sat down and put her head in her hands. She didn't know what she felt more, anger at Celeste for ruining Myla's cake or anger at herself for getting involved with Quincy.

"Paige, is everything okay?"

She looked up and saw her mother standing in front of her along with Meeko. She didn't want to cause any more of a scene than Celeste had, so she tried to play it off.

"Yeah, I'm just not feeling all that great, that's all," she said, wiping the tears from her eyes.

"It's okay, sweetie. It was just a cake, and the manager is gonna find another one. The kids didn't even really notice. They're having too much fun in the pool."

Paige began to feel worse. Her mother and Meeko were comforting her. She could no longer lie to them.

"Celeste was here."

"Where? I didn't see her. Where did she go?" Meeko began looking around. "I'm surprised she even came. You know how anti she can be."

"She left. She was here long enough to knock the cake out of my hands and leave."

"What?" Jackie reacted.

"Oh, hell naw," Meeko said. "What the hell is her problem? I'm going to beat her ass down when I see her. She'd better be glad she left."

"Meeko, watch your mouth," her mother warned.

"Sorry, Aunt Jackie."

"No, she was upset," Paige told her.

"Upset about what?" her mother asked. She took a seat on one side of Paige and Meeko sat on the other.

Paige took a deep breath then confessed. "I went to Jasper's last night with Quincy, and Aunt Gayle saw me."

Meeko shook her head. "Paige, you went out with Quincy behind Celeste's back? Why would you do something like that?" Meeko frowned. Paige looked over at her and saw the disappointment in her face.

"I know what you're thinking, but this isn't something that I planned to happen. Quincy and I started out as just friends . . ."

"And now you're more than friends? I can't believe you." Meeko stood up. "I don't know what to say, Paige. You know better than this. This is freakin' unbelievable."

"Just let me explain," Paige told her.

"There's nothing to explain. You just admitted to creeping with Quincy. You're wrong." Meeko folded her arms over her bulging stomach and walked off.

Paige couldn't hold back the tears. Her mother put her arm around her back and Paige put her head on her shoulder. "Mama, I swear, it's not like that at all. She didn't even give me the chance to tell her what happened."

"You know her hormones are going crazy. You can tell her later. I thought she knew. But why did you lie to me, Paige? You say it wasn't like that, but you seem like you were being deceitful. You should understand her being upset."

"I know, Mama. And I can understand if you're mad too."

"I'm not mad. I'm worried a little because you've never lied to me about anything. So, if your friendship with Quincy was legitimate, then why did you feel the need to lie? I know you, Paige and Meeko do too. We both know that sneaking behind someone's back with their man isn't even in your nature, especially when it's family."

After sitting in silence for a few moments, Paige opened up and told her mother about everything that had transpired between her and Quincy over the past few weeks. "And right after they sang happy birthday, Aunt Gayle walked up."

"Well, I guess we don't have to ask if she told Celeste." Her mother sighed.

"Obviously, she did."

"This is all Marlon's fault. If he would've married you and treated you right, none of this would've transpired," her mother teased.

"You're right. I should be blaming him." Paige leaned over and hugged her. "I'm sorry for lying to you, Mom."

"I understand. But don't do it again."

"I won't."

"So, now what are you going to do?" she asked.

"I don't know," Paige told her. "I can't see him again. It would cause too much confusion. It already has."

"What about Quincy?"

"What about him? I should've never gone out with him in the first place. Whether Celeste was his girl or not, I know she liked him. I was wrong," Paige told her. She knew that she couldn't talk to him anymore, although her feelings for him were strong.

"But I thought you said he made you happy."

"He does—well, he did."

"But is he worth losing your aunt and your cousin over, because you know this isn't going to sit well with them. I'm not telling you what to do, but I suggest you think long and hard because you know that men may come and go, but family is forever."

23

"So, you're just going to ignore my calls? Is that it?"

Paige looked up from the paperwork she was going over. Her first instinct was to jump up and hug Quincy, but she restrained herself. She didn't say anything, but shrugged her shoulders.

"I know you got my messages, so I'm not even going to ask. I was gonna say the hell with it and stop calling, but I wanted to see you face-to-face. I came by your house the other night, but you ain't even come to the door. I thought we were better than that."

She had received all of his messages and had watched him walk to his car from her bedroom window the night he came by. It took everything within her not to run down the steps, open the door and call for him to come back. She knew if she did, there was no way she could let him leave without having her. And if that happened, she knew it would be even harder to let him go.

"I've been busy," she told him. "You know how it is."

"So, now you're too busy for me?"

"Yeah." She pretended to fumble with some books on the counter.

"That's bullshit and you know it." His voice rose and she shushed him.

"This is a library."

"My bad, but you're not being straight up with me, and I'm getting a bit perturbed."

"Look, Quincy, I can't see you anymore and you know that. I'm sorry."

"I hear what you're saying, and I understand family loyalty, but what about how you feel?" He unzipped his leather jacket and she knew he wasn't leaving until he got an honest answer. "You're gonna ruin a perfectly good relationship because your cousin had a fake relationship with me?"

"It's more complicated than that." She sighed. "Celeste is my cousin, and she developed real feelings for you."

"And I have real feelings for you—not her—you!"

Paige's eyes grew wide. She couldn't believe he was standing here saying this to her. She couldn't take it. She had spent days listening to her aunt go on and on about how disrespectful she had been to Celeste. She finally had to tell her aunt to stop calling because it was turning into verbal harassment. But it had been almost two weeks and Meeko still wasn't talking to her. Her mother kept telling her to give Meeko time and she would come around.

"I'm sorry, Quincy." She looked down at her watch. "I have a meeting in ten minutes."

"So, that's it?"

"Yeah," she said and turned away from him before he could see her tears.

"All right then. That's cool. I'm outta here."

Pain engulfed Paige's heart and she walked into her office and closed the door. She sat at her desk and cried for what seemed like the fiftieth time that week.

She was beginning to feel like she was having a mental meltdown.

Telling her co-workers that she was ill and was leaving for the day, she grabbed her purse and left. The gray skies threatened to open up and pour out rain. It was as somber as her mood. She got into her truck and reached for her cell.

God, please give me the strength to make it through this day. I can't do it without You, she prayed. *Lord, You know what I need to do. Help me to do it.* She dialed the number.

"Come and get me. I'm in the parking lot of the library."

The cemetery was quiet and peaceful. Paige slowly walked through the tombstones reading the names of the deceased. She spotted her grandparents' gravesites along with a few more family members. In a way, taking notice of the others helped take her mind off the real reason she was there. But soon, she found herself standing before her destination. The small headstone read: Myles Michaels Davis, beloved brother and son. Beneath it was printed the day of his birth and death.

She knelt down beside the small, marble slab and thought about her son. Today would have been his first birthday. She buried her head into her arms and began to pray as she cried. She had stopped questioning why a long time ago, but the pain of knowing God had allowed her son to die still disturbed her.

She felt someone touch her shoulder. She raised her head and saw Marlon standing in front of her, tears streaming down his face. She stood up and embraced him, finding comfort in knowing that his pain was just as deep as hers. He was holding a small bouquet of carnations. She stood back as he carefully placed them on the grave and said a prayer.

"Hey, it's okay," he told her. She remained in his arms for a few more moments then wiped her face with a tissue he gave her. "I'm glad you changed your mind about coming."

"It was hard, and I have to admit I almost didn't," she said. When he called her that morning, she told him she wasn't up to coming, but later changed her mind. They walked hand in hand back to the parking lot.

"You want to grab something to eat, maybe go somewhere and talk?" he offered.

"No, I'm gonna head on home."

"Come on," he pleaded with her. Marlon touched her face. "You look like you could use a drink."

"No, I don't want a drink. But I could use a friend right about now."

"Well, you got one of those standing right here. Where do you wanna go to talk?"

Paige shrugged. "I don't know. But not anywhere like a bar or restaurant."

"I know the perfect spot."

They got into his car and drove for several minutes. As they rode through the familiar streets, she tried to figure out where he was headed.

She thought about telling him to take her back to her truck, but she decided to ride it out. After a few more miles, the houses became fewer and they drove into a secluded area. He turned onto a dirt road

257

surrounded by large trees. Paige had no clue where they were. Finally, he pulled over and stopped. She looked around and wondered if she should get out.

This looks like the perfect spot for him to kill me and leave my lifeless body. No one knows I'm even with him, either. It would be the perfect crime.

"Come on, get out." He tapped on her window.

She opened the door and climbed out. "Where the hell are we?"

"I call it 'The Spot.' I come here sometimes when I need to think," he said, taking her by the hand and leading her deeper into the woods. After walking about thirty feet, they came out near a large lake. It was stunning, even with the thick, grey clouds hanging over it.

"This is beautiful," she whispered.

"You should see it at night," he said, walking behind her.

"You come here at night? How romantic. I'm sure Kasey appreciates it," she said sarcastically.

"I've never brought her here, thank you. You always gotta go there, huh?" He frowned.

"Yeah, I do."

"It's nothing for you to be over, Paige. You just don't seem to get that. Come over here." He led her to a group of large rocks and they sat down. "Talk to me."

"I'm just having some family issues right now, that's all."

"You? Family issues?" he said. "I don't believe it."

"You're not funny, Marlon."

"I'm not trying to be funny. Your family is the strong, loving type. I just find it hard to believe that you all are having issues. What's going on with your family?"

"My family's not perfect, that's for sure. Let's see, Meeko, Aunt Gayle, Celeste nor Aunt Mildred are speaking to me right now. And it's all over a lie."

"Who lied?"

"Celeste did," she said then added, "and I did too."

He smiled. "You lied?"

"Shut up, it's not like that."

"Well, what is your mother saying?"

"You know Mama. She's been giving me sermons daily, but she's not choosing sides. You'd think that being in the middle of your nieces, sisters and daughter would be hard, but she just says what she has to say and that's the end."

"Ha, yeah, that sounds like your mother. But Paige, your family will work through this. They always do." Marlon stood up and walked close to the water. He picked up a rock and skimmed it across the water. "You know, even though you aren't speaking, if you needed them right now, your family would be there for you in a heartbeat. You're there for each other. My mother, I'm all she's got. She doesn't have any family. No real friends."

"That's her fault, Marlon, not yours."

"I didn't say it was my fault, but she's my responsibility. I just want her to be happy."

"So you're living your life for her?" Paige walked beside him and faced him. He didn't answer. She saw the tears in his eyes. "Then when do you get the chance to be happy? Don't you think you deserve that?"

"I blew my chance at happiness the day I let you walk out of my life, Paige."

"So, can you pick me up Saturday morning? My flight gets in at ten thirty-five," Camille told her.

"Yes, Camille, Myla and I will be there," Paige told her. Camille was spending spring break with them.

"Do you have everything ready for the shower this weekend?" Camille asked as she put her suitcase in Paige's truck.

"As far as I know, everything's set."

"You don't sound all that excited," Camille told her.

"Actually, I don't think I'll be going."

"Why not? I thought you were one of the hosts."

"Meeko and I aren't on good terms right now. She's not talking to me."

"What? Why not?"

"I've been seeing this guy that Celeste claims to have been seeing."

"What do you mean *claims?*"

"Well, Celeste says that she and the guy have been dating for months, but it turns out that they only went out once or twice."

"Hmmm, that's deep. So, what does that have to do with you and Meeko?"

"She found out I was creeping with Celeste's so called ex. She thinks I was being deceitful, and now she won't even talk to me."

"Who is he?"

"His name is Quincy. He's a really nice guy." Paige smiled.

"Do you like him?"

Paige thought about how she felt whenever she was with Quincy. "I think I more than like him."

"Then who cares what they think."

"Uh, they're my family. *I* care what they think."

"You're a hypocrite." Camille laughed.

"What? How am I a hypocrite?" Paige stared at her.

"Marlon wouldn't commit to you because of what our mother thought, so you left him. You said he wasn't man enough to be with you. But you're sitting here telling me you've fallen in love with a guy, but you won't be with him because of what your family thinks. Don't get me wrong, family opinions are important, but you said yourself that Celeste was lying."

Paige continued to stare, not saying anything.

"Take it from someone who knows firsthand. Sometimes you have to say the hell with everyone and what they think and live for yourself. You know that your family will be there for you no matter what. Don't mess up a good thing because you're worried about public opinion."

"Thanks, Cam." Paige leaned over and hugged her.

"It's no problem. Paige, go to Meeko's shower. You and Meeko are like sisters. She'll forgive you and you'll move past all of this. Believe me, just when you think it's over, more drama will be just around the corner. Isn't that how life is? And besides, whether you go or not, you better believe I'm going. Meeko knows how to throw one hell of a party, and I for one don't plan on missing this one."

The phone was ringing when Paige was unlocking the door. She decided to let the answering machine answer it. There was a few seconds of silence and she

261

figured the person was about to hang up when she heard, "Uh, look, I don't want you to think I'm calling for you because I'm not. I ain't lying. You already established that it was over and I respect that. A brother ain't about to start stalking you, either, so don't get it twisted. I'm actually calling for Myla. Hey, Myla, this is Mr. Q. Your birthday gift arrived this afternoon and I wanna get it to you, so . . ."

"Hi, Quincy." Paige picked up the phone. He didn't respond right away, and she wondered if he was going to hang up in her face.

"What's up?" he asked nonchalantly.

"Um, Myla's not here. She's at my mother's."

"Oh, well, do you mind giving her my number and having her call me? I'd appreciate it."

"Sure, it's no problem," she told him. Her heart began beating and she thought about what Camille told her earlier. She wanted to see him. "Do you have to work tonight?"

"No," he answered. She waited to see if he would continue with the conversation, but he didn't. She knew he was still angry about the way she turned him away earlier. If anyone was going to make a move, it was going to be her.

"I could come over and get the gift if you'd like," she offered.

"I mean, it's not a problem. I can wait for Myla to call me."

She inhaled, becoming irritated by his coldness. "Quincy, please. I need to see you. I want to see you."

"Paige, I don't know if you know this, but I am not the type of brother that's gonna be going back and forth with you. I came to see you and talk to you earlier and you fronted on me."

"I know, and I'm sorry. But I really need to talk to you. It'll only take me fifteen minutes. Just hear me out and then I'll leave." She waited in anticipation for his response.

"See you when you get here," he said. She smiled and double-checked her appearance in the mirror before she left. Her stomach flip-flopped the entire twenty minutes it took to drive to his condo. She tried to think about what she could say once she got there, but she forgot her planned speech once she was standing in front of his door, ringing the bell.

"Hi," she said softly. He stood staring at her, looking handsome in a grey T-shirt and a pair of basketball shorts.

"You got your hair done. It looks nice," he said, taking her coat. She walked into the dimly lit living room and sat on the sofa. There was a basketball game on the large television, but it was on mute. Erykah Badu was coming from the surround-sound speakers. "You want something to drink?"

"Do you have any tea?"

"Yeah, I do," he told her. He walked past her into the kitchen. He returned with a glass of iced tea.

"Thank you," she said, taking the glass. Her hands were shaking. There was a large, plastic-covered hanger lying on the loveseat with a bow on it. She knew it was Myla's gift.

"You wanna see her gift?" he asked, noticing her staring.

"Sure," she told him. He lifted the plastic to reveal a black leather motorcycle jacket with "Ms. Myla" in studs and rhinestones on the back. It was gorgeous.

"Oh, Quincy, she's going to love it." She touched the sleeve, admiring it.

"I hope so." He covered the jacket.

"I ain't lying. She will." Paige smiled.

"So, what's up?" he asked, sitting in the chair across from her. "You said you needed to talk to me about something."

He didn't waste any time getting to the hard part, she thought. "I need for you to know how I feel about you. I like you, Quincy. I more than like you. For the longest time, I've been worried about what my family would think or how they would react instead of focusing on how I feel. And in the process, I've totally disregarded what you felt, and I apologize for being selfish in all of this."

"And?"

That was not the reaction she thought he would have, and she really didn't have an answer. She thought for a moment and said, "And I want to continue dating you. That is, if you want to."

"I'll think about it," he said. "Now let me ask you something."

"Go ahead."

"Are you using this Celeste thing as a cover-up for the real reason why you don't want to take this thing further? I need you to be honest with me."

Paige frowned. "What do you mean?"

"Plain and simple, do you still have feelings for Marlon? If you do, that's cool. But don't use this Celeste situation as a scapegoat."

She took her time before she answered. "Yes, I have feelings for Marlon. I love him. I will always love him. I'm not going to sit here and lie. But my relationship with Marlon is over. That chapter of my life is closed and I'm ready to move on."

"Paige, I saw you get in the car with him after I left this morning."

"So, you have stalker tendencies too, huh?"

"I don't think so," he told her. "I'm not going to be the one you run to when you and he are on the outs. That ain't happening."

"Quincy, Marlon came and picked me up so we could go to the cemetery together," she explained. "We went to visit my son's gravesite."

"Your son?" Quincy looked confused.

She quietly told him about the birth and death of her son, which happened one year earlier. It was the first time she had opened up about it, and as she revealed her feelings to Quincy, she released tears that she thought were long gone. He moved and sat beside her, gathering her up in his arms.

"Why didn't you ever say anything to me about this?"

"I started to tell you that night at Jasper's. That's why I was crying. But I couldn't. It hurt too much to talk about, I guess," she sniffed.

"I am so sorry, Paige. Here I am acting like a total asshole all day."

"Yeah, you were. But I don't blame you. I've been acting like an asshole for a few weeks now," she said. "How did you know it was Marlon?"

"I didn't. But I figured I would peep your hold card and take a chance and tell you it was him. I mean, hell, it worked."

"You think you're so smart, don't you?" She straddled him and stared into his eyes. He grabbed both sides of her face and pulled her toward him. His mouth met hers and she closed her eyes. Their tongues caressed and she felt his hands on her back. She pulled his shirt up and ran her fingers along his chest. Her kisses went from his face to his neck, nibbling along his collar bone.

He turned his body and lay her back on the sofa then removed his shirt. She admired the cut if his body. He was beautiful, and she loved every inch of him. He stood up and lifted her into his arms, carrying her into his room.

On top of the bed, there was a pile of clothes, which he knocked off after laying her down. They explored every inch of each other's bodies with touch and taste. By the time he placed the condom on and entered her, Paige was so anxious, she felt like a virgin.

Their lovemaking was slow and intense. With every thrust, he would call her name as he stared into her face. His hands covered hers, and she held them tight as if this moment would stop if she let go. She tried to maintain control, but it felt so good that she couldn't. As she felt herself climaxing, he released as well. They lay in each other's arms, their sweat-drenched bodies clinging.

"That took longer than fifteen minutes," he said as he ran his fingers along her arm.

"Huh?"

"On the phone, you said you only needed fifteen minutes of my time."

"I guess I'll have to get a quickie next time," she told him.

"I don't do quickies," he told her. "Believe me, you get the whole workout every time."

"Every time?"

"Every time," he repeated.

"Prove it," she said, climbing on top of him and kissing his neck.

Ice cream was just what Paige and Quincy needed after making love for hours. They were standing in his kitchen, licking more butter pecan off each other than the spoons, when Paige heard her phone ringing. She escaped Quincy's attempt to swipe the spoon across her nose and ran to answer it. It was after two in the morning, and she knew that something had to be wrong. She saw that it was someone calling from Meeko's house. She quickly answered.

"Paige, I'm in labor!" Meeko wailed. "Stanley and I are headed to the hospital.

"I'm on my way," Paige said and rushed to be by her cousin's side.

24

"I can not believe they sent me home!" Meeko said as she climbed into her king-sized bed. Paige propped her pillows behind her head and covered her with the beautiful hunter green comforter.

"They sent me home three times with Myla. Get used to it. You need to walk," she told her.

"I've been telling her the same thing." Stanley sighed.

Meeko gave him an evil look and folded her arms, looking like a two-year-old. "I'm tired of walking."

"When do you walk?" Paige asked. "Going from the kitchen to the couch doesn't count."

"I walked the mall day before yesterday," Meeko snapped.

"Yeah, with all those bags she brought in, she looked like she walked three malls."

"Get out, Stanley, before I walk over there and knock you upside your head."

"I will be glad when this baby gets here so her attitude will get better," Stanley said. "I'm going downstairs. You need anything?"

"Yeah, this bowling ball out of my gut," Meeko whined.

"I'll be right downstairs if you need me, Paige." Stanley shook his head as he walked out the door, closing it behind him.

Paige sat on the side of Meeko's bed. "Why do you treat him so bad? You are so mean to him."

"I know, and I don't mean to be. I'm just so miserable, and he's the one that wanted this baby. I'm going through all of this for him."

"Meeko, that's not true and you know it."

"Okay, I wanted a baby too. But not right now. I wanted to do other things with my life, but I went ahead and had one now," Meeko admitted. "But I didn't know it was going to be like this. I'm miserable."

"I know you are. But this is just temporary. The first time you hold that baby in your arms, you won't even be thinking about how you feel right now. I promise." Paige smiled. "You know how miserable I was with both my babies. But all that was nothing the first time I held them in my arms."

"Would you want to do it again? Even after what happened last time?" Meeko asked softly. "You never talk about wanting more kids."

"I don't know. Part of me is scared to do it again, thinking maybe I did something wrong, like maybe it was my fault. But I also think about meeting someone special and having a child with him. It's hard to say."

"I know you'll meet someone special, Paige. You are a beautiful woman with so much going for you. You deserve happiness and you'll get it. But not with Quincy. He's not worth being with you. I called Celeste last night, and she had just made him leave. He's still trying to get with her."

Paige stared at Meeko. "What time was this?"

"About eleven, right before I got into bed."

Paige could not believe Celeste was still lying about Quincy. She decided to bust her cousin once and for all.

"Call her. Tell her to come over here now." She reached on the nightstand and passed Meeko the phone.

"Are you serious?"

"As a massive heart attack. Meeko, Celeste wasn't with Quincy last night. And don't get me wrong, if it were any other way, I wouldn't have a problem, even if she was. But I do have a problem with her always lying then playing the victim and causing chaos within our family. That's not right."

"How do you know she was lying?"

"Because I was with him last night. That's right, I was with him. As a matter of fact, that's where I was when you called me this morning—with him. I love Quincy. He makes me smile, and he's what I need in my life right now. Now Celeste has everyone around here thinking he's her man, and that's not true. If it were, I would never have fallen in love with him, because my spirit wouldn't let me. I love him, and right now, I'm going to be with him."

Meeko stared at her, not saying anything. Paige hoped she didn't shock her to the point that she really did go into labor. "Whoa."

"What? You have a contraction?"

"No, I just can't believe you just said all that. It's not too often you speak up about anything. All those times we dogged you about being with Marlon and putting up with what you put up with, you just sat back and never said anything. I know you loved him, and when I talked about him, it pissed you off. Most of the time I was just trying to get a reaction out of you.

"Paige, you're the closest thing I have to a sister. I love you, and I will love whoever you choose to be with. Don't ever doubt that. If you like him, I love him."

"How, Meeko? You completely shut me out when you found out I was dating Quincy."

"That's because you lied to me and I thought we were better than that. I was hurt. I don't ever want you to feel like you have to lie to me. I guess maybe my lesson in this is to keep my mouth closed. I shouldn't dog you like I do."

"Meeko, you don't dog me." Paige said. "You're entitled to your opinions and I respect them. But I can't continue living my life worried about what other people are saying or feeling—not even my family."

"Especially your family. You know we're an opinionated bunch. And Aunt Gayle is the worst. I can't believe Celeste's lying ass. She even has my mother taking her out to dinner and everything." Meeko dialed her aunt's number, not caring that it was seven o'clock on a Saturday morning. "Aunt Gayle, it's Meeko. No, I'm fine. Yes, ma'am, they sent me home and told me to walk. Yes, I know. Listen, Aunt Gayle, I really need to talk to Celeste. Can you wake her up?"

Paige stared at Meeko and soon she heard Celeste's voice come through the phone. "Hello."

"Celeste, it's me. I need for you to come over to my house right away. I don't care that you're sleepy. I don't care that you have a migraine. I ain't trying to hear none of that. I'll see you when you get here." Meeko hung the phone up and smiled. "She's on her way."

"She always was about getting attention. Remember the time she pretended to be

271

hyperventilating in church, right in the middle of Reverend Johnson's sermon? He got her, though. Kept right on preaching, even while the ushers were carrying her out the back door."

Meeko laughed so hard that she was crying. "Girl, I forgot about that. She was just so caught up in the spirit, but she paused long enough to fix her skirt in front of Donald Morris when they passed by him."

"Now, she's got issues—for real."

"I know. Always wanting to go out to eat in nice places, but don't never have no money."

They continued to laugh and talk until they heard the sound of the doorbell. Paige looked over at Meeko, who gave her a nod. They knew it was on.

"Come in," Meeko called out.

The door slowly creaked open and Celeste peeked in. "Meeko, are you okay?"

"Come on in, girl. I'm fine," Meeko told her.

Celeste walked further inside the room. She was dressed in a pair of blue sweats and a bulky white T-shirt. She still hadn't noticed Paige on the other side of the bed.

"But I'm not." Paige stood up. Celeste looked like she saw a ghost.

"Is this why you called me, Meeko? I thought something was wrong."

"Something is wrong, Celeste," Paige told her. "Why would you continue to lie about seeing Quincy when you're not? What's up with that?"

"What are you talking about, Paige?"

"She's talking about you telling me you were with him last night when he's not trying to get up with you," Meeko snapped.

"He is—I mean, he was. He came over to the house last night when he left his barbershop. But I told him that he wasn't gonna be playing me and my cousin. I told him that both of us were too good for him and to leave us both alone, and he left. Paige, I'm glad you left him alone. I'm sorry I let a tired brotha come between us. We family, girl." Celeste walked over and put her arm around Paige's shoulder.

"Wow, Celeste. I can't believe you did that. What time did he leave your house?"

Celeste shrugged and acted like it wasn't important. "I don't know, but he had to be to work at eleven. You know he works those weird hours."

"I really can't believe it." Paige shook her head and looked over at Meeko, who was just as astonished.

"Celeste, you need to stop," Meeko told her.

"Stop what? I'm for real. I know that I've been tripping these past few weeks, but I was hurt. I'm sorry, Paige, I really am."

"Yeah, you are sorry, Celeste, and I know your mama ain't raise you to be this way. How are you gonna stand there and lie to me in my face?"

"What? You don't believe me, Paige?"

"Hell no, I don't believe you. How could he be at your house at ten o'clock when he was with me last night?"

Celeste's eyes bucked and her jaw dropped. Shaking her head, she wailed, "What do you mean you were with him last night? So, you mean to tell me that despite the fact that he's my ex, you're still going to be with him? That shows where your loyalty is. This is some straight bull—"

"Shit. You're absolutely right," Paige finished her sentence. "Why would you continue to lie about him, Celeste? Why would you lie about being with him from the beginning? And please, don't even front like this is all a big surprise to you."

Celeste looked over at the bed to Meeko, who told her, "You lied, Celeste, for no reason."

"She had a reason. As usual, she wanted to cause a whole bunch of confusion and be the victim. It's been like that our entire lives and I'm sick of it," Paige said. "Poor Celeste, school was hard for her so she came home. Poor Celeste, she gets headaches and can't get a full-time job. Poor Celeste, Cofie broke off the engagement. It's always been poor Celeste! Well, guess what? I lost a child, a man and my home, but I damn sure ain't do it to get nobody's attention. Believe that!"

Meeko struggled to sit up in bed. Paige rushed to help her. "Don't get up, Meeko. There's no need. I ain't gonna hit her. That's what she wants me to do anyway, so she can go running to our mothers and tell them."

"Calm down, Paige," Meeko said. Celeste was standing in the middle of the floor blubbering. "Celeste, you need to stop with the tears and start talking. You had the entire family believing you had been dating him for the past ten months."

"I—what—she—"

"I don't even wanna hear it."

There was a knock at the door and Stanley stuck his head in. "Is everything okay in here?"

"We're fine, sweetheart. Paige and Celeste are just clearing the air." Meeko smiled at him.

274

"I promise I ain't gonna throw no blows." Paige rolled her eyes at Celeste. "At least not in the house."

"That's good to know," he said, looking around to make sure. "I was just checking."

He closed the door and Paige sat back on the bed. She realized that there was no point in even having this conversation. It was pointless. "Look, I think I need to leave. Call me if you need anything. I'm sure I won't have a headache."

"Paige, don't go. We need to finish this," Meeko said.

"I'm finished, and I mean what I said earlier. I'm living for me. I love you." Paige kissed Meeko on the cheek and walked out of the room without saying anything to Celeste. She said goodbye to Stanley on the way out, and he promised to call if they went back to the hospital.

She was dead tired when she got home, but thoughts of Quincy gave her a quick dose of adrenaline. She dialed his number.

"Hey you," he said as he answered the phone. "Is it a girl or boy?"

"Neither," she told him. "They sent her home."

"Ha, I bet she's mad about that." He laughed. "So, where are you now?"

"At home." She yawned. "About to get in the bed."

"Oh, so you ain't wanna come get in the bed with me?"

Paige blushed and her body became warm at the thought. "I thought about it, but I figured I'd let you sleep. I know you were worn out from last night."

"Hold on, hold on, hold on. I know you don't think you wore me out. I've been up for a while now. I had to clean up ice cream off my kitchen floor and make my bed."

"Oh, really? And are you insinuating that was my fault?" She giggled.

"I know my licking skills are on point. I didn't waste anything."

Paige cracked up laughing. "Hmmm, I don't recall those skills. I think you should come over here and refresh my memory. Pick up some breakfast on the way."

She quickly straightened up and jumped in the shower. While standing under the steaming water, she heard her doorbell. *Damn, he ain't waste no time*, she thought as she hopped out and grabbed her robe. She hurried to the door and opened it.

"Good morning."

Paige was too stunned to say anything. She blinked to make sure she wasn't dreaming. "Marlon, what are you doing here?"

"I came to pick up Myla." He smiled.

"She's not here. I told you yesterday that she was staying at Mama's and to pick her up from there."

"Oh," he shrugged, "I guess I forgot. So, are you gonna invite me in?"

"Uh, I was kinda in the shower, Marlon. The water's still running." She looked at him strangely.

"My bad. Well, I guess I'll talk to you later, unless that was an invitation to join you."

"Funny." She smirked. "No, I don't think it was."

"Your hair is wet." He reached out and touched it.

"I told you I was in the shower. What is wrong with you, Marlon? You're acting crazy."

In a split second, he pulled her into his arms and kissed her. She tried to push him away, but he kept a grip on her.

"Stop it, fool. Let me go," she cried out.

"Paige, I love you so much. Being with you yesterday, I don't know— it just made me realize how I messed up. I know that I should've married you a long time ago. I was too stupid to see how much you and I had when we were together." He stared into her eyes. "I want you. I want to be with you."

Paige maneuvered her body out of his grasp. "Marlon, you're tripping, you're tripping, you're tripping."

"No, I was tripping before. I was stupid. I know now that our friendship is what I need. You're what I need in my life."

"Okay, listen." Paige knew she had to take control of the situation before it got out of hand. Marlon was serious and she knew it. "Marlon, yesterday was a very emotional day for both of us."

"And we got through it together." He took her hand.

"You're right, we did. And we did because we are friends. We always will be friends, Marlon. But we . . . our . . . there will never be another *us*. I guess that's what I'm trying to say. It's over, it's been over, and that chapter of our lives in closed now."

"So you don't love me? Is that what you're telling me?" Marlon looked hurt, and that wasn't her intention.

"No, Marlon. I keep telling you that I'll always love you. But I acknowledged a long time ago that it was over, and I'm not turning back. You decided that I wasn't worthy of your commitment, and I accepted that. Maybe it's time for you to accept it," she told him.

Just as he was about to respond, the sound of a motorcycle caused them both to turn. Quincy pulled into the driveway. He got off his bike, taking a plastic bag off the back. He quickly walked to the doorway, where Marlon and Paige were standing.

"What's up." He nodded to Marlon after he removed his helmet. He kissed Paige on the cheek. "Hey, baby, I didn't know if you wanted pancakes or French toast, so I got both."

"Thanks." She smiled as he walked past them and into the house.

"You ain't tell me you had company," Marlon said.

"I didn't have to tell you, Marlon. Well, I gotta go. I'll call Myla and tell her you're on your way," she said, turning and leaving him standing all alone.

"Everything okay?" Quincy asked.

"Everything's fine." Paige walked over and kissed him. She was glad that she made the decision to be with Quincy at all costs. She got the feeling that standing her ground with Marlon, no matter how hard it was, was definitely the right choice.

"Goodbye, Marlon," she said, waving as she closed the door.

After breakfast, she and Quincy were lying on the sofa watching cartoons when the house phone began ringing. She eased off the sofa and walked into the kitchen to answer it. "Hey, Camille. What's going on?"

"Nothing much. Just a friendly reminder call to not forget me next Saturday," she answered.

"You just reminded me yesterday, Camille." Paige laughed.

"And I'll be reminding you every day until Saturday, right before the plane takes off. Where's Ms. Myla?"

"Probably with her dad. He picked her up a little while ago."

"I take it she's going to spend time with her new stepmother, huh? I can't believe he married that cow."

"Stepmother? What are you talking about, Camille?"

"Marlon and Kasey got married at the courthouse the other day. She's knocked up, of course. Not only that, but Mama sold the house and is moving in with them, so you know I won't be coming home for the summer, unless I can stay with you."

After she hung up, Paige grabbed the side of the table before she fell. She could not believe what Camille was saying. There was no way Marlon was married. He was just on her front stoop begging her to take him back. She was furious. He was trying to play her again, but this time she was strong enough to resist. She walked back into the living room and sat on the end of the sofa.

Quincy rose up and looked at her. "What's wrong?" he asked.

"Marlon got married the other day," she told him.

"Cool," he said and lay back down.

She folded her arms and her leg began shaking. She didn't know what to do. She wanted to jump in her truck, drive to his house and slap him. "I hate him," she said, not realizing she was talking out loud.

"Why?" Quincy asked.

"Huh?"

"Why do you hate him?"

"Because he's such a liar and a manipulator."

"That's no reason to hate him."

"He just stood outside pledging his love to me and he's *married!* She began to cry. Quincy slid over and held her. "He married her. He says that he loves me, but he married her. I can't believe this."

"Baby, what's there to believe? That he's an indecisive bastard that can't think for himself? That he made the biggest mistake the other day by marrying a woman he doesn't love to please his mother? You knew all this months ago. You told me about it. You thought he was screwing her, so even the pregnancy shouldn't come as a surprise. You should be tickled pink knowing that your job is done. His wife has to deal with him now—not you. What's her name? Katie?"

"Kasey." She couldn't tell if it was the smoothness of his voice, the safeness of his touch or the sensibility of his words, but she felt herself calming down.

"Kasey has to deal with his mama, too. All that nonsense is behind you for good. All you have to worry about is making me happy." He kissed her forehead, laughing. She sat up and elbowed him in his chest.

"Stop it, Whitney! I keep telling you to stop beating on me."

"Bobby, go get me another waffle and bring me some whipped cream, too," she demanded. She kissed him full on the mouth and once again, she swooned. The sound of Teddy Pendergrass began singing in her head and she knew for a fact that it was good, so good, loving somebody, when somebody loved you back.

Epilogue

"Hi, Mommy."

"Hi, Myla. What are you doing?" Paige asked one Sunday morning when her daughter called. She and Quincy had gone to church with her mother and were in the car, headed to Jasper's for brunch. She hoped they would have a better experience today than they had on the night of her birthday.

"Nothing. Savannah and I are about to go in the backyard and play."

"Oh, Savannah's at your father's house?" Paige was surprised. She supposed Marlon had finally come clean with his mother about her and she had gotten over it.

"Yeah, and Mom, guess what? You know that lady that lived down the street, Ms. Kasey? Well, she and Dad got married and she's having a baby. I'm going to be a big sister again."

"That's great, Myla." Paige sighed. She was no longer upset about Marlon and Kasey's nuptials. Quincy was right, they deserved each other and whatever Ms. Lucille had to give both of them. Paige was over all of them. She had bigger and better things to deal with in her life.

"Mom?"

"Yeah, Myla."

"What's thrash?"

"What?"

"What's thrash?"

"I don't know, Myla. Why?"

281

"Because Ms. Lucille gave me and Savannah a thrash test," Myla told her.

Paige turned up the volume on her phone to make sure she heard what her daughter was saying. "Cut the radio down. Now, what are you saying, Myla? What kind of test?"

"She made me and Savannah open our mouths and rubbed the inside with these big Q-tips. Ms. Kasey is gonna take them to work with her tomorrow. But Ms. Lucille says if they come back that we have thrash, we can't come back to their house, because it's contagious."

"Turn the car around," Paige said. From what Myla was saying, she knew Kasey and Ms. Lucille had given the girls DNA tests. They had gone too far, and she wasn't having it.

"What?" Quincy looked over at her like she was crazy. "What's wrong?"

"Myla, where's your dad?"

"He went to play golf."

"You and Savannah get your stuff together. I'm on my way," she said and hung the phone up. "Get on the Interstate, Quincy. I'm 'bout to handle this once and for all."

Believe me, just when you think it's over, more drama will be just around the corner. Isn't that how life is? Camille's voice played in her head. But this time, Paige was ready and willing to take it head on.